LAUREL

Herbert Gold
A GIRL OF FORTY

"Mr. Gold has invented memorable characters and evoked a time that coils and recoils around San Francisco. He has done so with such accuracy and sympathy for the characters that it is possible to imagine that the personal events could be shifted to New York or almost any other American city. His people—their truths as well as their deceptions—are universal."

—Herbert Mitgang, *The New York Times*

"The best novel Gold has written in a long time: tough, funny, worldly, smart . . . very much in the tradition of Nathanael West: He has a sharp eye for the revealing detail. . . . *A Girl of Forty* is fun; it is also chilling."

—*The Washington Post Book World*

"Suki is no more to be missed than was Sally Bowles in her time . . . a shining little tale, entertaining all the way while offering biting commentary on some California follies in our time."

—*The Washington Times Magazine*

"Gold somehow manages to maintain a precarious balance between social satire and the recounting of a real tragedy. He has written a novel that is often surprising, occasionally stunning and, ultimately . . . touching."

—*USA Today*

ALSO BY HERBERT GOLD

A GIRL OF
FORTY

Herbert Gold

Published by
Dell Publishing Co., Inc.
1 Dag Hammarskjold Plaza
New York, New York 10017

Laurel ® TM 674623, Dell Publishing Co., Inc.

ISBN: 0-440-32887-X

Reprinted by arrangement with Donald I. Fine, Inc.

Printed in the United States of America

August 1987

10 9 8 7 6 5 4 3 2 1

WFH

FOR JUDI AND GORDON DAVIDSON

ONE

"Why does everybody talk about the Virgin Mary?" Suki asked me. "What about the Virgin Joseph? If Mary never got around to doing it, neither did Joseph, did he?"

When I first spied her across the room at a St. Valentine's Day party at the Old Spaghetti Factory & Cafe in San Francisco, the fixed gloom on my face told my friend Victor that I thought her wonderful. I was myopic; I was powerfully taken. "What are you thinking?" he asked, following my gaze and knowing the answer.

"What a terrific woman."

He studied the blond, jumpy, grinny, skinny, laughing lady toward whom my various troubled ions and bions were directed. He had been married, as had I; he had learned from experience, as I had not. It was clearly a skiing-and-workout lady, a health-and-diet lady, a person who liked men and enjoyed being liked by them; a lady with giggle lines and nice pokes toward a fellow when she talked with him. An active helmet of pale blond hair stirred when she threw her head back, just for fun. She touched it down into place, then laughed again. What could be bad here? She was terrific—my very words.

Victor has a cautious streak in him. "Remember," he said, "no matter how wonderful she is to you, to somebody she's a pain in the ass."

But by that time my leg muscles were twitching and I was on my way, planning remarks like, Whose guest are you? Whose friend are you? I'm Frank Curtis and you're—

"I'm Suki Read, I'm a software programmer, no, I'm not—wine promotion, *really*—I came by myself because I wanted to, can we get through all that boring stuff fast? I know who you are."

I was California stringer for the *London Telegraph* and *La Prensa* and *Politikken of Copenhagen* and, occasionally, in my native American, for U. S. magazines and newspapers. I taught journalism at Berkeley. I ran a West Coast ham-and-eggs word factory. In some ways I was enterprising; as to women, I had been both an enterprising winner and loser. I remained undiscouraged. This seemed to be a defect in my metabolism due to healthy arteries and a lazy, busy, distracted life. Given the facts of my history—mine and almost everyone's—my lack of discouragement in love indicates a degree of stubbornness amounting to a failure of intelligence.

When I saw Suki—well, my nose twitching, trying to pick up her scent across the room—I was once again happy on the road to being stupid.

And then, since this was the day devoted to lovers, we were having that conversation about the Virgin Joseph; that is, I was listening to Suki impart her modern woman's intelligence in the matter—sharing with me, as we say in California, the database: *clever Suki.* "So that's the perfect family I was raised—do you say reared?—to admire. The woman gets pregnant by a miracle and the man steps aside. Oh, boy."

"Theology's a weakness in my small talk."

"You think I'm not serious. Why do men think that? Maybe you're Joseph, maybe all men are Josephs. But I'm the kind of Mary finds my own miracles, fella."

"Hey, what did I do to you? We just met." But then, being friendly (anyone for small talk?), and sincerely trying to be up on things, I told her about the sperm bank in Berkeley that serves lesbians exclusively, although for legal reasons it claims to be an equal-opportunity impregnator. The daddy lesbian brings home the bacon and serves it on a spatula to her bride. The donors are as anonymous as God, except they are chosen from a roster of non-sexist gay males, just in case there's something to the theory of inheritance. There just might be.

Suki was laughing and nodding and enjoying my little briefing from across the Bay Bridge in Berkeley. "Want to be God?" she asked. "Or maybe you prefer to play Joseph. Personally, it's all the same to me. Why are you sniffing?"

"I like your smells."

"It's cologne and white wine—want to get me another one, or should I get it for you?"

"Yes. Yes," I said.

Up close, Suki had quick and urgent moves. Pretty soon she was touching my arm to emphasize essential further points in the conversation, such as speaking of love, here it was Valentine's Day again, the day of the saint who specialized in Cupids and low-fat chocolate and hearts pierced by arrows, but we both had come unescorted to this festival for lovers. You and me! All alone! How funny!

We touched glasses and drank. The mini-ceremony made a pause in the torrent of Suki spilling over me.

The world is blessedly full of coincidences and happy accidents of nature. Flashing narrow white thigh beneath slit folds of slithering cloth, flashing small pink and white breasts in a silken blouse with an extra button undone, showing tips of teeny-tiny white teeth as her mouth came open with laughter, Suki was a small bright package of delights. She smelled spicy and good; it was more cloves than sweet; she moved around a lot. She was very active, awfully nice—that smile urgent and changing. How sure she

was. Bright, even in theology. An innovator in
contemporary religious thought. She knew she
could arrive with nobody and go home with almost anybody.

I preferred that she go home with me.

She did; terrific!

Alas, she did.

I'm not going to write dirty unless it's essential, but it seemed to be a lucky evening. She was
funny and fun, she was quick and able, she was
devoted to pleasure in the way someone who
likes massage is devoted to massage. Love was
good for her, it relaxed the body and spirit, the
soul could go on soaring in its own blessed privacy, the voice making sentences and little excla-
mations. I didn't feel our souls were talking pre-
cisely to each other, but that's a mere detail.
There were utterances. She was jolly.

No physical details, please. But a barnyard element was missing in Suki. The sweating was so
clean! And the urgency was so healthful and
neat. Although, like me, she was past the middle
of the journey of our life, perhaps even for California she had a bold teenager's matter-of-fact-
ness. Athletic stretching, yes; soul to soul, no.
But body to body? Whatever's right. Anything
that pleased. "Go ahead, try that, too," she said.
"My last lover, the orthodontist, liked to do that.
Go on, go ahead, get wild. It's nice."

There seemed to be a fastener missing. I
guessed she was put together with Velcro, not
with blood, lymph, sinew, a past and griefs, a

13

future and hopes, a heart—of course, I was wrong. But she was different. Not crazy, just lacking the normal melancholy, doubts, nostalgias, hesitancies, wonderments. What you saw was what you got, and how splendid it was! And how foolish not to be content with something so spicy-smelling, eager, delighted, frank, open, and eager to be of use to itself. And merry and bright! Knowing it had to be of use to others in order to get what it wanted for itself. Can't all those qualities make do for tenderness now and then?

"My main man is in Chicago on business this weekend," she told me. "I suppose you could spend the night, but sometimes he comes back early. But we won't have breakfast this time with my son Peter, the light of my life."

This time: I wasn't a one-night stand for Suki.

Happy slightly complicated St. Valentine's Day.

She was boarding temporarily with her main man in a long railroad flat on the Kearny steps up from Broadway in North Beach. Her main man was an architect and city planner. Just at that moment, while her house in Cow Hollow was being painted, she was staying with him. Her son was with his father in the (vaguely) East Bay. Sometimes she thought she might rent out the house in Cow Hollow—call it Pacific Heights and charge a little more—and use the money for travel. Or she could go on staying with her main man—leave Peter with the stuffy father—but other times she thought it would be more fun to go back to her little house in Cow Hollow in a week or two. The kid should finish high school in one place. She liked his company, a dear bright boy, terrific mechanical aptitude. Pretty soon she planned to make up her mind.

I was a few seconds behind this getting-acquainted postcoital rush. "Why do you call him your 'main man?'" I asked.

"He's black," she said.

I suppose that was as good an answer as any. It was a Suki answer.

I didn't spend the rest of the night there, but the next evening, Sunday, we met at Enrico's cafe. There was no logical reason for this except that I wanted more of her and she was a person who liked to hug an Irish coffee between her hands at Enrico's during the misty San Francisco early-spring evening. It was a nice way to end the old week and begin the new one. So we came together with different but intersecting desires. On the evening of the Sabbath she also liked intelligent conversation about herself.

Suki's life story was crowded and she was willing to fill in the outlines. One divorce; one child, Peter, light of her life, supposedly shared with her former husband, but really her entire responsibility; good earnings in the p.r. trade, specializing in California wines. There's work to be done and a person does her work, helping to move the white wines and hoping the red ones can get going again. Taste is not permanent, whatever people say; even fashion in as basic a commodity as varietal grapes can alter for no good reason—the stock market, wars, real estate values, demographic bulges, any damn trivial distraction can cause people to go from sweet to dry; some people even drink rosé.

Suki's philosophy in such a discussion on the terrace at Enrico's was fairly strict coastal California stuff. Keep healthy but have fun. Guard against trouble but don't let caution dominate your thoughts. Life must be a festival and never finance your house with a variable-rate mortgage. Hidden from view, she also kept another philosophy, leaving the unanswerable questions unanswered. She said what was appropriate to the time, place, and stranger.

"Were you cautious about me?" I asked.

"A little," she said. "I hesitated. Before my friend Sherrie, um, she asks men their sign—"

"Before she goes home with them."

"Before she lets them go home with her." She touched my hand and grinned. "I tell her people who believe in astrology are total idiots, really out of it, but of course I'm an Aries and you know how skeptical they are—"

We laughed together. It felt cozy. The outdoor gas space heater was singing and spitting softly. "Mine's Visa," I said.

"Well, anyway, first I hesitated, then I saw truth and honesty in your eyes. Earnestness. Maybe a little lack of, oh, maybe—don't get mad now, Frank—devil-may-care. So I thought if you had herpes, you'd mention it."

"Thank you," I said, "for that confidence."

I also appreciated her not leveling with me. It was her secret un-California side. She confined her confidences to the practiced and manageable ones, such as career and sex.

"Your eyes weren't too shifty. The whites are really white, but the pink is a little pink. I think that's interesting. You're not too unattractive, Frank." She was silent and thinking, reconsidering, as the waiter offered her "a splash" of coffee (she nodded), and then she said: "Actually, the question of caution hardly comes up, dear. Since I haven't needed to think about it yet, have I?"

I spread my hands to apologize for my presumption. Not everybody is looking for love, for solutions. I definitely needed to understand this lady and, before I understood her, to realize that I never would unless she decided a measure of understanding fit her plans. And she would measure it out herself.

We watched the world of Sunday night float by—a pair of hookers (one black, one white), a cop, a pink-hatted pimp trailing after; some beefy tourists; kids finishing a weekend in North Beach; Hube the Cube with the early edition of the *Chronicle*. There were glints of silver in the air, like dew, and the buzz of the outdoor heaters on Enrico's terrace. Suki asked: "You tired? The end of the week and all?"

"No."

"Then," she remarked cheerfully, "I live—well, sort of stay—right up the steps over there, don't I?"

Wasn't it interesting and lucky that she was temporarily encamped just around the corner from Enrico's cafe on the Kearny steep of the hill?

I knew I shouldn't have. I knew I wanted to. I did.

I knew all good people on this misty spring evening in San Francisco should be discussing whether Richard Nixon would be rehabilitated in exchange for justifying the poisonous interest rates of the Jimmy Carter administration, and whether Ronald Reagan, who was too much of an actor to be taken seriously as governor of California, could really be accepted as President, Master-of-Ceremonies, and Best Friend of America—or at least, if we were serious people, we should be discussing the state of the newspapers of San Francisco or the destruction of architectural scale downtown or the release of the violent crazies on the streets; and Suki agreed with me about what we should be discussing, except that she had a few more ideas—the aimlessness of adolescents like her son, for example, and the blandness of most of the people she met, the white-wine-and-Brie people for whom Armenian flat bread was a big adventure, because they were too scared to take any real chances, and, ah, the other big ideas.

"Which ones?"

"Tell you later," she said. "Let's hurry."

Tugging each other up the stone steps, touching and bumping, this was passionate intensity heavily shaded with the giggles. Later that evening I decided our haste may have saved me from serious harm, assault, injury, the embarrassment of being murdered. First the Kearny steps, then the wooden stairway that led to the flat she shared with the distinguished black architect and city planner not scheduled to come home from his professional meeting in Chicago until tomorrow. Into a kind of guest and workroom we fell, wriggling and twisting. Clothes off, impatiently helping each other. A futon unfolded on the floor. My clothes in a careless heap beside the Japanese foam mat. . . . I remember a spindly drafting table, the struts of track lighting equipment, a vague gleam of enlarged photographs of buildings and a lavender plan, slightly askew, tacked to a cork board on the wall. Since we were using natural light—that is, the streetlamp through the filmy willow leaves outside—I didn't examine Jarod Howe's professional equipment in any detail. This time it did not have that healthy massage feeling. Either the Irish coffee had had a distinguishing, specifying effect on her or I had done her an injustice or last night she had just been shy, didn't know me, expressed herself by a certain abstention. Tonight was different.

Afterward, a few hums and murmurs and general praisings of life as the festival it was meant to be. We let the words fit our breathing, however it came out; we had been intelligent enough for one evening. We began the swift fall into sleep.

Didn't get far. A sudden rattle of doorknob down the wooden stairs, a bump of traveling bag and briefcase, and Suki hissing into my ear: "Jarod! He wasn't due till tomorrow, oh, he always *does* this to me!"

"Unh." My breath must have smelled of pure terror.

"Don't move," she commanded. *"Don't move."*

She glided off and away, silent, swift, and intentional. At the moment I was impervious to the grace of her narrow and silky behind. I heard a deep laugh of surprise. He sounded powerful. I heard welcoming sounds, heartfelt greetings. Through the half-closed door I heard and saw lights flash on, flash off; refrigerator door open, shut; a can popped. More giggles and murmurs and the architect and city planner's surprised words, "Bare-assed! Sometimes you get kind of affectionate when you miss me, don't you, baby?"

As their bodies thumped toward the bedroom, I ran through my several emotions until I found gratitude. Clever, sweet, considerate Suki. She was tucking him into sleep as she had done to me. And all to save me from embarrassment—what a nice person she was.

Of course, she really cared for me. Jarod was just the man she lived with these days and he had a nasty habit of coming home early from his business trips.

I lay there thinking. Soon the sounds subsided. It didn't take too long. Conventions, meetings, travel, late Sunday nights are hard on a practicing architect and city planner, I suppose; tuckered him out, all those time zone changes. There was deep breathing, slow, rhythmical, peaceful, restful; two kinds of it, his and hers— restful for *them*.

I lay there not finished thinking. It was time for some sort of action because, in the way of all flesh, I felt an urgent interest in relieving myself. Real life is like that. I couldn't rehearse all my options in detail, had to be a doer and a mover. I slipped into my clothes, hearing the hiss of thigh against corduroy like a storm in my ears; everything but my boots. It took a few minutes. Well-worn though they might be, my Sunday evening jeans were not equipped with silencers. Cotton corduroy was the loudest sound in the room. I carried the boots. Slowly, slowly, down the stairs, settling with each incipient creak, hoping to be taken for a cricket. At the doorknob I paused. Turned it slowly. Surprising how slowly and silently a person can turn a doorknob when his life is at stake. Outside, under the willow tree that grew in the little worn patch between the house and the Kearny steps, I glanced upstairs. No noise, no light, no scurry or rush. A bent moon overhead, plus the streetlamp, plus the adrenaline that had replaced most of the blood, plasma, spleen, and saliva in my body, cleared my eyes. Not having peed, I still had to pee; and here in the middle of the night, I didn't think like a good citizen. I peed under the tree, but since it was the steep slope of Telegraph Hill running down to the Broadway strip in North Beach, a narrow river began coursing and twisting and bouncing down the steps. It caught the moonlight, steaming in the coolness. In my selfish need I had neglected to consider the force of gravity. I finished and hastened to the other side of the street (just a visitor in town, not responsible for plumbing errors, sudden showers; who, me, Officer?).

By the time I reached my Fiat, ready to head across the Bay Bridge to my cottage in the Berkeley hills, I was ready for sleep again. I glanced out over the middle-of-the-night stillness. A dog poking in some trash; a cat; another. A Chinese kid either traveling on Hong Kong time or looking for an automobile to hot-wire. A stir of branches in fresh streamlets of fog heading east out of the Golden Gate. I remembered the definition of the bachelor—comes home from a different direction every morning—and decided this was a tiring procedure. Fatigue sets in. The poking dogs and cats are better equipped for it.

I drove home with a yellow one-dollar-off pizza notice flapping under my windshield wiper. Free soft drink of choice with purchase Tues/Thurs.

I slept deeply and gratefully, with perhaps a little resentment submerged down there someplace. I was awakened by the telephone. "Where'd you go?" Suki inquired.

"Where'd I go!"

"I mean, when we got up I figured the best thing was to tell him. He didn't mind too much. I made breakfast for the three of us, but then I went in to wake you—it's like you were never here, Frank. And I warmed these nice bran muffins for three!"

"Got home alive," I said.

"Well," she said, "then we'll just have to have breakfast with Jarod another time."

"Jarod," I said. "Jarod?"

"Oh, it's all right, dear. We have a faithful relationship of total fidelity within a radius of two hundred miles. I mean, if either of us is more than two hundred miles away, we can do anything we want. So how was I to know he was wending his way home a day early? After I explained, he understood. In fact, I think we both learned something from the experience."

"What did you learn?"

"Keep each other informed of changes in our travel plans, darling."

I apologized for not joining them for breakfast. Instead, I chewed at a three-day-old crust of whole wheat bagel with instant coffee and bachelor milk from the box. The morning was shot, and I'm a morning worker. Sometimes education and the independent life get in the way of morning working.

Trying to summarize the problems of savings and loan mergers in California while thinking evil thoughts about Suki was difficult, but finally, toward the middle of the day, I told myself that people who call other people names are stupid, vindictive creeps. Gradually I calmed down. I lied to myself. I told myself it was morning, not afternoon, and did my day's work.

When next I saw Suki, she cheerfully filled me in on the news. She and Jarod had come to a parting of the ways. There had been a debate about the radius theory of fidelity, whether a person measured from his office in the Embarcadero or her house in Cow Hollow, and how to factor time into the deal. What if, for example, a person was not two hundred miles away, but was gone for more than three nights? What can a person do for health and fun and spirit under such circumstances? Why should geography be the only criterion of fidelity? For example, five hundred miles away, but only for a day? Or one hundred miles for three long days? A person could get lonely. Another person could get tuckered out. How to measure these things sensibly?

"In my opinion," she said, "I don't want to be tied down—"

Suki's opinions were vivid and pressing. I didn't need to hear the entire analysis. I accepted the spirit of her quest for justice, comfort, and grace.

My friend Victor was worried about me. He felt I was losing ground in some competition which he saw and I didn't. To me it was not a battle; it brought the vividness that had been missing in my life. I didn't enjoy the doldrums, the middle-aged doldrums, and here was Suki to lift me out and give me the kiss of life, or the slap, or the bite, or just the eager and urgent clutch of her intelligence. How could I not be grateful, how could I not follow as long as I could?

"Be careful whom you marry," Victor said— he had these little sayings, "because marriage is only for a little while, but divorce is forever."

"I'm not marrying. I'm not even—I don't know if I'm even in love."

"Bewitched then. How about fascinated?"

"Granted. I stipulate that."

"You'll do whatever she wants."

"She doesn't mean me any harm, Victor."

"Of course not. Does the avalanche decide to bury the skier?"

I liked her son and the boy liked me. Since I didn't have a son, it gave me a peculiar twinge of desire, of nostalgia for what I didn't have, to watch Peter playing with his tools in the garage —little motors, radios he took apart, a bike he cleverly put back together. "Peter, I could never do that, it's just amazing."

He blushed and swaggered a little. "Mom gave me a clock when I was young"—he had just

turned fifteen—"I got it all out on newspapers
and then I made it run again. I still have it. The
alarm works. It's got a face on it, Frank."

"I'll bet everybody you know has digital."

"Some of my friends had to *learn* to read faces,
they grew up with digital."

"Listen," I said, "you could come to my cottage in Berkeley and spend a day and I'll bet
everything would work again. I don't understand that stuff at all. Do you fix leaks, too?"

He looked up from his electronic motor kit,
his hands smeared with oil, and said, "When?
When can I do that?" He touched his face and
there was a light smear of oil on his cheek.
"Frank, when can I spend a day at your place?"

Suki came out through the garden to call me
in for afternoon tea. She didn't call Peter, but he
assumed he was invited. She didn't ask him to
wash his hands and face but she asked him if he
was bothering me. The kid shrugged and looked
at me until I said, "How could he? You see how
he's attaching that motor to the bike? He's a ma-
gician."

"Mom, Frank says I can go to Berkeley and
spend a day—"

Suki told him to watch out for being ridiculous, and then what she gave the boy as examples
of ridiculousness were Gerald Ford and waffles.
She told him not to expect her friends to spend a
whole Saturday or Sunday entertaining a kid,
even if he was terrific with household and yard
machinery. "I mean it," I said, "Peter and I are

friends. I could use some help, I could." He flashed me a brilliant and grateful smile.

Suki told him the reason she hadn't asked him to wash up before his snack was that he could take his waffles out to the garage if he wanted to. Also he could stay in the house if he wanted, but then he would have to wash up. The choice was his.

"I guess I'd like to finish and put everything away before tonight," he said.

"Good fellow," she said. "You're the best son a person could have."

She watched him carry his plate out through the garden. She ran after him with the honey and jam and melted butter. Then, when she came back, she shut the glass doors and pulled the curtains and gave another example of ridiculous. "Lovemaking is the worst," she said. "Why should I have two breasts and you two balls? I want them, Frank! But I don't have to take them from you, do I"—the glint of grin and teeth, the light pressure of fingers and nails—"since I've got them now."

"Hey, watch it. Isn't Peter likely to come back into the house?"

"He *knows* when I shut the doors. *And* pull the curtains. Stop being so nervous. Now as I was showing and telling, dear—"

She liked to play with peoples' parts. She liked people to kiss around the place where her invisible parts hung.

"Another thing," she explained. "I like gay

men to make love to me. They have a good attitude. Sometimes two of them. Of course, there's the medical problem—"

"Okay," I said, "maybe we should get up and make some more waffles."

"No, really." She sucked her lower lip, she kissy-kissed me back down. "I like it not to be deep, Frank, but then I want it to be deep."

"That's a problem."

"That's really a problem, Frank." And she was lost in thoughts that were none of my business. She said what she wanted to say and then she stopped. Those were the rules.

Peter stayed out the rest of the afternoon and finished attaching a motor to an old balloon-tire bike he'd found in a junk shop down on Turk Street in the Tenderloin. He too seemed to know the rules in Suki's household. She allowed him his freedom because he was so bright, so capable, and they lived in the real world. She wanted to give him the same respect she gave herself.

"Hey, Frank?" she said. "Get up, wake up, go talk to Peter while I have a shower, okay?"

Groggily I went out to admire his work. "Maybe I could ride this across the bridge," he said. "You think they'd let me?"

"I don't know the vehicular code, but it's terrific. You might need a license."

"Did you mean it?"

I understood what he was asking. "I really meant it, Peter. You're invited."

He watched me, plinking spokes on a wheel.

Suki had a theory about Peter. Since he was the most important thing in the world to her, she owed him the same respect she gave herself. She tried not to interfere with his raising of himself. Her theory was part of the general deal she made—noninterfering consistency. To smother him, as so many mothers did, was a tendency she did not have.

In your own way you have it, I said.

She answered with her usual friendly firmness: In my own way I *don't*.

If she insisted she was not overpowering, who was I to try to make a case for it? Anyway, she didn't live by theories; only offered me one about Peter because I seemed so interested. Personally, she preferred to live by her knowledge that the past was past, the future was whatever she made of it, and today was the vivid and crucial part. She allowed her son to follow his own path. It was my fault for almost bringing it up.

"Almost," I said, and laughed. "You're the biggest thing in laissez faire since—"

"That was a good song," she said. "Let it be, let it be. But I guess you're right, since he's my love, I do have a theory about Peter."

It seemed to me that I could hear the squeak of crisp little hearts breaking all over San Francisco, including Marin and the Peninsula, as Suki trampled down the regiments of men. I tried to keep alert and cautious, but vividness in a time of doldrum is hard to refuse. No pain no gain, I told Victor.

"There's a lot of gain?" he asked.

His question had a point. As time went on, there was a different kind of doldrum for me—hurt, loneliness, something that used to be jealousy—that's what it would be in a man less resolute than I was determined to become. My attitude needed to rise to Suki's standards.

Our love affair came to a halt without any quarrel. We went to bed—or in our case, to futon —a few more times. Things began to oppress me; her relentless good cheer, maybe. So much intelligent lightness weighed heavy on me. Maybe it was my fault. My own good cheer is occasional and fugitive. There were others in her life, probably several, all trimmer, cleverer, and richer than I was, but even if I acknowledged the inappropriateness of jealousy, it didn't lift my spirits. "I want to be your friend . . ." I said.

"Naturally! And we are! Good friends!" she cried. She took stock of what she had just said and lowered the brightness a little. She was aware and made sad little corners at her smile. It was something like dimples or parentheses or fasteners, closers. "Peter liked you better than anyone, which I think is a sign of character in both of you. You're two of my favorite men, always will be."

So as it worked out, Peter didn't spend any Saturdays looking over the household machinery at my cottage.

"Frank," Suki was saying, "it's been nice."

TWO

I wrote to my sister back in Detroit, only to say hello and we hadn't been in touch. This was a fact of which Dorry was fully aware. Suki had an unsettling effect on me; not jealousy, not desperation; she stirred up the old animals. "No reason," I said to my sister, calling her the same day my letter arrived, "just hello, hello."

Dorry replied that she now had three children and why didn't I have any? I ignored the jab and tried for the other side of family feeling. Our parents were long gone, we're all we have left, Dorry, shouldn't we meet?

"We *have* met," she said.

"Oh, come on, Dorry," I said. I promised to visit her and the three children and the husband any day now. Any year now, is what I thought.

"Thanks for the Christmas card, Frank," she said. "Cutest one I got, whenever it was."

I also remembered the woman I almost married in Detroit and almost called her, too, but didn't want to hear about Palmer Park, the Caucus Club, and that clever little bowling alley on Woodward near Wayne State where we hid out from the man who had actually been her husband at the time. Our love was served up along with thumping bowling sounds. She didn't divorce him. I asked her once or twice, but maybe I didn't insist. Then someone else pushed a bit and she did divorce and remarry and I considered revisiting what I had lost. After the call to Dorry, I decided to save this excitement for another time.

I even looked at the masthead of the *Detroit News* to see who was still there. Fresh down from Ann Arbor with a B.A. in Sixties Head and Sit-In Studies, I had thought I was destined to be a star of daily journalism—thought it so brightly that the paper did, too—and I moved into ten years of feature writing, three or four broadening, expense-accounted trips a year, and the promise of someday taking on the column vacated by W.K. Kelsey. But punditry was not my line. I waited till I got my year as a Nieman fellow at Harvard—more broadening. And then California and teaching and an occasional freelance piece seemed not an unworthy destination for a journalist who lacked that blood taste in his mouth, too much preoccupied with his orphaned youth, his notion that a good woman might make him vivid to himself as he entered his forties. It turned out to be no woman for quite a while. Someday, when the haze cleared, I would take charge of a big subject. That was the intention.

I agreed with myself that Suki had unsettled me again. She was what California was supposed to be, even if she wasn't what I was supposed to be looking for in California. More than ten years in San Francisco and Berkeley and I was still the unborn pundit from Detroit who would someday either achieve all the fine things in life, such as love, useful fame, and a settled condition, or maybe not achieve them. In an unsettled state I had found a settled condition. At least I liked my work, it was useful, and I liked being healthy. I was lonely for a family.

Suki changed that. I gave her full credit.

Suddenly folks noticed that I had become a more devoted member of the academic community. I actually attended a meeting of the Faculty Senate. Fred McKnight, my dean, said, "Well, Frank, I'll be. Are you here as a reporter or do you really care about the future of journalism in this university?"

Deans are taller than people. I crouched a little and said, "Don't hit me. Maybe I'm just bucking for whatever there is to buck for around here."

"Some of our regents think journalism belongs in the trade schools, you know, not the Mother Campus."

"Don't expect me to agree, Fred."

He chuckled. This dean was chucklier than people, too. "Not to get me wrong, Frank. You personally are an ornament to this institution. Only trouble is, we've got so many ornaments, we could do without some of them—only kidding, Frank."

What good old Dean McKnight meant: It didn't seem right that, with an academic salary plus freelancing, I might pull down almost as much as a dean. (Wrong about that, Fred.)

I also accepted an invitation to a department barbecue in honor of a distinguished member of the *Columbia Journalism Review* board. I would probably have attended anyway, being fond of barbecue, all that good grease running down the face, but Suki left me a bit lonely, like an orphan again, and I found myself looking forward to any distraction, to my classes, even to my conferences with students. Since my old Detroit insomnia had returned, I bent over my students' papers in the middle of the night. The raccoons were at the garbage, the future reporters were at the word processors, and Suki was not there for me.

Yet she was a generous person, a good cook, an assiduous friend. She believed in conserving the ecology of her affairs, even those too weak to survive on their own. As she floated through lovers, or burrowed through them—each lover required a different engineering—she transformed them into companions. I was one of a collection. She invited an ever-increasing crew of lively folks to her little house on the edge of Pacific Heights for well-garlicked spaghetti with clam sauce, white wine, laughter. She majored in social graces; sexual avidity was only a minor, perhaps a subcategory of social graces. She spoke of hot tubs, racquetball, skiing, tennis, and working out in the same happy fashion she used for talking about love. Sex, for her, happened to include physical contact, relaxation, comfortable sleep, a buzz of contentment, a moment of meditation with the brain turned off, and a happy appetite for light munching. So it ranked right up near the top with massage. There was a touch of lust buried in there someplace, and I suppose some men, Frank Curtis, for example, might harbor a secret hope of igniting it. Suki herself didn't harbor that hope.

So be it. Occasionally, as a good friend to Suki and also to various male friends who were going through marital disasters, I introduced her to someone new. Everyone was impressed with her clean lively look, her quick spicy smells, her eager laughter. She was a listener, a talker, but not an interferer. She knew what she liked and she liked things a lot. She always announced very early that her son came first. She was clear when it came to values. No one failed to be grateful for clarity and fun, even Sam Webster.

But Sam Webster was different. "I prefer to transact business," he said. He was rich. He was smart. He was black. I knew him because he set up a minority media project in the journalism department at Berkeley, just drove over from Oakland one day and said, "Everybody in the papers tell lies, it's even worser on the TV, I want some of my own people get a piece of this action. What do you call it, interns? We get these kids off the streets and teach them a trade. Tell their lies and the Man say, 'Okay, great, good lies, you can type, go work for the *Oakland Tribune.*'"

I had laughed and asked him if he really wanted better press or television coverage.

"I got none, that's the beauty part," he said.

"Then what's the problem?"

"No *problem*, man, everything copacetic. I just mean not every kid can be a runner. I mean some of them wear glasses, you know what I mean? Kid got a good voice, don't want to sing in no Baptist choir, let him be an anchor man. Hey, you want my money?"

I liked him. I thought he might like Suki and he did, and I thought she might like Sam and she did. They took to preferring each other. This could be another "main man." "When I'm not occupied in my transacting," he said, "I appreciate a good time."

His transactions seemed to require South American and European travel. I had a sense that the business part was in South America and the European leg of the journey was just a nice way to get home. Suki liked to transact a little skiing in Switzerland on the road back from Colombia and Peru. Sam was willing. A sweet-tem-

pered person himself, he appreciated Suki's good
nature and how she didn't pry too much into his
transactions, past, present, or future. He wasn't
used to women who had their own agendas in
mind—unlike others who sometimes wanted to
carry things they shouldn't carry and be cut into
his profits. It was a good deal for both of these
independent souls.

Neither of them would have fallen in love,
grief, or special pain had it not been for Suki's
one little habit of liking to include the entire
known world in the long-running dinner theater
and operetta of her life. She had fine, bare,
tanned shoulders and arms; her gesturing was
wide and inclusive. At a pool in Montreux, Switzerland, she spied a skinny little Italian blond
with whom she thought she might have a lot in
common. It turned out she did. The skinny little
Italian blond, with her round blue eyes, liked
Sam and zapped him with her baby looks.
Though they had no language in common besides their distant outposts of English—East
Oakland elegant and Turino finishing school
Holy Sisters of St. Bridget of Liverpool—they
managed to exchange addresses.

Sam remained the complete gentleman he always intended to be. He delivered Suki back to
San Francisco before he began taking Gala on
his business trips to South America.

Something about this new transaction—her
time in life, Peter growing up, a blip in the
soul's spansule, a sudden leakage of jealousy

from the watertight compartment—brought
Suki to fierce pains and fevers. She realized, or
thought she did, that it had been true love between Sam Webster and her. Retroactive love is
ruthless. She was desperate with loss, she cried,
cursed, she wailed with rage. Since I was responsible for introducing them, I listened to the details. She adored him now. She wished to destroy him. I was unwilling to arrange the latter
and could do nothing about the former.

Instead, I tried comfort and distraction. I offered to take her to dinner. She could talk about
her problem. She was pale, stricken, deprived of
appetite, but consented to order a little food and
leave it untouched. She sipped her white wine.
Her lips and eyes glistened. Rage flowed. Sam
was a rotten lover. People think black guys are
special, but in her experience, only some of them
are. During the time she was with Sam, she continued to see other lovers, who were much better at getting down to it, at quilt-and-pillow talk,
at hugging and snuggling, at all the good stuff
that does its part to make life worthwhile. "Even
you," she said, "were better than Sam."

I murmured protest. Such compliments and
rankings were not what I sought from her. I suggested that sex has something to do with the
meeting of minds, that one person's great lover
might be mediocre with a different partner.

"He's so *cold.*" she said. "He just doesn't care.
It's rush and go with him. I never enjoyed him
that much."

"So you're well rid of him," I suggested.

"But how could he do that to me? We had such fun together. Nobody was ever as good to him as I was"—exaggeration of history is a mark of retroactive sincerity—"as I wanted to be, anyway, if only he'd let me. He's the man I truly wanted."

"You have a problem?" I asked. "I mean, if he was rotten in all those ways, why do you want him?"

"I don't!" she cried. "But I did. And oh, I still do."

Oh, she still did. There was no means of avoiding sympathy for her. Grief is real even when the occasion seems not what another, non-grief-stricken person might consider appropriate. The code for how people should tell about their sadness is not strictly defined. There is still individual initiative here. Light Suki, mother of one, disappointed lover, was discovering the common pains.

I thought to lead her to different thoughts by taking her on a tour of San Francisco, a little walk, a meal, maybe a coffee or a drink in the picturesque lesbian village off Mission on Valencia. I thought she might be interested. Just for a change. It wasn't to offer her new pleasures and sorrows, but simply to call to her attention that there are many ways through life, how time rolls forward, there are other people in the world with their own issues and concerns, which they take seriously. We are not alone. Suki was not alone in the universe to suffer her pangs.

She didn't seem to be paying attention.

Notice the redwood shingled office of the Feminist Prison Collective. See how the police patrol cars have women officers. Pay attention to the Bent Can Food Surplus, "All-Organic Damaged Merchandise." Those women with their arms around each other really care. "Legal Services, Single Mothers and Job Harassment." Suki, there is turmoil amid the resolute new peace. "El Salvador and Nicaragua to the Fore! Latinas Arise!" What do you suppose, Suki, that storefront is about?

Her pale brow was furrowed with thought. How sweet and sad she looked in her Esprit T-shirt, which hung a little loose these days. When a person weighs just the right amount, to the ounce, she mustn't lose whole pounds.

Suki was sharing no insights this evening concerning the march of socialism and the betrayal of the revolution by China's male oligarchy. "The Koven of Four Speaks for the Broad Masses?" It was immaterial to her.

"He's petty," she said. "He's small. He has lots of money, but what if he has no class?"

"Look at that bookstore," I said. "They allow children—no men. Do you want to go inside? Poems, stories, personal accounts, even geography, all about the Problem. I'll wait on the sidewalk."

"He's infantile. He's not a real man. I gave him a chance, but he destroyed it."

"How about a cup of coffee?" I asked.

"He may be doing something illegal. We both know that. He kept a lot of secrets."

"Are you thinking of revenge? Is that really like you?"

"I never really cared for him. He's not my type. Frank, I can't stand being without him."

Tears. Predictable Suki always managed to surprise me—tears flowed. Her eyes were red and swollen. We sat near the ferns in a sunny corner of the Alice James Coffee Matrix. A lovely young waitperson in a sixties grannie dress glided back and forth, serving cappucino, serving fresh-squeezed orange and carrot juice, serving homemade oatmeal raisin cookies, serving the People, not serving us. She was truly a nurturing person, but not for me. After we sat awhile in this real estate of revolutionary statement, I said, "I don't think they're going to—can you think of a reason why, Suki?"

This was a test of her awareness of surroundings.

"He's good at making money, but not at being a genuine feeling caring responsive individual."

After a while, with no check to pay because no food or drink had been offered, we moved on. Suki failed to notice that she had not partaken. True love is unaware of the petty appetites. The lovely femme in the nurturing Sixties granny dress bestowed upon me a smile of heartbreaking sincerity and vengeance.

As we strolled down the street in the early evening, Suki took my arm. She fit her step to mine. She put her head close to my shoulder and surprised me by seeming to know in what year, city, continent, and district of San Francisco fate happened to have dropped her. "These women around here, they're missing something," she said.

And then she began to recite how happy she had been with Sam and how he had ruined it all by his foolishness.

Like a spreading stain, Suki's fanatic disappointment in Sam Webster surrounded and washed over me. How could I suggest it was a waste when I had judged her for failure to allow the darker feelings in? This loss could mark the beginning of something fine; she didn't like it, didn't require that kind of fine. Telling her that loss and grief are good for the soul was a time-tested, unproductive procedure. She had other plans for her soul and didn't require interruptions.

I too was made uneasy. Always effective with what she set out to do, she was good at making me feel accountable. But after I gave her the chance to talk, tell about her hurt, let it up the chimney again, and she was thinking I could be a conduit—that I could convince Sam to return —we temporarily suspended our friendship. We

Herbert Gold

would avoid each other for a while. Someday, of
course, we would resume.

She sent Christmas good wishes printed on a
color photo of herself and Peter smiling in front
of the fireplace. I sent her an American Greetings card.

She gave her large New Year's party without
me. I understood.

Nella Rodgers, who had a tavern in North
Beach, closed the place one Monday for a wel-
come-home-from-Baja party for Suki and I was
not on the list. Well, returning from Baja is not
one of the great traditional religious festivals.

She telephoned. She wanted to talk. She described missing me in lively, happy, reproachful
terms; I meant so much to her. I'd heard she
now had a psychiatrist lover and interrupted to
ask if all was going well. "I have four of them,"
she said.

"Four psychiatrists?"

She trilled with her cool, slim, annunciatory
laughter. "Four lovers. Only one is a shrink."

"Oh, sorry."

"And funny thing, he's not the one who
knows the most about me."

"That's normal, Suki. Maybe he's the serious
lover."

"They're all serious, my dear. It's interesting
how they don't find out about each other. Three
of them don't. But one knows about all the others—not the shrink, the carpenter. He's the one
I can talk to. He's not very jealous."

"You probably picked the right one to confide in."

"Not a regular carpenter, Frank. He does fine cabinetwork. He gives great veneer. He'd be a rich man, a world-famous artist in restoration of French provincial, except he stays up late."

"Stays up late and that hurts his career?"

"Stays up late doing coke and that's expensive. But he's so understanding most of the time."

"Terrific."

"Too bad I don't like him best except to talk to."

She was wrapping me into her life again on the telephone, weaving her spells of charm and complication. I began to limit my answers to agreements and assents. When she asked how I was, I said fine. "Can't we meet?" she asked.

"We *have* met," I said.

"Oh, Frank, that's what I like about you—independent. I need a man like you in my life."

Since she already enjoyed a quartet, she thought she might engage a quintet, including a retreaded baritone. She had so much to tell that a telephone could no longer do justice. Peter was growing up, for example. The light of her life was attaching bigger motors to bicycles these days. He had a secret social life. He said he missed seeing me for breakfast now and then—Peter really liked me.

I invited her to meet me at the Old Spaghetti Factory & Cafe, but it had finally closed forever, so we sat at an outdoor table at the Savoy Tivoli

on upper Grant, talking over recent old times.
Had it really been two years since we'd first
met? Or three? The Spaghetti Factory was gone
and Sam Webster had departed and I was still
leaning forward across the table to catch the
least laugh from Suki, to breathe the perfume of
her breath, to marvel at the teasing, self-depre-
cating conviction of her gossip about herself.
The years were going by and time didn't matter
and life must continue to be a festival and it was
especially very important because now that's all
there was.

"My God, you don't remember if it's two
years or three, Frank? I remember the date."

"It was Valentine's Day."

"So maybe it doesn't really matter which year,
does it? If you haven't lost too much protein
mass."

"They say Ronald Reagan still loves to arm
wrestle. One of my students did a story about a
bar in Richmond—"

"We're just as much from California as Ronald
Reagan is, probably more so." She looked at me
with narrowed eyes across the table. A thought
had struck her and she was amazed. When life is
a festival, there are bound to be surprises.
"Frank, I can't believe it, have you been brooding about me?"

"No one forgets you, Suki."

"Oh, boy, if only! I admit I brood about myself sometimes, but that doesn't mean other people have to."

She held her cup and tasted the foam on the cappucino and didn't say anything about how cappucino foam was a thing a person could never get too much of. She was also silently tasting our meeting of minds. She didn't have to speak; words are not sufficient for old friends and lovers, anyway; the fondness was part of the sizzle of outdoor heaters, the smell of coffee and cinnamon, the low murmur of other conversations. She wanted to be a bit sad tonight and here I was, all ready for her. There was a sharp speculation and measurement in her glance and she waited before making her confession. She hoped I was worthy of it. Sadness was okay, but moroseness would be going too far. "You're okay, Frank?"

"Fine, just fine. Missed you, Suki."

"That's a help. Missed you too, but—"

Her shrug. That's just how it was. I wanted to live in hope and desire, and now desire and memory had come to be on her mind these days. People had their seasons, they passed each other going in different directions, but then it turns out the world is round and you see each other heading back.

She wanted me to catch up with her life. Because I was steady in a world where many men didn't know about the roundness of things and seemed just to fall off the edge, she could tell me a piece of her truth—tonight she could, anyway —and trust me to know there are limits. I wouldn't press her. It didn't give me any rights.

47

She didn't put up with being pressed; surely I had learned that much about her in these years of following my routines, watching her from Berkeley and gossip and a distance, trusting her to remain what she was.

It didn't mean she would always be the same, as a former lover in his foolish moroseness might think. Even Suki knew it was necessary to move with the changes that could not be stopped. Festivals can darken because of matters beyond a person's control; weather, health, a son, a quirk of metabolism, a momentary failing like her error with Sam Webster. Although ease and balance are supposed to be normal, fevers exist and a person can't deny them.

She was learning, it seemed. History was writing its messages on the perfect fair envelope in which Suki was wrapped. She had a crucial birthday coming. She was a person who admitted her birthdays. Openly defying the years was a matter of ardent deep principle, was a rock and foundation. Everybody should have at least one such principle.

She continued the conversation. "How can a person—?"

"You look wonderful."

Impatiently she shook her head. "No, please," she said. "I'm getting older every year, just like everybody else."

"That's only a rumor, Suki."

She tapped her fingertips against the table. She did not want me to make nice. There's a

time for flattery and flirtation and this was not
it. She had forgiven me about Sam. She had forgotten him. Here is how much she had succeeded in forgetting him: Sometimes she even
chose to remember him, if she happened to want
to bring a little ridiculousness into her life. It
was healthy to mock herself. It even threw other
people off balance, like a yielding aikido move.
Well, it was more important than a clever move.
It was a reminder. She didn't choose to be ex-
empt. Even if life is a festival, some of the festivals must celebrate disasters. That's history, and
Suki was in favor of it.

She allowed Sam to be her disaster and then
she allowed Suki to celebrate her convalescence.
She knew about love and loss, loneliness and the
midnight regrets, and she was brave about these
things, and she wanted other people to understand her. The master-carpenter coke-sniffer was
a good listener, but she wasn't sure he was jealous enough to be a good lover. He paid attention, but he didn't rant and pout. "How can a
person find a person who really cares?" she
asked.

"I can't say."

"Have I got a ways to go?"

"Think so, Suki."

We touched cups with this modest contribu-
tion to understanding. She had reached the time
of philosophy. It was a temporary condition perhaps, but no less real. "People who don't love are

missing something," she said. And then she lowered her eyes, her face closed down, her lips damp and trembling with a terrible suspicion. "Do you think it's better to miss it?"

THREE

As sometimes happened, even after our love affair ended, when she was lonely and I was lonely and one of us thought of telephoning the other, and neither of us had any better plan in mind, I spent the night with her. I guess this is why, for me, the months and the nearly seasonless seasons of San Francisco slipped by almost like the time of a long marriage. She had a fixed location in my life. I didn't even need for her to know how important she was, and if she had known, she might have ended it. Perhaps for her time didn't move either, but her reasons were Suki's, not Frank's. No obligation, no responsibility; just what felt right and helped clear our separate orbits through the solar system. My way was mine, a secret to be kept from her, since her procedures were hers and only Suki set the rules for herself.

I assented. We were kind friends, interested, alert, enjoying each other's company—it couldn't have been love. I tried to understand Suki's procedures. Only people who were *not* lovers could be so comfortable together here and there, now and then, easing each other into sleep under cozy quilts, with fine linen sheets in warm weather and flannel sheets when the January rains pelted down.

Then in the morning she bustled about, always lively before her coffee, as if the mere smell of it brought her up into full enthusiasm. Coffee, good Graffeo Colombian, was a more reliable pleasure than love. She trimmed grapefruit for me and her son with a twisty little grapefruit-trimming knife. She liked tools—also a shinier and more reliable pleasure than men. The boy watched her with his proud, shy, clever little smile. And then, on this day, she hurried off to work—"Bye bye! Bye, all!"—clattering and swift and gone. She left me to finish breakfast with Peter.

I gave Peter the sports and the comics. He handed me the news and the business sections. Neither of us read the cereal boxes, because Suki had also left poached eggs as a little surprise. She liked to distribute nice surprises like poached eggs in the morning.

Peter stared at the shivering eggs on the counter with adolescent distaste. "She makes these things in a gizmo looks like a diaphragm," he said.

"Now how does a sixteen-year-old know what a diaphragm looks like?"

"Seventeen," he said. "You missed my birthday, you owe me a shirt or something. I saw one over in the Women's Museum in Berkeley."

"I didn't know you liked museums."

"Everybody I know uses the Pill, that itchy foam, or"—sarcastically—"the male learns to take responsibility."

"The boy, in your case."

"Mom had her tubes tied, so you don't have to do anything for her when you're acting like a boy, Frank."

"I'm not so old, Peter. So far I'm only forty or so—forty-three, to be exact."

He looked at me with amusement. *Typical.* All the middle-aged farts in his experience tried to be young—the guys who fluttered around his mother, coming and staying for breakfast and going.

I think he really meant it about wanting to collect his birthday present from me, although he had a repertory of clothes with snaps, zippers, epaulets, and the pockets within pockets that the Teenage Fashion Police had prescribed for that year—a combination of Bolivian Air Force officer with Japanese tea ceremony gown. He had set up rules of behavior for his mother's former lovers; a lover-in-law three or seven or a dozen times removed, which was my category, owed him, minimum, an all-natural-fiber item of costuming.

It was a school holiday, Martin Luther King, Jr.'s birthday. This meant that Suki went to work anyway; I went to read midterm papers and meet students anyway—the assignment was to hang out in an all-night diner in Oakland and describe what they saw; and Peter went to work on his cycle in the backyard. "Got to make some changes," he said.

At first I thought he meant the little Suzuki motorcycle, pedals or gears or electrical connections, but I didn't know exactly what he meant to change and maybe it wasn't about the Suzuki. Well, why not, to pay tribute to Martin Luther King, Jr., I might as well take an hour to talk to a poor oppressed white boy in the Cow Hollow-Pacific Heights section of San Francisco while he worked on one of his toys. That's a time when he doesn't have to meet your eyes, when a kid might lay out what is really on his mind.

Perhaps I didn't really want to know what was on Peter's mind. It turned out it wasn't the Suzuki after all. It was his old Schwinn bicycle he was playing with. The kid had mechanical aptitude, no doubt an inherited talent, shared with a mother who zipped around the daredevil routines of her life, putting a breakfast, a garden, or a love affair in order with skill and pride in workmanship. He had the same cool eyes with higher geometry encoded into the genes. Suki never even kissed bumpers when she fit into a tight parking spot.

I watched him attach a tiny device to the

Schwinn. He was continuing to motorize his fleet of bicycles, the hobby I'd seen him start a few years ago. He had sold a dozen of them already. When he tested it, the engine went spinning and buzzing. It looked like a whirring nest of hairpins. Peter's arms were shapely and tanned, his eyes were dark and intense, the brows furrowed; the fuzz of adolescent mustache above his tensed lip was pathetic. This beautiful boy would be a gangly creature for a while, and then a too-handsome young man. He had abruptly grown older behind my back, perhaps behind Suki's, without giving notice. I remembered my invitation to spend a day at my house in Berkeley. It should have happened. Now it seemed too late; the kid was tough, gleaming with teenage secrets. I should have persisted, but the permutations of friendship with Suki made it unclear what connection I had with her son. By now he had other things on his mind besides fixing my old Zenith FM radio and taking apart the refectory dishwasher.

He had bought a new kit by mail, he was constructing a faster motorbike; he was rediscovering the wheel. He liked figuring it out. The motor had been designed for something else. His feet crunched on gravel—as close to a snow sound as he knew out here. Since he skied, snow was only a resort pleasure, produced, as far as he knew, by snow kits for the enjoyment of ski consumers.

The bicycle spokes twanged like guitar

strings. He said under his breath, "Shit, shit," and then glanced up at me with a dazzling smile. He jumped on the seat in his faded Levi's, bouncing up and down, reaching for the little insect of a motor to see if it was cool, if it was cool to reach for it like that; and then swung his long legs off and bent to go on fiddling and adjusting and praying: "Shit, shit, shit."

Some of Suki's gay friends found him cute, all right. Even I could see he was cute, although he was too old for me to use the word. I was in the other, heterosexual category of Suki's occasional companions. Each of us served in our various fashions—some plowing and irrigating her garden, some confiding, telling the gossip, keeping track of the new pleasures in town. I trusted Peter knew the difference.

Yet he flirted with me, wearing crotch-torn jeans, after I spent the night with her. I wondered if he had any luck with her previous one-night tenants, or the occasional week-long tenant, and if such luck was good or bad.

He was not effeminate, just desperate for love, like a girl needing a father. And like his mother, Peter wielded his brightly acquisitive eyes for both seeing and being seen; and then sometimes, when they fluttered away, for being not seen. No, he was not a normal boy who was not yet sure if he wanted to make love with men or women. He was a boy who was sure he wanted to be as successful with men as his mother was. I doubted, even with all his prettiness, he could manage that trick.

"My mother's fishy," he said, and made a fish mouth, a kissy mouth. "I'm her pet aquarium."

"Actually," I said, "the bowl is the aquarium, and the fish are inside it."

He stared at me, fluttering his fish mouth, clever kid, showing the fleshy, fishy quiver; did not acknowledge the correction to his vocabulary. Maybe this was an acknowledgment.

"Is it hard for you?" I asked. Like a pale, owlish, psychiatric uncle, feeling pale and psychiatric, I leaned on the bicycle seat. Nonchalant, was I?

He grimaced. "I just wiggle my lips together, fold my tongue over, it's not hard for me." And his laughter was high and shrill.

He knew that wasn't the question. Clever lad; nice tricks of a boy in the morning sun. Since he had picked me to be his special friend among all his mother's friends and occasional breakfast companions, I had better think carefully before asking questions that would encourage him. Watch out, Frank.

"Lots of things are hard for me," he said, bending to the bicycle saddle and poking at it with a tiny wrench. "I mean, when you were young, they just had sex. Now they got Safe Sex. We got to get organized and think about it. We got to figure out when it's okay to work up from Safe Sex to Good Sex."

"Yeah, there are some new diseases. Is that

57

something the kids at school are worrying about
these days?"

"Hey, no. I just like talking to you, Frank. Nobody lives forever, I don't waste my time worrying, I just like talking to you."

"Maybe we ought to talk about what's on your
mind then."

"Okay, okay," he said. "Main thing is, Frank:
You're a big fraction for Mom and a big fraction
for me and that makes you a *big* fraction."

"What does that mean?"

He grimaced at his hand where the wrench
had slipped and drawn a little blood. He grinned
and licked it. "Okay, main thing is, I stop making my best fraction nervous, so we'll talk about
business, Frank."

Before he took up bicycle motors, Peter had
thought of franchising breakfast restaurants,
Castle of Krispies, with a menu from Post, Kellogg's, and the Granola Bros. Once I asked him
if his high school started kids on MBA's and he
said, "Hunh?" as indeed he should have. "We'll
use real melocream or dairy substitute for diet-
ers," he said, "and there's a sweetener too—not
sugar—'LoCal Breakfasts All Day.'"

"It's an idea," I said. "I never wanted to go in
business, but lots of people do."

"What would you think of a bicycle motor in-
stallation and repair service?" Peter asked. "Lots
of kids, you know, they don't need a license for a
moped or these things I can do, cheaper'n
mopeds. I'll bet I could sell every kid in school."

"What about the parents? It isn't safe to buzz up and down these hills."

"Safer'n coke, man. I bet it's safer'n spending your money on street drugs and *then* go buzzing off the hills."

"If that's the choice, Peter."

He grinned and winked. "This is outdoors. It's, well, pedal-aided, so it's exercise, go to the store for things, have fun. It's the choice, *Frank.*"

Somehow he was managing to turn a nice conversation into not so nice. This is a skill some people have.

For years Suki's son had been reviewing the parade of men at breakfast. Usually, I supposed, they tried to be friendly, sometimes sleepy or curious or even, the way men are, just wanting out so they could begin another part of their lives. For Peter, there may have been a kind of grace in this company. At times, anyway, and with some of the men. Perhaps I imagined grace to please myself. But at thirteen or fourteen, when he began to feel the greasy needs and to dream of pleasure, he could hardly have matched his own desires against what his mother was doing with her regiments of good soldiers. Could his mother and whoever—Jarod Howe or Sam Webster or Alfonso the detective or Frank Curtis or any of the others—have felt together what he felt?

I tried to remember what it was to be his age. Like every kid, he was dangerously unique, a peril to his own dreams. I imagined the soft light

of the sunrise through his curtains, waking him
to find new strangers having breakfast with his
mother. Sometimes an old stranger returned, or
stayed a while, passed through on Suki's road.
Some even came for light suppers with her, patted the boy on the head, showed tricks with
coins or smiles, told riddles, slept elsewhere.

Like the other men, I hadn't thought too
much about Peter. He wasn't on our minds
when Suki anointed us, invited us to avoid the
night drive home, awarded us a good breakfast
in the morning. We had other priorities.

Peter mostly seemed cheerful, a good kid who
giggled when tickled. Then he grew slim and
handsome as if to rival the prettiest of her men,
dark like them around the muzzle from sunlight
and sun sports. If Peter was already bent over
his bowl of breakfast cereal, granola or Wheat-
ies, he glanced up at the new man and said, "Hi.
Mom up yet?" and went on reading the back of
the cereal box. If it wasn't a school-day, he might
not take breakfast until nearly noon, just drinking juice out of the container in the fridge, and
then might hear his mother giggling and throwing her hands on the mouth of a lover if the
visitor took to groaning or shouting too loudly
for the morning. Sometimes we forgot when it
was a school holiday.

Since the thought troubled me (but jealousy
was not allowed), I wondered how much the
facts of Suki's life were a vexation to Peter. He
was allowed to be vexed by unannounced com-

pany at breakfast, as long as he didn't show it
and shared his cereal and wasn't jealous. A permanent son like him might be troubled in a different way from a sometime lover like me. I
couldn't be sure how my non-jealousy compared
with his.

I looked at the boy's gold-flecked eyes, the
dark healthy sleek adolescent hair, glistening
like a seal's pelt, the narrow athletic California
rump in jeans which his mother made him wash,
for cleanliness' sake, every night. He didn't wear
shorts beneath them. He liked tightness; he
didn't like the seam-line from Jockey's. Suki
thought that was kind of cute of her son, beginning of a sense of style, and pointed it out to me.
Light of my life, she said. Another mother, in
the same way, might have boasted of a son's pi-
ano playing or his gift for languages.

He was squinting and reaching for little bolts
under the saddle of the bicycle. I admired the
desire to get it just right. His Nikes looked pro-
fessionally trudged in; his fingers were greasy
and agile. He enjoyed equipment and technique.
Like Suki, he seemed to know what he was doing, and watching that childish hardworking
scowl in the sunlight, I thought about how he
was the son of a woman I liked a lot. There was
something to learn from what he was becoming.
He was at another entrance to his mother's place
in the world, and mysterious in his own way.

He snapped the little pliers shut and glanced
up, lifting his eyebrows as if to say, You still

61

here? "I'd like to smile like a cheeseburger, you know, if a cheeseburger wanted to make nice. Mom's friends all have those French Brie smiles, that white wine drip in the corners. You know, don't you?"

"I don't know any smiling cheeseburgers," I said.

"That's my point. You're one of the smiling Bries. Good Frank. Nice Frank. Frank doesn't bite."

I felt the heat against the capillaries in my face. It was like a rush of niacin. "Peter, are you going into creep training?"

"Hey, I like that."

"But you don't know anything yet."

"I like that too, it's so ignorant. Don't you write for newspapers or something?"

I put a restraining order on myself. "I used to be a kid and mad. I'm still mad sometimes."

"Hey, Frank, you asked me a question, if things are hard for me. Okay, lots of things. I'll cop to that. But lots of stuff is easy, too. And here's what I'm trying to do—take the things I can do pretty easy and help myself with the stuff that's hard."

"Can I help you?"

"Probably. But I told you I'm taking charge now. So I don't think I'll actually be *asking* you if I'm taking from you."

"If I can, Peter—"

"I'll bet you can," he said.

Why me? I was wondering. That was the

question I used to see in the defendants' faces when I covered criminal trials. Why did Peter like me? It also seemed that he didn't like me. He only chose me.

He knew I was deeply interested. He seemed to have the modem for access to my dreaming. When I slept, I dreamed of Suki; and below the reverie line, when I thought I was attending to the traffic across the Bay Bridge or showing my students how to put themselves into magazine pieces while keeping themselves out, I went round and round about Suki. And around again. I was infected with her.

Peter and I shared something, both of us available and susceptible, and that gave him reason enough to care for me and to feel contempt for me and to need me and feel spite for me. Every boy deserves a father. Like Peter, I deserved a family.

I wasn't sure this was the family I needed. Surely this was the very family I didn't need. But a person doesn't always get to choose what he cares for.

"Brie," he repeated softly, daring me to make something of it. "Mom should have been a less bean."

"What?"

"*Less* bean," he said. "Fool with ladies, wouldn't have to fool with you. But she only fool with them on rare occasions one of you ain't around."

"That's a cute remark, Peter."

"Well, I'm changing my life. I can say what I want to say."

"We'd all like to change our lives. We'd all like to say the cute things that come to mind when we—"

"I hate my life. I'm changing it as soon as I could."

"You mean you can?"

"I could," he said.

He pulled a kind of cord and the motor started. *Vrubb, vrubb.* The old Schwinn was now a motorbike that could drag up San Francisco hills, wobbling a little, needing the pedal on the steeps, and Peter had done it himself. "Congratulations," I said.

"I knew where to go for the kit. Easy if you know where to go and what to do when you get home."

FOUR

"I wanted to keep things as they were," Nella explained, and she was describing the tavern she had bought in North Beach—remodeled, redecorated, refinanced, "repositioned"—and it sounded like Suki explaining about her life on the happy occasion of her fortieth birthday.

Not every woman is honest about this event. "I've faced the facts and they are mine," Suki said. "I want to keep things just as they are."

"She really does," Nella said. "She's such an inspiration to a person."

Nella and I stopped to watch Suki floating off in her springlike, bridal, virginal white frock shot full of antique crocheted perforations and layered with a dozen tiny veils of lace. Her hair, sun-bleached and near-natural, tossed as she laughed and ran, barefoot at her party. Her toenails were pink. Her nails would have been pinkish even without the polish, the armored halo blondish without its fairness-extender, its hair-helper. "Love is blond," Nella murmured, and then, in response to my grin: "Okay, you can't expect me not to be a little jealous. I've got feelings too."

There were many guests. The circles of friendship had drawn together for this occasion. We could choose to intersect if we liked, or to share nothing but our pleasure in Suki. Jealousy was inappropriate. Nella and I would have to do without close attention for much of the evening. Now and then Suki would be sure to find us and touch us with a caress, a light stroking of the hand or cheek, which stated we were very important, we were most essential, really very super and marvelous, even if she didn't have time for us just now—so many old friends in the house this evening.

"I'm giving this surprise party for myself," Suki had explained at the door one more time, giggling sweetly with the game of it, welcoming another guest, repeating, "Put your coats in the room with the big Peter on the door."

He had a supergraphics "PETER" stenciled on his door because his mother thought he needed his own territorial rights. He was at the age when a mother begins to think of such things for her son. In her own way, which was different from the way of others—but Suki never pretended to be like other women—she understood about privacy. In the midst of intelligence and fun and careful consideration, Suki's privacy drew us all to her, so many friends and suitors and former lovers and perhaps future lovers and men and women whose loneliness she relieved by making herself the center of their lives. When she was silly, she was still brave and unpredictable. Beneath her open astonishment in events there was a hidden surprise. There might even be pains which haunted her private hours; Sam Webster had been only a game of sorrow, a rehearsal at most. That play was closed. So far I felt safe against Suki's troubles, although I didn't know what she could do to me if a chance at defeat or real loss came her way. As she did with Peter, she gave all of her friends the chance to make our marks in her world.

"I thought I'd give this surprise party for myself—no presents—oh, you shouldn't, take it back with you!" She sighed. "You always did violate my rules, I have to resign myself because you're so wonderful, but thank you anyway, thank you—"

Nella went on telling me how she kept things exactly as they were in the traditional old tavern. "You know, the Barbary Coast and all that funky spirit, so what I had to do was I got rid of the Puccini on the jukebox, who listens to *Carmen* anymore, and put in a little Willie Nelson, Merle Haggard, that kind of ethnic country ilk, eighty-six the old Eye-talians who used to hang out there, smell up the place—nice people, though, lovely wonderful people, so good to their children, especially their rotten sons—get some terrific ferns in the joint so it looks like home, attract a better class of singles, not your yuppie singles, just the high achievers in software, data processing, advertising, active in your middle management situations—"

"Traditions are irreplaceable," I said.

"You got it." Her gun hand, her trigger finger shot forward from the hip in the television host punchline gesture. "Without tradition there is no history, not in SFO—you *got* it," she said. "I've been networking with the tavern keepers from the Feminist Saloon Guild to dialogue how we can keep the faded old worn-out shtick vital and alive while preserving the modern contemporary shtick. Do you have some input for me, Frank, speaking as a today's male?"

Now Nella had moved in close. She had worked herself up. She was jabbing a finger straight at my heart. I had strong bones in my chest, calcifying a little more with each passing year, a legacy of earlier eons on all fours in the savannas and forests. Surely my ancestors were both hunters and prey; I called on instinct to survive Suki's birthday party. Nella was waiting for an answer.

At this point in time the input was in my quarter, near the food source, on my floppy disk, if only I could keyboard some dialogue. Nella made me feverish. "Downtime," I murmured apologetically.

Nella was a people person. She was born fond

of them. She knew when a male was totally useless.

I drifted away to regain my senses in the sunny aura of Suki, to listen to the music of her voice, that lady of my preoccupation who could even arrange a party to surprise herself. Nella found other partners to dialogue, finger food to pluck, traditions to uphold.

Preoccupation? If I was preoccupied with Suki, then what's obsession?

Peter, where the coats went, Suki's son, was now seventeen. Used to be seventeen, as his mother and everyone else used to be and then were more. Today, still seventeen, Peter was earning money for his fleet of motorized two-wheeled vehicles by subletting his room for use as a coat depository.

As she held a cluster of new arrivals at the door, Suki's gaze suddenly grew still, without expression, expectant. For an instant this could be mistaken for rest and peace. I was about to speak with her, nice party, oh happy birthday dear friend, really nice event, when I saw the cloud thicken over her face, a spreading procedure of darkness; yes, the word cloud is correct this time for the shadow on those healthy pink cheeks. Peter had come in with two girls, two Marin County moth creatures who could have been anywhere between fourteen and forty-four but were probably gathered around the Tamalpais High School end of the age scale.

Suki had told him she would be using his bedroom for coats and things. People would be using his bathroom. He had promised to be elsewhere that evening, maybe spend the night with a friend; it was an agreement.

A similar cloud slipped over Peter's face as he explained he was just stopping by to pick up some shit out of his sock drawer, the Jello Biafra tapes, and to borrow the keys to Suki's BMW because his motorbike was a little small for the three of them and she wouldn't be using the wheels tonight anyway, would she? Pink Cloud met Dark New-Shaving Cloud and the storm back and forth was of this order: How could you be so inconsiderate, Peter? . . . What's the big deal, Mom? Feeling the crux of the crisis today, Mom, getting into the low forties and all?

"Frank!" said Suki, as if I had just unexpectedly surprised her, arriving from a distant place. "Peter, say hello to Frank."

"Hi, what's happenin'?"

"Okay, the keys are on my bureau. Don't smoke till you get wherever. Drive carefully," she said, "this is not a scooter."

The boy ambled off with a little smile on his face, like the little smile of his delicate mother. Suki was neat and thin, thin nose, thin mouth, all very clean and healthy and neat, racquetball and running and yoga, and she was celebrating her birthday by wearing an antique white bride's dress, perforated frequently by those starry veiled ventilations, so that since she wasn't wearing a bra, it would have been extremely clever of her to hide her nipples. She was clever, but didn't choose to be that clever. Her eyes followed Peter and the two Tam High wraiths as they trooped into his bedroom.

"He's a handsome kid," I said. "This is a difficult time for kids and their parents. Whatever happened to that moped sort of thing he had last year?"

"His father was sweet looking," she said, watching the bedroom door close. "Some people think his father is still attractive. Maybe he'll develop a little more discipline than his father— pay support on time, for example."

Peter's father, a software genius—that's going too far: a software innovator and promoter (that's still going too far: a pretty good salesman) —was terrific at start-up in peripheral, IBM-compatible companies. He lived down the peninsula in Burlingame and would probably not be attending his former wife's birthday party. He was too busy trying to bring his latest company out of Chapter 11, which was not bankruptcy, he had explained to her. It was just a federal way of saying a person needed a little more time to straighten things out with the banks. His ex-wife and ex-son could try to be equally understanding.

Instead of the check, he had sent her an assortment of California nuts and dried fruit. Since Suki could have used a little tuition for Peter and Peter was fighting the battle of oily follicles, this was not child-support-compatible.

Through the open gate leading to Suki's house, and into the garden behind it, and over all of us, the weather report was favorable, as usual. It was San Francisco forever-springtime weather, a little warmer than expected for this universe of Pacific Heights, Cow Hollow, smelling of flowers and green and clam sauce and cologne and the healthy thin sweat of runners. Someone hurried past in an invisible cloud of Johnson's baby powder, one of the caterers. The colors of Suki's house were pink and yellow and bright. The sky over the garden on Filbert Street showed jet strips of fog; later it might grow cool with the July evening billows sweeping through the Golden Gate. Japanese koto played, and a flute—Jean-Pierre Rampal. Suki and I had made love to this music a year or two ago, and she had given me the record afterward. She bought herself another. I wondered how many men here had made love—had made like—to that sweet Frenchified Japanese music, and received the record as a prize afterward, and then I asked myself to stop wondering. It could only be called love in a few cases.

Due to her former husband's business difficulties, which were due to his impulsive and irresponsible character, Suki was obliged to survive without live musicians on her fortieth birthday. The dumb tinkerer, who tinkered mostly with financial statements, called himself *enterprenoor*, should have understood that, although he was supposed to be a quasi-genius in Cupertino and

San Jose, the bankers in San Francisco were really smart.

Forty years old today, with the pink of breast
peeping as she flowed in her antique white
bride's confection of cunning perforations,
gauze, and etched petals, Suki looked pure, innocent, girlish, nothing sullen and congested in the
lip, nothing swollen with blood or lymph, all
flowing lithe and athletically in the here and
now of her new decade. Even after her mini-
quarrel with Peter, even with the stress of or-
ganizing a birthday event for herself, so many
old lovers present, so many possible future lovers waiting, she looked astonishingly young,
pretty, and fragile; I guess hopeful does it—her
secret and unquenchable hope.

"Have you talked with Peggy?" she asked.
"You've met Peggy—that's Peggy—she needs
cheering up."

"Don't you?"

"Never!" Suki said, laughing. "What good is it
to need cheering up? No one can do it anyway."

"People try," I said.

"*People try,*" she repeated, and twisted her little mouth at me. I had said something stupid, as
people do at parties. At Suki's parties I was
worse than usual; she upset my precarious social
balance. I wasn't jealous or possessive. I was
sometimes lonely, but lots of people are lonely at
parties. Peggy over there, engrossed in looking
through the little stack of videocassettes, moving
her lips as she read the titles, was lonely. She

may not have intended to spend her time at a party reading movie titles. Suki, too, must have had doubts at times. Although just a moment ago she may have wondered what Peter was doing with his two little Tam High moth persons and why he needed the keys to her BMW, she was not going to upset herself by asking him. Those were mere details. She had social balance. This was too nice an occasion, and a person only has one fortieth birthday, whenever she chooses to have it, perhaps even when she turns forty years old. Silly to violate this aura of good cheer by bickering over details with a son. "Have you met Alfonso?" she asked. "Alfonso! Come here! Alfonso Redd, Frank Curtis."

"We already know each other," I was saying, "not necessary—"

But the bulky black man had gracefully turned, smiling, big-gutted, and asked, "Suki?" She crooked her little finger, hithered him, and he swam toward us through the crowd. Alfonso was a San Francisco vice squad detective with a law degree. "Night school at Golden Gate, but I passed the bar," he had told me, chuckling at the amusement of this, "first the Connie's Kan Du Bar and then the California Bar." Suki explained how he had broken several mass murder or child perversion cases, something like that, and was working on many more, pure logic plus careful reasoning, and smoked a little dope just like a regular responsible person. He was making the streets safe for people, but he was socially aware. He was a terrific natural talent.

Alfonso chuckled. He carried a Responsible Negro Leader belly and chuckle machine; the light in his eyes was bright and famished. "No sense just burning it all up," he said, evidently referring to the dope, "not when it come all the way by sea or by land from Maui or Guatemala. "Burn *some* of it instead. We don't sell it. Would be illegal and unadvisable. Logic tells a person that. We burn the rest of it in cylinder form, little by little—the birds get high, the rats get high—"

And that Santa Claus chuckle rolled over us, deep and warm, causing several of the women to look up, blushing with the confident pleasure in it. "I got a stake in integrity, both for my law degree, in case I ever want to practice, but mainly as a *de*-tective, good benefits. Ho, ho, ho."

He saw me jump at the laugh, its deep rich volume, and gave me a shrewd look out of the brown face with his brightness of eyes carefully protected by full cheeks and forehead. The laugh had worked for him over the years. My jumping wasn't going to change the facts. Suddenly he grabbed my collar. "Listen, buster," he said, "since I was a bitty boy I always want to root around in nice clean things, just root around till she hands my balls back to me. So don't you go squint at me like that."

"What?" I asked.

Ho, ho, ho again. "Jiving," he said. "When I

75

play bad cop, I grab the accused like that. I keep the accused off-balance like that. It's how I do it. I thought I'd show you how detection works logically."

"It's very interesting," I said.

This time no ho ho ho. But a little wink from Alfonso's heavy, smart, engorged face with its rolls and creases and protuberant forehead protecting a whole lot of brain.

Alfonso turned a funny purple in his head equipment. He would be blushing if he had chosen to be a white man. He looked capable of doing what he liked to do. If he had chosen to be white, he probably could have managed it. We must have been talking, but I was thinking about how I was conquering jealousy, another great victory. "I used to be into Afro, about ten minutes I got into that," Alfonso said. "Now I'm into myself. Don't need conk, dreadlocks, none of that. I like getting into myself, works better for me."

"I appreciate your—" I began, but he was cutting through the waves, not needing me and my struggles any further, following Suki to the table where the sushi lay, all clean and glowing and slimy and shiny, tuna with a smile, rice in seaweed-girt morsels of ferment. Alfonso was after Suki, not sushi. He speared a curl of raw tuna with a toothpick. Not raw; marinated. He beamed at me across the room as his fleshy mouth enveloped the morsel, slipping it directly past the strong yellow squarish teeth. He knew I was a former alleged perpetrator around here.

Our conversation might continue another time. Now I settled for gossiping with Ted Keneally, the criminal lawyer, stiff with pride and his neck brace. He had dived into a pool that was a little shallow for him. God and fate and the hunger of American jurisprudence for his special interest in both the justly and the unjustly downtrodden had saved his life but given him a severe wound to the vertebrae. Nothing, however—certainly no trauma to his spine—changed his celebration of the many plots revealed daily in his vocation. "They set him up. The pigs set him up." I didn't need to ask who or whom. It was the standard conspiratorial pigs, the usual societal victims. It used to be George Jackson or Huey Newton; now it was Bob Avakian. With the aluminum support-band holding his head on straight, giving him a rigorous and prideful view of the world, who could dare to tell him nay?

"That's lots of stuff we can use, that's my talent," Ted was saying. I think he was talking about the Revolution. I knew he also went over to his ex-wife's house every Sunday and mowed the lawn for her. On her birthdays and religious holidays he made sure the lawn was neat in St. Francis Woods; sometimes, for old time's sake, he tried to have sex with her—not to enjoy it, just to celebrate their past. And always, for old time's sake, as usual, she refused. So who could deny him a revolution when one was so much needed?

"That Alfonso. He moves so easy." Was Ted also jealous of Alfonso? "You got to hand it to a guy off the streets who moves so easy."

Alfonso's parents had both been teachers, but it was true, he did have a corner-boy style along with the plump game of Tomism he played. Ted and Alfonso probably did business together in crime prevention and law prevention. "Like he says, and his granny said before him, and now I say after him, quote, Things that go around come around. Alfonso says."

"Unquote. You know, Ted? I never heard him say that."

"Maybe not to you, but I'm his friend. For an Oreo he's one straight dude, man." This guy went to Corner-boy Berlitz. He repeated for emphasis: "He's my friend."

So Ted was also worried about Alfonso. Jealous and scared and sweating at night. Another one for me to worry about, if I decided to go back to worrying.

For different reasons I decided I was going to like Alfonso and not like Ted and withhold permission to be jealous of either of them. I was old enough to make this decision. I may not have been old enough to be sure I would live up to it.

Suki liked to put people together; it gave her energy to feed the combustion between strangers, supervise the throbbing and swelling of gases within a Pacific Heights compost heap.

"I'm up for watching the sparks," she said. "Don't you like parties, Frank?" Suki had a way of sparking in public; it was a thing not everyone can do, and she did. She grew warm in this heat. She leaned against my shoulder in a hostessy way and waited for Ted to finish. You would think she didn't have a care in the world, or even better for a grown-up person, she took the measure of all care and rode triumphantly through (in her BMW, if Peter wasn't using it). She knew about care. She just didn't permit it.

"What's the reason you're giving this party?" I asked her.

"My birthday, probably."

"Is that really all?"

"No. Like to see my friends together."

"It isn't your birthday?"

"It is. Probably. Why should I tell you?" And she refilled my glass with Wente Brothers white-something wine. I was already a little dizzy; not jealous, not worried, not sweating except a little with the wine. I shouldn't have asked whatever question I had just asked her. She had given me the answer I deserved. "Be happy, Frank," she said, "I've hit the barrier."

And was determined to go right through like a daredevil driver. She didn't believe in going around to come around. That was Alfonso's and Alfonso's granny's way. Impatient grace was more Suki's style.

Suki looked young, easily young, but Sherrie looked younger. Thin seems to look young, and

Sherrie was lanky, thin, and girlish, another dieted and exercised forty-year-old, describing the tragedy of her life to Ted Keneally, perhaps because she thought he could find a nice lawsuit in there someplace. "The molest happened when I was six to sixteen," she said. "I'm a case of six-to-sixteen molest. Dad did it to me because Mom was frigid. So was I, but of course a six-to-sixteen child isn't *supposed* to get it on with her dad. Not with any enthusiasm. It was a case of pure molest by Dad."

"Sherrie, you told me last time," Ted said. "I'm more into politics these days."

"But I didn't tell you how I got unfrigid, due to this kid," Sherrie said. "This is just personal, not legal. He hung out in the park near the Mill Valley library, selling a little dope, merchandising, and I just happened to tell him my story, and zap! the same thing happened to him with his mom, it came up, so one thing led to another between us—"

Sherrie had been a flight attendant but now was a therapist, specializing in flight attendant problems—anomie, alcoholism, anorexia (the Three Big A's), plus jet lag, still being called stewardess after it was practically in the Bill of Rights that they're flight attendants, and molestation on the job by pilots and a few straight male stewards, flight attendants, and old-bag female ones. The union has seniority rules so the women tend to get older. It's not a growing field anymore.

"Are you still seeing the young man?" I asked.

"*Seeing?*" she said, incredulous. "What's to look at?"

"Whatever," I said—an apology.

"Mm-me, that's good," said Sherrie, lifting a cracker with caviar and sour cream from my plate. "I adore *black* caviar," meaning not the red. "Can I have one of these, too?" The caviar on the cracker with the sour cream left my plate and entered her fingers, then her mouth. She was the sort of reformed anorexic who lived off other people's plates; it pulled her from the brink of starvation. In her practice with the Three-Big-A's women, what she called the Triple-A folks, her clients, Sherrie advised them to graze wherever they found a wholesome snack. It's not the same jungle out there anymore; men love it when you pick a cracker here and there; sexy. Sherrie presented herself, brave little bony chest forward, as proof that it worked. The way, in my childhood, some women loved to feed men, Sherrie loved to be fed by them. "Isn't it great how Suki always lays out a spread?"

"Best I know," I said.

"And keeps her figure. Do you want to bet she eats any of it?"

I had heard this line of discourse before. I happened to know that Suki ate, ate greedily, burned it all in sport and thinking and disregarding sleep as a waste of wonderful time, but I wasn't going to try to convince Sherrie. I was hungry. I bent to the pasta salad—this was a test

—to see if Sherrie would take that, too. I dipped a serving spoon into the hot eggplant casserole. I decided to save the towering green and erupting fruit salads till later; there was so much, and all arranged for color and carefree design; even food was decor. "You know, if there's a fly in the salad and you find it, you know it's good—"

"The protein."

"Oh, Frank! No, no, we get enough protein anyway, flies don't even have a heck of a lot, that's middle-America prejudice about we need protein—you ever see anyone in Pacific Heights with kwashiorkor, those darling little swollen bellies from Africa? That's *sick*. Pay attention to little Sherrie now. Flies and worms and little white icks in the salad mean"—triumphantly—"they didn't use pesticide!"

She had not only been violated by her trusted dad and yet grown up to be very attractive to a healthy, well-balanced, nineteen-year-old Mill Valley dope dealer, not only graduated top third of her class from therapy school and gotten her certificate come loudey from the Burbank Institute of Psycho-Dynamistics, but she was also into green salad ecology. And she had this in common with her nearly closest friend, Suki: Nothing stopped her. Sherrie was still sharing her insights about nourishment with me: "My opinion, only it's more like a truism, is sushi is a passing fad. It's tasty, it's healthful, it's ethnic, it's got a tang, but it's just a fashion. Don't get me wrong. I like it."

"It's a will o' the wisp."

"You said it, I didn't. I was eating sashimi when people thought it was only raw fish. I was playing Vivaldi when my friends thought bossa nova was advanced. I was hip to incest when nobody else—"

But I was protecting my plate from her delapidations by moving swiftly toward the garden. I was stopped on the way by an old acquaintance. In my Aquarian student days, he'd have been called a friend—we were looser about definitions in the sixties.

Wirt Olmstead, the collagist, had opened a cabinet, found a bottle of Courvoisier brandy, did the reasonable thing, poured, and was sipping it over ice. "This koo-vwa-say," he said, "it's from the heart of France. I don't eat anymore, don't have to."

"I heard."

"From deep in the heart of France, the little town of Cognac, they send me this concentrated sunlight, Frank." He held the glass up to the light. "You can practically see the history of the universe here, Frank, if you have eyes to look and a lung to breathe it in. Not everybody does."

Wirt had given up politics and sex to become a Breatharian. He had adopted a faith which enabled him to draw his nutriment from the air and sunlight. It could solve the world's hunger problem better than the Hunger Project. All the broad masses had to do was get the chlorophyll going in their systems. He sipped the koo-vwa-zay and said. "That junk food'll kill you. Even the philosophy of it is bad."

"Okay."

"And that Sherrie with her balanced diet, listen, Frank, I want to issue a warning from a friend, she'll kill you as sure as God gave us waste products to beware of."

"How come you drink?" I asked, knowing I shouldn't.

"I don't," he said. "This is just celebrating Suki's birthday. I'd be a fool to eat or drink, so I don't. I just stand in the sunlight and breathe. I take water though—that's why the ice cubes in my koo-vwa-zay. In the Sierras, God freezes'm, too."

"How's your wife?"

"Left me. You didn't know that? What kind of friend're you? I left her for Suki, but Breatharians tell the God's own truth, even to old friends that don't give a shit. Honey left me first."

I remembered Honey well. She was as devoted to rear views as Wirt was to breathing. She sold microminis in the little shop in North Beach called Bottoms Up. When she greeted folks, she turned pertly and presented her rear parts like a prairie dog. Oh hi, she would say, I didn't see you coming. She was looking the other way and saucily twitching. She too had a religion; stimulation of the haunches was what she believed in.

Wirt was still explaining about the breakup of his marriage. In one way or another, that's always a source of grief. "She left me because of my philosophy. I hadn't met Suki yet, so that wasn't the part she couldn't take. And I was only breathing part-time, still couldn't say no to a barbecued rib or those criminal French fries with all the animal fats. Honey said it was because I stopped fucking her, but that was only her theory."

He waited for me to contribute to the discussion. I had no philosophy to offer. Soothing remarks don't help in cases of tragedy; wisdom isn't much better.

"So it was all for the best. She don't pull my string anymore, man. Takes more like Suki to jerk my cord, only I still can't get her to see the solar system like it is. You can get food from the correct deep breathing in the sunlight, but not sex. Honey was hung up on the stuff other people tell her. Suki's good. She tries to get me to eat again. I tell her to breathe profoundly, not shallow. We don't agree about everything, but that's what makes the world go round, doesn't it?"

"If it's not gravity," I said, "the pull of the moon."

"You're kidding. You mean the sun."

"Sure thing."

"Hey, man, she keeps my *Empire of the Air* collage piece hanging proudly in her garage. Right next to her BMW. Used to be in the bedroom, but we're not going together seriously anymore."

"But she spends a lot of time in the garage—

parking, unparking, plus watching Peter work on his cycles. That's a good place for it."

"Right. That's what I say, Frank. Next time you're helping her in with the groceries, check it out. There's a piece of her undies I ripped off glued in the lower, no upper right-hand corner, where the universe meets the solar system, it's the wing on the angel up there, the primal myth. . . . So Honey moved to Ellay, took the kid— Fairfax, I think. I don't need her anyway. Suki doesn't agree with everything, but she admires my art. I think she's gonna take care of me. Hey, you notice how this ice turns to water in the koo-vwa-zay? You hold it in your hot hand and it just turns to water? So I'll pour a little more of the French sunlight over my ice."

Suki liked to take care of the lost if they were interesting lost souls. Like Honey, she might have an opinion about who was interesting and it might be different from mine. She sought a maxi-family in San Francisco in which she could be the maxi-mother, maxi-mistress, maxi-wife. There was no convincing rumor to advise me how to take this. I was only Frank Curtis, wanting more of her attention.

I left Wirt discussing breath, sunlight, and never eating anything again with a dentist who wanted to look at his gums sometime, just out of curiosity, for the sake of science. Suki had noticed our conversation and murmured to me as she darted past, "He's a dear. Some would say starving, but he's an artist. My goal is to see him painting again. Gluing."

"What about eating?"

"Oh, that. I don't think he realizes he's a muncher, not that pretzels and potato chips and finger food is what a grown man should . . . ever since Honey left him . . ."

But she was already gone, counting on me to complete her thought for us both.

"Is that lady weird?" somebody was explaining, and answered his own question: "From the planet Debbie."

Someone else whistled. "That weird?"

"Strange. I mean *strange.*"

A repeat on the whistle. "That weird. Maybe the elves from the planet Debbie will come and take her away."

"On the planet Debbie, pal, they've only got planetary space people. No elves."

"That weird."

Suki, who had left me to lean her head against some other guest's shoulder, and then to touch the hair of a woman guest, and then to make sure her college-girl helpers were keeping the kitchen going and the bowls and platters filled, came back to fit her neat narrow head into the spot on my shoulder which remembered, nerves tingling, where her head had sometimes rested. That gesture brings and evokes tenderness, doesn't it? The shadow of her hair had never left me; the touch of her forehead still radiated warmth. Such sensations are true; they can't lie;

they have weight, don't they? I wished to be happy and she assented, at least to my wish.

The yellow-and-red sunset glow off the daylight-saving's sky, down from the skylight and through the doors and windows, made everyone look tan and smooth; healthy, tan, smooth, and beautiful; a party at this hour in the summer took off the pounds, the cares, the years; maybe only the years. At one window a flower was preserved between two sheets of amber glass and the light poured through; a butterfly and a strawflower pressed together. Down below, San Francisco Bay sparkled. We could see Alcatraz, the Rock now a national park, and a few sailboats ducking and soaring while the nearly invisible dots on board flirted and enjoyed their beers. And I knew, amid so many blessings, drenched in sunlight and Suki light, that Suki really cared for everyone and me. Liking so many people didn't mean she couldn't make room to care for me, too.

"Ladybird Johnson beautified America. That's why it's so beautiful," Ted Keneally was saying. I didn't join this conversation.

"Cynics like you don't help."

"I'm not a cynic. I'm a revolutionary."

"Revolutionary lawyers in a top bracket with Wilkes-Bashford suits like you don't help with their cynicism—"

"Okay, then America is beautiful."

"Okay, Ted, today she's a nice old lady even if her husband was a crook who killed hundreds or

thousands or so. I'll give you that. I remember
Vietnam."

It was Sherrie's voice giving the right answers. I still didn't join.

"Sherrie, you win," said Ted. "As long as you
keep it in perspective."

Sherrie had a puzzled expression on her face.
Suddenly there were doubts. "What makes me
think Ladybird might be in good shape?" she
asked. "Last time I saw her, she was hefty, bal-
loony bazooms. In fact, now that I try to remember, what makes me even think she's still alive?"

I turned when Ted Keneally brushed past and
Sherrie caught my eye. Ted was committing an
act of revolutionary escape to the bar.

"Frank!" Sherrie cried. "Something I want to
ask you! What would you think of a man whose
ex-wife wants something more than anything
else in the world?"

"Don't know what I'd think."

"She wants a catamaran. That's what he told
me she wants. What would you think of such a
man? Can you be bothered with their problems?"

I tried to say I didn't have the criteria for
judgment, but my lips wouldn't form the words.
Instead I moved my mouth around in a determined way, working toward a significant moment of balanced party affability: "Suki has a lot
of different friends, including me, doesn't she?"
and finally succeeded in getting the words out,
but by that time Sherrie had tired of my shilly-

shallying and was offering the catamaran enigma to Jerry Whiner, a screenwriter whose stuff had been stolen by all the great stars. "The stuff of my life, man," he said, "they play but they don't wanna pay."

His real name wasn't Jerry Whiner. I could never remember his real name because, in my heart, he was Whiner. Fortunately, since this was San Francisco and California, I could always just introduce him as Jerry and wait for someone else to come up with his real name. "Whiner," he would say, "Gerald Whiner," but I'd always forget in time for the next time.

I was thinking: Suki does everything for anybody except validate their parking. And all someone would have to do is suggest it and that, too.

"You what?" said Jerry.

"What what?"

"You were saying something."

"Oh. What's your name, Jerry?" I asked. "Someday I might need it."

Jerry handed me a card with a grin. "Suki always says you have a sense of humor. Of course, everyone does, only some are more hostile than others. But we both kind of like yours. Give me some advice. I tried not shaving this afternoon, for the Unshaven Look—you think I have the Unshaven Look?"

"Another day or two."

"You see? A sense-a-yumer," Jerry said. "You may proceed."

Suki was running to and fro on her little cheerleader's thighs, rounding the turn into a miraculous middle age. She believed in happiness; she believed happiness was a treat. "I have a special surprise for *you*," she said to someone. She wanted to have a surprise for everyone and she wanted it to be Suki.

"I'm not angry," someone was saying in the garden—it was a man, maybe, or a boy, or a hoarse woman, saying, "it doesn't matter, it's unimportant"—it was a male person speaking—"but don't do that again."

"I thought you said you weren't angry."

"Now I'm getting pissed."

"So you were lying to me."

I heard a scuffle, a rustle, a snap of flower stalks breaking, vegetables getting pureed before being picked. Alfonso leaned out the window. "Hey, you guys! Watch Suki's garden, willya?"

The bowl of fresh fruit salad was humming in tune with the excitement. No, it was the ice-maker humming just behind the fresh fruit. No, it was a juicer, making something healthful. Suki was laughing and saying, "What's a party without a fight between two or three lovers? What's love without a lovers' spat?"

"Is spat, in this case, the past tense of spit?" asked Jerry, because he was a writer with a sense-a-yumer whose stuff was frequently stolen by the top Bay Area stand-up comics, some of them with tentacles that extended all the way down the coast to the Coast.

The fellow playing Spat in the garden was not what he sounded like; he was sturdy and short, with plump thighs, plump and prominent nostrils, a lock of purplish hair falling over his plump forehead. His partner in Spat was more like it: dark, pretty, slim, and sulky, his lower lip reflecting his lover's blood-swollen plumpness with a delicate puffiness of its own. The two separated for a cooling-off period as they entered the house. The young man ran to the bathroom. The sturdy one, Hossein Farassian, brushed back his lock of hair as he approached Suki.

"Didn't I just see your son," he asked in his caramel-flavored voice, "that handsome lad? You must be proud, my dear friend. I don't see him. Where is he? Has he disappeared into some secret place?"

Suki made Motown movements with her arms and upper body. "Girlfriends," she said.

Farassian's smile had enough goodwill in it to erode the plastic enamel of false teeth. The purple of his hair, the heavy violet of some tropical flower, took the light and smothered it. His voice rumbled and cajoled. "That fine lad, he's the Standard of Excellence in young men, as far as I can judge. Is the girl worthy?"

Suki looked at him with a half-smile. She hadn't thought of Peter as the Cadillac of sons, but Farassian dug earnestly into his imported stock of compliments. Although he personally was immune to her Motown upper-body moves, it was the least a guest could do. "If I were to sire a lad like that, I could die happy. But who knows, my dear, if I will ever enjoy the bliss of a son?"

"I hope you find one," Suki said, and slid off with hostess murmurs. A motorcycle from outside filled the space between the Iranian exile and me with an uphill scream that blended power and hysteria and undone mufflers, a jerky sob of gears shifting, a kid no doubt not wearing a helmet and courting premature brain damage at a San Francisco intersection. Farassian would have liked a son like that, too, nursing him back to health.

Alfonso glided alongside like a ship into dock, loading food with both happy hands. "Frank, you're not eating," he said. "I know it'll be here when we're gone, all this tasty chow that don't leave stains. Normally I like food leaves stains."

Alfonso chuckled.

I chuckled.

Alfonso rechuckled, evoking barbecue. Enough amenities. Then where was Peter, where were his girlfriends with their goods and services, where was Suki's major automobile? All the amenities—nice friends—were on the scene; Suki was trying to paper things over, anyway. The motorcyclist was humping his gears up and back, back and up, screaming his energy into the fading daylight.

Not many of the guests could have noticed the little problem with Suki's son.

Since they hadn't noticed about Peter, and

they were here to celebrate, that was their mission, no reason for Suki to worry. No excuse for fretting on an important birthday. No jitters were on the program. The boy was just acting like a regular kid, which a mother also likes to do sometimes.

Suki had obligations to keep life a festival, as it must be. She had made the rule long ago.

Suki's most intimate friends, some of the finest amenities a person could want in the friendship line (not Sam Webster, though), plucked carrots and zucchini, avoided the deviled eggs, stuck to the slimming and health platters. They tended to avoid the deeper dish nutriments, quiche, calzone, the delicious olives wrapped with bacon, which served mostly to shed spicy smells into the air. A few were tempted, Hossein for example, and a person had to provide for them, too. Maybe lukewarm or chilled, the deep and dark dishes might later serve Peter and his friends, who required calories for that final push into their adult sizing. Sherrie, so deeply committed to anorexia and the Triple-A's that she could eat caviar with sour cream and her metabolism wouldn't even recognize it, was talking about a friend, a Mill Valley film director, Terry Tuna, whose new movie had "opened wide"—twelve hundred theaters, counting the plexes—and closed within the week, probably making it impossible for him to finance another film. It was his karma. She too, in a brief acquaintance earlier, had opened wide for him, but closed within a weekend when he showed his true self. All that Hollywood smooth slides right off a person—Mister Terry Tuna was a stupid vindictive overweight asshole with no kindness in him at all. In the crunch, that's what emerged. As a therapist with a diploma specializing partly in southern California character disorders, Sherrie should have known, but mostly she did women and Terry sneaked up on her. She tried to be open with a man who said he needed love, understanding, a caring and sharing relationship— oh, the fucker sure knew the words—someone to fly down to Beverly Hills and go to dinner at Jimmy's on Little Santa Monica where they just sent the check to his office and he didn't even have to show his American Express Platinum card and then to private screenings at the Director's Unit and meet a whole new world of fascinating creative people. To do these things with. To be proud of the lady who had her own diploma, her own field of creativity in the Triple-A's. A line like you wouldn't believe unless you went through it yourself.

Sherrie paused a moment. She frowned and let her lashes fall over the pain in her eyes. She didn't want to leave out too much, but on the other hand, perhaps I could profit from a mistake in love which provided a learning and growing experience. "What's the new form of AIDS, Frank? Hearing AIDS. From listening to assholes."

I winced.

"I don't blame you," she said. "I'm a driven person. He made me that way." Terry was a shitface with a dropped pair of buttocks, absolutely lapsed, a total cellulite disaster—pardon her French—from riding around in limousines and listening to workout tapes but not doing them. What more could she say? The truth was, Sherrie didn't really want to get involved in explaining about him, it wasn't worth our valuable time together. Mister Terry Tuna thought he was a Hollywood hyphenate, a cineaste, an auteur, but to Sherrie he was as previously described. Need she be more specific? Had she already sketched the general outlines?

"Let's have a bite," I suggested.

"That's what Dracula did," Sherrie said. Her brows were knitted together. She was wondering if, in my vanity, I was jealous of so much attention paid someone else, the famous cinema auteur.

A new tray was being passed and it was only right to give it our concern. The pretty helper girls, teenagers, looked Greek. Their mothers were Swedish cousins who had come for a year as *au pair* girls in California and stayed; their fathers were black brothers from Oakland. It was a family of caterers now. The mothers did most of the preparation, the almost-Greek daughters did the graceful serving, the fathers sometimes helped with the driving, the loading, the valet parking. The mothers had arrived late for the Aquarian flower period in San Francisco history, but unlike most transplanted cut flowers, they had taken root in the gourmet food preparation game. Exogamous had worked out fine.

Big Watkins, a visiting law prof from the University of California at Davis, was trying out a witticism, probably someone else's, because he was nervous at parties and didn't know most of these people. "You know what an economist is? Fellow who doesn't have enough personality to be an accountant." Poor Watkins must have been an acquisition Suki made on a Wine Institute trip to Sacramento and, in her careless and kindly way, decided to invite to her birthday party.

I tried to guess what she saw in Watkins. Big fellow, fit and rosy and nervous, probably bright in some statutory way. Needful, divorced, content with a law school job—that's probably what she saw in him. He would see her as a miracle of ease, sweet smells, tinkling laughter, and not a kid like the ones at Davis. Suki would be grateful to Watkins because he was so grateful to her. To be loved by an awkward but amiable and decent depressed law professor could easily be construed as a compliment.

So what if Suki had spent a night with Watkins in his little divorce condo off the Davis campus? What if she had? Of course she had. Probably after Sam Webster. In her grief. Passing the time. It was no more significant than Peter's riding around and parking with a Tam High girl,

or a couple of them, or a boy, or a couple of
them. That's what a person does in the evening,
especially a businesswoman with a lot of nervous energy and trouble getting to sleep without
a warm breathing body at her side. I imagined
her pushing her muzzle against his hefty back,
kissing his shoulder blades as she had mine. . . .
I commanded myself not to imagine this.

Or maybe it was before Sam Webster.

Warren Loup, the old movie producer from
Los Angeles, charging off his visit to San Francisco by taking a meeting with Terry Tuna, was
sitting in a chair and reminiscing about all the
yachts he had owned. "More than some South
American navies," he said, "more than all but
the top-drawer dope dealers." Suki bent swiftly
to sit on the floor beside his chair, along with the
rapt young women. Peggy was listening; so were
Sherrie and Nella and someone else whose name
I forgot; Peggy was entranced—this was so
much more fun than reading the titles on videocassettes. With his grizzled white beard, the im-
mense sad bags under his eyes, the steady rasp of
his anecdotes, his terrific esteem for himself,
Loup was an enthralling raconteur about yachts,
houses, pools, and former wives. Then Suki was
up, flashing her skinnied thighs and her Victo-
ria's Secret lace panties, both to show how
quickly and alertly she could respond to the
command Up! or Down! and to continue on her
way to pleasing every guest at her party. *A toast!*

someone had cried out, but the hubbub rode over this suggestion.

Warren Loup glanced at the place where Suki's thighs had been, sighed, and said, "Fiberglass hulls make it too easy. What I really like is lots of wood for the crew to clean and paint." A savings-and-loan millionaire and the young men who had inherited their money were not sitting on the floor beside his chair, fascinated, but their ladies were. Warren didn't mind. If he couldn't have Suki, he could at least have a nice studio audience.

The former spatters had now made up. Suki enforced her own good feelings upon them. "Look at these greens!" Hossein was saying to his friend, now indoors, sharing the same glass of white wine, passing it back and forth, their quarrel ended, their spat a mere glitch of history, which only brought them closer. "Her garden, her greens! She really really ecologizes, doesn't she?"

Suki incubated her vegetable sproutlings in a miniature greenhouse alongside the garage. Then she planted them in intricate rows and circles. When she worked on her knees in dirt, she was praying for life, for all natural creatures. (Not the snails.) She was praying for herself. She admitted it. This was acceptable, even if it ignored a lot of the facts and wasn't really natural —a work of art and determination. It ignored the snails.

One quiet Sunday morning, while Peter

rinsed and stacked the breakfast dishes in the dishwasher and I helped Suki pluck snails into a bucket, snatching them from the dew before they could retreat for the day, Suki had explained to me that a garden is not peaceful and natural—a bank parking lot is more like that—a garden is a struggle against aphids, mites, snails, mice, even raccoons out here in the jungle of Pacific Heights: "Come on, Frank, just pick 'em up, they won't bite, these are the same ones the French eat." There has to be fencing and poisoning and trapping and ferocious weeding (now there's a natural thing: weeds); her garden was a hugely unnatural effort to keep a vision she had. Sherrie had convinced her to try garlic, parsley, and territorial spraying of expensive imported all-natural camel piss to keep the predators away, but it just meant she lost a whole season's crop. A garden was a struggle for dominance, Suki against nature, and she had to find her own way by stubborn persistence.

Of course, the sun and dirty knees and exercise were nice. There were lovely things about a garden, too, and that's why—

The savings-and-loan executive was waving his arms around. "Attention! Attention here!"

"I think someone is striving to get our attention," said Hossein Farassian to his fellow former spatter in the garden. "Here, you hold the glass, dear. I disapprove of those party photos in someone's family album which reveal a person raising his cup of cheer for all eternity, as in those English plays, don't you know—the Love That Has No Name."

"Let's call it Fred," said his friend.

The intellectuals of dining were gathered in a tight feeding knot. A woman named Barbara, a design consultant, was saying, "We went to dinner at my cousin's last night. It's not so much she's my cousin, she's my *friend*. First there was a lobster bisque, followed by celery remoulade—superb, an adventurous concept—and then the fish course. She's not into California cuisine, she's into Traditional Norman I think it is—and then there was a—"

Alfonso and I had found each other again while the savings-and-loan executive sought to put his long-range plan into action. Alfonso was saying, "My job is a play to the securities market, or you could put it, the insecurities market. That'd be another way to put it."

"I guess it's a growing field."

"Man, it ain't topping out yet. Ever since Cain and Abel business been good, money or your picture in the P.O. or just plain jealousy, and then you input Sodom and Gomorrah, the sky's the limit. Sodom and Gomorrah weren't brothers like Cain and Abel, but they had theirself some hot old times—"

Alfonso had been thinking. He was mid-career and still thinking.

"—I don't wear the entry-level green Industrial Security uniform, warehouses, offices, check off names, stuff like that. Now I'm the

Man in Blue—but in sport coat. What I do prefer is I'm the man in blue in plain clothes. Because rank is definitely more better, pal," he said with his wide wet grin, rivulets in the creases of his lips.

It was the grin of someone who knows all the lies and enjoys them fully. Knew youth ends in ruin, life in death, love in not-love—and yet was willing to go for all the final things that come after the first things. I liked the detective. We both liked Suki, had maybe enjoyed a little run with her, and Alfonso was saying, "Some people fall in love and right away they try to make over the other person—stop smoking, get rich, carry out the garbage. Other people fall and what they do is they make over their *own* heads. She's perfect! She's magic! The good God gave me this here blessing and it smell nice besides!"

"What does Suki do?"

He sighed, grinned, and patted me on the shoulder. "Maybe she smart. Maybe she don't fall in love with but one person. You lucky, fella. She so much in love she don't have to bother changing nothing."

"With herself?"

Alfonso slapped my hand. "See, getting smart already, after only about forty-five years or so, isn't it?"

Alfonso was a California winner, but he didn't know everything and asked my opinion. Was it classy of Sam Webster not to show? In my opinion, was it classy of him to leave town and just send those flowers over there? Did I have a view in this matter?

I looked at the bright jungle, enough to support a small population of parrots and hummingbirds, and said that—in my opinion, Alfonso, for what it's worth—he sent *too many flowers*.

Alfonso opened his eyes wide and spread his huge hands. "Man, you white folks got your *ways*, you got your funny *moves*. You keep on *'splaining* things, Frank, and one day soon I'm gonna *unnerstan'*."

"Alfonso, stop it."

"You my buddy, Frank. Can't stop it with you."

But we had to pay attention to other matters. The savings-and-loan executive was tirelessly gesticulating. He knew he would have his victory soon now. Eventually courtesy would win out, even in polite society. "Please!" he cried. "Everyone, please!"

At last there was a gradual hush, a falling away, an expectancy, a new part of the evening ready to begin. Suki had disappeared in order to make her return. I saw her through a tropical bead screen, interrupted by color and shimmering in the motion of air, wavering and lovely as she parted the strings of Mexican beads.

She walked through with the pride of a bride. As she passed, she took my arm as if she loved me, and then moved on to take other arms. I saw a look on the men's faces when she passed.

Those who remember losing in love have sad eyes despite their smiling. This bride was traveling alone through her husbands.

"Toast! To an outstanding lady!" the savings-and-loan executive cried out.

"Or if not her, to Suki!" said Jerry Whiner, covering his mouth and looking for a laugh from the Greek caterer girls.

There was a pause in the clatter and chatter. We could hear the music—Japanese strings with Jean-Pierre Rampal's flute—and then the voices came up again. "Read the box," Jerry Whiner was saying. "Hey, gang, this is America. Suki, where are you? Where *is* she, gang?"

How had she managed to disappear in a moment of our inattention, just at the time when the graceful kiss thrown toward the crowd was all that was required? I went to look for her in her bedroom where some of the sweaters and jackets had been deposited. Suki stood there with the back of her hand peculiarly turned over her mouth. The clothing on the bed had been dumped onto the floor (parquet, patterned and polished wood, a small Afghan rug). The bed was in disarray. The quilt had slid off. Peter was in the bed with the two Tam High girls, pink and puffy and mussed, odd pieces of clothing still clinging to their bodies, one girl burrowing her head in his armpit, her face shut down, the other defiantly, with little red stoned eyes, staring up at Peter's mother. This one was wearing some of Suki's bracelets and a blouse on one arm.

Peter moved the sheet off the body of the red-eyed stoned girl. The red-eyed stoned girl, with the bracelets and one arm in the sleeve of a blouse, was a boy.

Suki was only standing there with the back of her hand across her mouth, in her white frock with the clever jagged ventilations, in her forty-first year. "None of your fucking business," Peter was saying.

I backed out of the room and away. Peter saw me, but liked to see me; Suki didn't notice me; the girl and boy in the bed with Peter didn't care.

From the carpeted dining area where the food had been set out, and the table with the wines, and the caterers standing with their Afro-Swedish smiles on their happy faces, I called back to the bedroom. "Suki, come out! Suki, we're trying to propose a toast!" and felt the stinging flush in my face.

"Suki, we're ready! Come out, Suki!"

The food, the garden, the charm, the fun she brought into the world. All her friends, new and less new, waited. She appeared and put up her hands in protest. She stood there, making just a little curtsy, then a little bow in her wisp of a white dress.

"To Suki!" I said. "To the lady who would rule our lives if things were right with the world —and she does!"

Everything must have been right with the world, just as I said, because there was applause and cheering. Alfonso beamed. Jerry Whiner shut up. Suki reigned.

Didn't she?

A city hawk was swinging gracefully overhead in the garden. Maybe it was only an oversized gull. Suki's eyes were filled with tears; the fine lines about her eyes came of laughter and occasionally too much sun. With so many men who adored her, she really shouldn't need Peter, who was younger than most of the men she liked. That door was closed now, anyway, and all her friends were out here.

"Oh, dears, by the way," she said when the cheering and clinking of glasses had stopped. It was an odd thing to say with the eyes wet. "Oh, by the way, I guess we continue, don't we?" And she smiled, her entire small face smiled through the wetness, a person who had the upper hand on the mere details of life.

FIVE

"I need to tell you about my best love affair," Suki said one evening in her garden, one of those evenings in San Francisco when the air is warm and dry, the fog not in yet, the scent of flowers is light; she said she just wanted to share this pasta salad she happened to have in stock, a glass or two of white wine, some coffee if we decided to stay up late. "I want to talk, Frank. It's show-and-tell. You tell me about yours, too."

"My what?"

"I'll tell you about my best, my best very best, and you tell me about yours."

"What if *you* are, Suki?"

"Oh, sha! You're *impossible*. Your *best?* Don't lie to me about something so important, dear, this is serious."

I sank into the creaking French wicker chair. The air, the smells, the evening, everything was

soft and graceful. If a garden is a place of struggle against nature, this garden had won a battle.
I didn't want to hear what Suki wanted to tell,
but as usual, just this once again, I followed
where she led.

She understood. A person could always count
on her understanding. A person could count on
her understanding and then on her going right
ahead anyway. "Don't you want to talk to me,
Frank? Be sincere together?"

"Suki, suit yourself."

"I do. Shouldn't I? So will you pay attention?"

"I'll listen."

"You're jealous. Oh, dear, I can fix that."

She touched me. She reached for me. I believe
she even, at that moment in the San Francisco
summer, yearned for me.

But reaching and touching and not yearning
more than necessary was her idea of fixing
things, and then going on with what she had
planned for her summer evening was still her
chief idea. The agenda was that she needed an
audience for selected top moments from her all-
time hit parade. Making love, she knew, was the
antidote for the blues and also to elation. It
brought a passing melancholy and peace, a comfortable sinking into soft slow words, despite
that tense spasm which didn't last long enough
to break a friendly mood. Well, elation was acceptable at times. But it was not so good as her
own stylish peacefulness.

Making love was the all-purpose elixir. Just

now it was designed to open my ears. Magic! He'll listen. She stroked and caressed me considerately, gently, expertly, her mind elsewhere.

Suki liked to talk, but she explained herself better with glances and catches of breath, invisible enclosures of perfume, knee and thigh gesticulations that provided the offer of more sources of sweet and strong Suki scents. She liked to tease, but she preferred the humor of winks, pouts, jiggles. She enjoyed conversation, but agility explained life better. She understood about emanations; it was one of her arts. Her cool blue eyes had a use for all the good distractions.

So on an occasion like today, a day like this one, an evening which just came tied together by springtime, summertime, whatever's right, in order to bring the past into the present, and to cover the future with suggestions or plans or patience or kindly acceptance—whatever might be right for the future, too—now when conversation seemed to be the correct act to perform, Suki really wanted to talk. She wanted to explain. She wanted to tell her history and what it meant or didn't mean. She wanted: to make me listen to her other love affairs. That shouldn't be too much to ask of a dear friend. But because she was considerate: only a few of them.

A person learns from what happens, she explained. For example, the Swahili for clap—

"Pardon?"

"Gonorrhea, dear. The Swahili is *kissini*, or

maybe it's *nokissi*—now I forget because you're not being responsive, Frank. I had this friend from West Africa, Ghana, brilliant, brain surgeon and soccer captain. He had to give up studying for brain surgeon because he was afraid it would hurt his soccer—takes up so much time. What a kick he had!"

I had heard of occupational injuries, but until Suki explained the fine points of pre-occupational distraction, I didn't suspect how much becoming a brain surgeon could hinder a person's soccer.

She kept a bullfrog paperweight on her desk. Now she ran with little steps to find it—pop eyes and amphibian reptilian flattish baby paws to caress whatever might need to be weighted below it against the breeze. The bullfrog was made of lead, coated with bronze; a great rouged penis hung beneath its chestiness, printed with waxy lipstick, giving another dimension to the thin-lipped snouty smile. "Cyprian gave me this —my Ibo—when he came home from his safari to Atlantic City. Hoped he'd find the ancient ruins of the Playboy Club. Brought me this present."

She waited while I turned it over in my hand and returned the objet d'art to its rightful owner.

"That was my African phase," she said.

"What you use it for?"

"My phase?"

"The frog."

"Froggy keeps my papers from blowing away. It's a kind of a charm, I think. Reminds me of Cyprian, he's a minister-in-exile now, I think that's his title—minister-in-exile—made about ten million dollars in Swiss francs while serving his country in Health and Welfare. Lives in London. Gets off on pink blonds. Can you blame me for movin' on up, like Jesse says, after my African phase?"

"How do you feel about that? I mean, you're a pink blond, too."

"I'm a tanning blond, but let it pass. Frank, you've got to observe more closely. I'll admit, even we tanning blonds should use sunblock and I'm beginning to pay the price. I face that now. I don't want skin cancer and I don't want those Porcellana spots, either. But does it really *really* matter? Sometimes I can just touch Froggy underneath, you know, underneath here"—she had picked it up again, and I was afraid she would kiss it, and she did—"you know, underneath, where Cyprian adored to be kissed. I can get off on that. On my good memories, Frank."

She smiled and shrugged. She worked the long nail of her index finger against the comical lipstick on the undercarriage of the frog. Now her fingernail was pink with a sliver of waxen lipstick. Now her busy thumb had peeled it off. Now it was gone.

"Sometimes I like to remember Cyprian, no good reason, I just feel like staying in bed and remembering him. Suppose you or some other good lover didn't call yesterday, Frank. Just suppose. So I go get Froggy on my desk. I don't think Cyprian looked like that, who can keep those details in mind forever? I'm not sure anymore. He was black, most of him, that marvelous blue-black of African students, but one part of him was sort of pink or purple when it—"

She stopped, lowered her head, and the pale helmet of hair shook with the silent giggles. She bent her head to the frog, attentive to a thought. Her finger was working on the lipsticked phallus, scraping at some earlier joke or pastime. There was a heavy, almost torrid beach smell off her flesh, that pungent reek which a long afternoon in the sun might give her; beach oil, regret, and cum. Suki was a clean woman, one of the cleanest, pure and scrubbed; yet all at once the world and civilization, uncivilization and her thoughts, drenched her, as they do.

My heart worked hard, finding not enough place in my chest to hide. I didn't know if this panic was for love and pity or with fear that she might suspect I loved her, pitied her—didn't love her, despised her, needed to run away, couldn't bear to be without her. Animal dreads and hormones flooding, electrocutions and circuits flicking, I simply stood still for her. She printed her will upon me, striving for frivolity with all her heart. Out on the street a kid was skidding back and forth on a motorbike, yearning to kill, learning to destroy, preparing for his accident.

"Steve. Brat two doors down, worse'n Peter ever was," said Suki. "A few years ago he didn't know how to wipe his nose without help. Now he's got toy wheels, it doesn't matter if he wipes his nose. He's got everything he thinks he wants. Stupid family—mother, father, teenage hood. Peter doesn't even bother with him anymore."

The bullfrog's penis was wiped clean of lipstick.

"What does that have to do with it?" Suki asked. I didn't know what she was thinking of. She ducked her head toward the buzz outside. She was thinking about Motorbike Stevie. "I'd like a little quiet. I prefer bees buzzing"—she brightened—"or your heart thumping. I can hear it, Frank. I love natural sounds, but should you have a checkup? Or is it just you like me and I make you nervous?"

I laughed. "Modesty's not your strong suit, Suki."

"Oh, come on," she said. "You're my favorite person in the whole wide world. I can almost call you a friend."

New lovers stare. It may be the glaze of glands, but so what. They reach into each other's eyes, yearning and merging for a while. Later, when one of them loves less and perhaps the other loves more, the one who still loves a lot hunts for the eyes and the other is looking elsewhere, impatient or embarrassed by so much attention. The lover cannot find the loved one's eyes anymore. He still wants that truth of love;

the other will not yield it, or knows it exists no longer, if it ever did. Oh, surely it did. But it is gone now.

The conflict of eyes continues—this sad miscomprehension. Fondness forever is an aspiration few have but it might be a worthy dream, if we were not so drunk with that painful ambition to drown in eye-strutting and soul conversation and urgent infinite merging.

Suki was fond of me.

That was as far as she went.

I'm only discovering what I thought and think of Suki.

My body throbbed with the need to possess her, my heart pounded in her presence, I guess I wasn't just fond. "Mentor me," a young woman in the journalism department at Cal once asked, "then I can network you, and we can input each other." So I know what it's like not to be fond, also. Suki had insinuated herself by means of that power that I have trained myself to deny. I craved her; she didn't need to want me. I searched out the foolish ancient reasons for my stubborn longing: What point in being alive in May if you're not in love? And how about the rest of the year? Aren't all the months alike? Are the days and weeks and months only for dying in?

"No," I said.

She knew enough not to ask what I was saying no to. "Would you like to make love sweetly?"

she said. It was as if she had forgotten, or perhaps it hadn't been sweet. "I'm lonely, dear."

Maybe what was will be again.

Or maybe, I thought, what wasn't can't be brought to life. The black gloves will close on her throat no matter how lovely the May in her garden, the bird in the high branches. It circled, it was graceful, it was a hawk.

"Hold my hand as if you care for me. Just hold my hand. Then even you can make me do anything."

A miracle, I thought, a hawk in the city, if it isn't a gull.

"Did I tell you I'm worried about Peter? I did my best to be a good mother, but now what? I'm not sure."

"I'm not sure either," I said. "At this point, there's not much you can do. Do you want to know about him?"

"Didn't you say there's not much a mother can do? He needed more of a father than anyone gave him. Surely not *his* father." She sighed. "Oh, why should I bother you with these problems? Oh, Frank, life is so beautiful!" she sighed on a sunny afternoon of trying to feel good. "Why die? Why not make love?"

We did so.

I dreamed of possessing her even as it might have seemed I possessed her. There was a negative lightness in her soap and cologne cinnamon smells—the lack of calamity. When I told her this, she grinned like a child and said, *Blonds*, but it wasn't blondness. She had known disappointment, maybe even a few kinds of grief, but she was still a stranger to calamity. She sometimes acted like one of those salty crustaceans who drift without backbones, held together in the sea by their shells. I was sure the spine was there, I rubbed my hands down her back, I counted the articulations under the silky skin. She was held together in some fashion of being a woman that I couldn't fathom.

When she cried out, it sounded like a sob and she was laughing with that speckled flush on her forehead, cheeks, her breasts. She or I or both of us said, Good, good, good, and it was about our bodies, not about whatever else there is of us.

"Why grow old?" she asked during the sleepy time, sleepy for me, afterward. She rubbed her nose against mine (friendliness), tapped my shoulder (dismissal), and said, "You nap."

She got up to perform her yogic procedures, stretching like a cat, opening her mouth like a lion, running through the diagrams in the book open beside her little Japanese foam mat, held open by a bullfrog paperweight.

Only then did she take her bath, followed by a cold shower.

Only then was she ready to ask more questions about age, death, her son, and the meaning of life: "Should we have some pasta for dinner?"

And to finish her agenda for the day—to reminisce, now that I had been given my reward in advance, about her life in love. A young woman

of forty who has lived for adventures in love deserves a reward in lovers and friends who are
willing to listen, doesn't she? In a world burdened with time, she can't always be young and
forty, can she, no matter how she stretches, re-
laxes, curls, stiffens, opens her mouth to the future in the silent yogic lion's roar. She has
earned the chance to make her life real by telling
the best partial truth she can.

Nobody earned the right to be humble, at
least nobody Suki could recommend to herself.
Everybody wanted all he could get, maybe love
or power or money, surely improved grace and
beauty, maybe even just sweetness, sweet days,
tasty times, or another glass after the chilled
wine went down nicely—*something*—all of it, as
much as possible of all of it. The humble ones
out there were trying for less pain, less life, and
that was wrong, they shouldn't, and Suki didn't
need them. She had no use for those who strove
for less. Only the stupid and the unsuccessful
earned the right to be stupid, mad about it,
stumbling through their days, getting hurt, failing God and San Francisco.

Suki avoided these defeats. Steadily she
wanted everything. If she was sad, and of course
sometimes she was—she would be missing an experience if she missed sadness—she grew angry,
which piles strong chords upon the melody of
sadness, and then of course it's not sad at all.
One ran, one danced, one made fun, one found a

new friend. She had learned these words: Anger is an *empowerment*.

Mostly she did quite nicely without emergency fuel like anger, trouble, no way to turn. Crazy Wirt with his Breatharian religion, draw your juice from the great chain of being, no need for anything dirty, almost had a point there with Suki. If anything could check him out, Suki might. Solar power suited her better than burning fat. Mostly she was simply in love, a kind of love, which solved and then unsolved everything, in a rhythm which echoed the turns of the moon and her menses.

Tegrity, she called her desire. *In*-tegrity sounded too negative.

"Got your own ways," I mumbled, eyelids heavy, trying to listen, wanting to listen, wanting to sleep, wanting to close down the day with her, breathing with our arms around each other.

She was kind. This time she granted my wish. It's the powerful who know how to be kind. It's a part of tegrity.

That lonesome click-click-click and high-pitched whistle in the night of a train of thought continued as we lay curled together. Suki was still trying to make sense of things. She was also trying to let me sink as I needed to. Gradually she let go of her thoughts. We slept in a tangle. My heart was calmed. Suki's edge was softened. She was letting go, she was letting go, she was joining the world of men and women who can live at peace. In our dreamless passage we touched and, for different reasons, it was the comfort we needed.

Probably it wasn't later than midnight when I heard the noises and sat up. Dangling and quivering in the air like a marionette, Peter stood in the doorway, screaming, "Whore, whore, whore, whore!"

Suki's despairing wail: "What did I do?"

"What you always do, whore." And then he grinned at me, cooing with a marvelous gentleness, "You're just doing what comes natural, man. But listen, Frank, don't go talking about me to women anymore, okay? Not any goddamn woman or mother of mine or any conversation man to man."

"Maybe you shouldn't be ripping open doors—"

"Peter," said Suki, "my good little boy, what's the matter, Peter?"

"I mean, Frank," he said, "I mean you're old enough so you probably know it, a man's got to feed himself what he needs and eat all the cunt he can and watch his ass. Mom thinks she can't use hers up."

"Peter," Suki said.

"I think you better close that door," I said.

"G'night, folks."

SIX

My college roommate in Ann Arbor eloped with
a prof while we were still planning our summer
together. ("Hi, Frank, I just fell in love—sorry
about that!") Even then, like other solemn young
men, I had a yen for chipper young women, un-
burdened by gloomy responsibilities for the future. Now, like other solemn middle-aged profs,
I fastened onto a university career partly because of its memory of uncompleted college
days, its never-ending hope of liveliness, its dili-
gent irresponsibility, and when I stood off and
looked at myself—which I tended to do more
often than was useful—I saw the false youth of a
tennis-playing Berkeley campus personality.
("That's Frank Curtis at the net, used to work on
the most important paper in southern Michigan,
he turned down a column." "Southern *Michigan?*" "I think it's near Detroit or Chicago, isn't

that where they had the riots? He was into print media from the beginning. I had coffee with him once, he's not that bad when he gets going—")

In my retreat into northern California, my cottage above the campus, my routines of instruction and distraction, I lacked some needed risks. I used to crave wildness; I still did. Suki taught me discontentment with the comfort in which I was hiding. Peter's rage and wildness reverberated in me; I didn't have a son of my own; I knew I still craved vividness, although I was trying to answer both Peter and the craving with appropriate patience. I was a bit smug and wise, wasn't I? Undeservedly planning to be helpful and unhurt?

Disaster seemed to be some of the attraction around here. There was still a lot of boyishness in the neighborhood. Peter was reverse-imaged in the gloomy, physically fit, adjunct professor of journalism.

I sat on his bed and tried to put a space of heavy silence into the conversation before I began it. I was looking for adult advantages. He was tapping his foot and watching me sideways. Suddenly, as if he didn't have much time to waste, he picked up a TV remote-control device and began unscrewing the back of it with a tool on his pocketknife. He exposed a nest of transistors and wires. He looked up, wondering if I was planning to get started or just to sit there all day while he lined up the red wires, the green wires, the yellow wires, a little clip, the screws, the batteries, on a strip of white paper.

There was no advantage in waiting. I couldn't find the edge on him. I might as well just stop trying to out-silent him and begin. I said: "Your mother asked me to talk with you about the other night."

"Can't Suki talk to me herself? She speaks English."

"Is that what you call her?"

"Isn't that her name? She used to tell me to say her name like everybody does. Used to worry it'd scare her boyfriends hear a kid yelling, Mom, Mom, Hey Mom, around breakfast. Used to think her boyfriends wanted a girlfriend, not somebody's mother."

"Your mother asked me to speak with you," I repeated.

"I'm here. Speak."

"Why are you sore at her? What's your gripe about me?"

Silence. He was trying for cool and easy; didn't make no never-mind to him. But there was a web of tiny sweat drops on his upper lip. It was not a hot day.

"Because if you are," I asked, "sore, why don't we talk about it?"

"Go ahead. I don't mind."

He slid the strip of white paper under the chair with the lineup of electronic innards. He got it out of the way. He shrugged, leaned over,

set the folding knife on the far edge of the strip
of paper, sat back up, and smiled helpfully.

I sat on his bed and concentrated on breathing. He watched me from the chair in front of
his tape library. On the wall there was a poster
of two naked brown people draped in leather
straps, one showing a thin strap pulled tight between the buttocks. With the strain of the faces,
the disposition of the flesh, the pulling of the
straps, the gleaming and shadows and cropped
hair, I was not sure which, if either, of the figures was male, which female. These were not
personality portraits.

Peter observed my sighing, that this was difficult for me, that I was letting him know it was
difficult for me, and he grinned. He decided to
put me at my ease. "Usually I like the spades
better, but you're one of Suki's studs I also like.
The spade guys are neat, especially that cop,
what's his name, Alfonso, I really like him, too.
Sometimes I don't like his stink in the morning,
but that's not his fault. I'm liberal."

"Peter," I said.

"Well, Mom and him get that jism-cunt smell.
They like their coffee before they shower. You're
going to say it's my fault, aren't you? I mean, I
could stay in bed till after they shower, or take
my cereal to my room, couldn't I? Well, it's my
house, too."

"That's not what I wanted to talk about."

" 'Course, maybe it's not, since Dad owes me

so much child support and he never gonna pay. And I'm a big kid now."

"Peter."

"Funny, you came here to lecture me, and I'm lecturing you."

"I came more to listen to you."

"I'll bet," he said. "Oh, boy. I bet."

He was dressed in a blue denim uniform with patches of white where the threads showed, the knees came through. This was not the careless jeans-wearing of another time. His shirt was blue, his pants were blue, his socks were white, his running shoes were blue. His jeans jacket was blue. His calculating eyes were as dark as an IBM screen. He raked his hands through his hair, which was long and fine, unlike the butch punk slices of hair on the male or female leather people in his poster. Peter, like Suki, had his own ways of doing things. He leaned against the metal wings of his chair and looked blue and unperturbed at me. It was up to me how long I stayed. It made no difference to him. His slouch and lean said he might have something better to do—listening to his tapes, say—but he could spare the time.

I simply waited. One of us needed to talk. Finally he said, "Is there any reason besides what I think you might have a special interest in me? Since I'm a minor, a minor's welfare? Since you're not a shrink or a social worker, some special reason such as fucking my mother?"

One excellent option was to walk, and immediately. Another option might be to follow this through like a good dog. I chose not to walk. "Are you asking me, Peter?"

"Don't make no difference, does it?"

"You asked. It does to you."

"A difference," he said, thinking this over. There were so many things to consider. "I was just wondering. Take away a little of the edge you got on me 'cause you *think* you got an edge. I already suppose to have a father, in case you didn't know."

"I think," I said, "I've got a disadvantage against you. Because I think I should be talking to you. And you see no good reason. So I'm not—"

"You're not in a strong position," he said cheerfully. "Okay, I like to laugh."

"Are you laughing now?"

"Can't you tell? This is—Mom would say—delightful. Is that what she says? *That was delightful, Frank. That felt good, Frank, really delightful. Do it again please Frank.*"

"I can go right now, Peter. I don't need this."

He answered something. I didn't hear him. He was looking inside someplace, his eyes seeming to darken, as gold-flecked eyes sometimes do, as Suki's blue ones did when reality flooded over her even though she had already proved that reality is not really real.

"What did you say, Peter?"

In a whisper he repeated, "Don't. Don't go yet."

What I then thought: If he needs to beat on me a little, I'll let him. I'll just remember that whisper, this need, and let him. Was I not supposed to be the adult around here?

I stretched my legs and waited.

"Mom thinks trying to be young makes her more viral," he said.

The kid was so smart and swift in his moves and just a kid. "I think you mean virile," I said. "Viral refers to diseases. And with women they don't usually use that word, it's considered to be a man's word."

He shrugged. "That's cool. It's a disease and it's a man's word, but that's okay for Suki. Why don't *you* call her Mom?"

"Your mother's my friend now. Suki, the way things go around here, she's an old friend. That's what I think about her."

"Congratulations, occupant, you may have won a three-hundred-and-forty-thousand-dollar dream house for subscribing to Suki. Now all you have to do is make it with my mom and see if she likes you best. At her age, she might could want to settle down—"

"Your mother runs her own life, Peter."

"—or are you just . . ." He grinned and thrust with his hips and sang, "Are you just a vagabond lover? Da-dah!"

White seams where the jeans were washed and worn, worn through, threads showing. The Cloroxed thread-showing white-bleached look was still popular in certain sophisticated teen circles.

"Peter, why are you so sore at me?"

He thought that one over. He took that one under advisement. He decided to correct it. "No. What I think is I'd like to sing with you, talk with you, maybe dance with you. You into dancing? with me? Suki's boy?"

An intelligent person would have just walked away. An intelligent person might have thought to himself, Well, Suki was fun but this is unnecessary. There was no need to keep this going.

I thought he might just blow off his froth if I waited. Like other impatient men, I've learned a false calm.

He was smiling at me. He enjoyed my patience. His smile lit up the world like a strobe light—first here, now there, then gone, then here again, and it's all for dancing. Like Suki, he had not yet decided if the world deserved a steady light from him. There was a silver twinkle on Peter's chest, a chain; would it gradually, as Peter grew hair on his chest, turn golden in color, and double and triple itself in new links and chains? The boy had probably never in his life buttoned the three top buttons of his shirt. Snaps; no, they were snaps. He was of a generation that didn't know much about buttons.

"My mother's the big sexpot, isn't she? Well, I tried that. I can still do it—made it with a lot of girls. All my friends do. I don't try to get ahead of Mom."

"A kid never can. That's what it is about being someone's child. When you grow up, you stop rivaling."

"Neat, *child.*"

"It'll come in time, Peter."

He was fidgeting, something on his mind. He had another hope. "Frank?"

"What is it?"

"One thing I can do, Mom can't?"

"I'll bet there are several."

"Pee standing up—that's a start. Hey, Frank?"

"What?"

He stretched out in the bleached jeans so the seams drew tight and the threads whitened like capillaries and the flesh was showing and bulging through, no undershorts, and he was making sure I noticed.

"Don't be dumb, Peter. I know you're a smart kid. I know you don't like me and you like me. I know—"

"Man, do you know a lot. Do you know everything, Frank?"

"Okay, Peter."

"Okay, *Frank.*"

The look on his face was boyish, sulky, jokey, ingratiating, that complex talent of the teenager in California or anyplace, the one with his own room, stereo, tape deck, video equipment, wheels, secrets, power, a history of getting his own way but not getting what he wanted. He had done his laundry and the pile of sorted, balled-together sweat socks, clean but with permanently darkened toes, lay at his feet like fuzzy snowballs. He picked one up and threw it at me.

I threw it back. Catch. Silent snowball fight in his bedroom. He giggled.

He pelted one at me. I caught it with my fingers. He frowned.

He reached into the drawer—white-painted metal filing cabinet furniture—and pulled out a slingshot. It was an evil metal transaction, no joke. "What!" I said. He aimed it at the window, which was open a few inches. "Don't!" I said, but he did and a metal pellet, capable of killing a bird, breaking a window, blinding a man, shot through the narrow open space.

"Good aim for a *child*," he said.

My heart was thumping and my head felt empty and adrift in panic. He lifted another weapon from the drawer, this time a rosary, blackened beads on a chain. "Cover my ass," he said. "I can protect myself. But just in case."

"You like to blaspheme, too."

"Right! I do! What does that word mean?"

"Don't you read?"

"If I have to. I get most of my news from the machines. I got other things to do. I got things I like to do."

He waited for me to answer. It wasn't a question; it needed no comment.

"Like a little detail," he said. "I got something might be in your interest."

"I don't think so and I doubt it."

"Could be wrong this time, Frank. You tried a fresh stud like me yet?"

"For what?"

He considered his answer. There seemed to be a tape delay. Things could be spliced together in the editing process. Having thought, he stood up, one knee came forward and was bent, the index finger jabbed toward me in the TV-host air-poke of enthusiasm, and his mouth began to move. "Go for it!" he cried, wiggling. "You got it!" He paused. "Or we could just sleaze around for a while, smokin' a little dope, watchin' MTV. Yours is the choice."

"Not much of a decision, is it?"

"Okay, question for you," he said.

I decided to ride this through to the end, or whatever it came to, even if it wasn't the end.

"What if . . ." He stopped and grinned. It looked like embarrassment and it wasn't embarrassment and it was to get my attention. He had that natural trick of not looking at me, making me look at him; he put the space over my shoulder on notice, he squinted at my knees, he made his little smiles. He had my attention, but I didn't plan to wrap it up in gift paper and ribbons. I was going at it wrong. I sat back, pulled at my socks, pulled my eyes away from him. He would have to settle for that. "What if, Frank? What if I tell Mom you made a pass at me?"

He had a little more of my attention.

Peter was making little sniffing laughs

through his nostrils, or maybe he had a cold, or maybe he had found a way to get too much coke.

"But I'd have to be crazy to think of a thing like that," he said. "Unless it was true."

And now his laughter was free and boyish and cute. He liked how I didn't move, didn't turn, didn't speak. If I were an animal, I might be hibernating, but since I was not, and there was no winter here in San Francisco, I was merely sleepy.

"The trouble with school is everything's in general," Peter said. "Let's go into a few details. If we get down, what do we find?"

"What are you trying for?"

"We, Frank. *We* trying for. I got my whole life ahead of me and you, man, you only got, max, some of it. I know Mom looks at it like that, too. She tries to say every day is her whole life, sunrise her run—she runs on the Marina—and nights of, you know, white wine and a little crotch aerobics, but I do believe she knows it's going by. For her and for you, too."

"We can probably agree on that. I'm not surprised by the news."

"Then what I'm saying. What I'm offering is do you want to taste what it's still like for me? I'm making this offer, Frank."

He had told me that the old-style hippies were now called granolas. He had slipped me samples of teenage information for several years now. He still had an edge on me. He liked that detail, knowing things people didn't know, controlling a person by surprising him.

Since he wanted to hold me here, he decided to ease off with a little gossip.

"I'm not like other kids around Sa'Fracisco. You know, good time, steal Daddy's dope, taste Mommy's ortho creme, wait it out."

"Wait *what* out?"

"Getting to be not a kid anymore. I didn't wait. Figured out the worst things can happen. They can. Even worse than the worst."

"What about the best?"

"You think? Oh, man, I'm not really stupid. Not that. Non ess possiblay. No, man, I don't play those games with anybody."

"Let us stipulate you are sort of like a grown-up already," I said with full pomp, and he laughed, which must have been part of what I had in mind. I wanted to change our routine.

"Discouraged, you mean? It doesn't discourage me. I'm not discouraged. Nothing gets me down."

"You learn that from—"

"From heavy metal," he said. I wasn't sure if he meant music. "So since I know"—he looked down to my belt, and then at my face, and then finally met my eyes—"I *know*, so you can do me."

"Know do what?"

"Do me, Frank. Do me. Do me like you do my—"

"Stop it!"

"Does my mother the family friend smell like new grass with dew on it in the morning? That's what one of her faggot lovers said to her—I heard them one time—one of her faggot poet boyfriends who can't tell she stinks like anybody else all smeared with sweat and cum."

"Enough, Peter."

"Enough what?" He pulled at his T-shirt. "Just to say hello, we're friends, we're kind of related, now will you do me?"

I jumped out of the chair; this was no time to be sleepy.

"Just once or twice hard? Because you want to?"

"Not funny, Peter."

"Just to fool around a little, do me?"

This was beyond what I had intended with Suki.

He shrugged; the grin was slow. He was being a cowboy now. "Tight 'n juicy, is my mom tight and juicy?"

I was standing, but all at once he was very quick. With a compelling urgency he reached with his hands, he wasn't unbuttoning his jeans, he was ripping the worn material along the thigh, he took out his penis, which was long, thin, ropy, bluish, erect. "This came out of my mother!" he shouted as I fled.

He leaned out the window.

"Hey, mister! Hey, *you!*"

SEVEN

Suki couldn't remember too well what it was like to be married to Cal Crowell, but she had a clear, blue-eyed, indulgent, exasperated picture of her life with him as ex-spouse. "Let me share it with you," she said in the California style, and as she told it I could imagine their meetings, his tenseness, her impatience, even a little of the fondness she almost felt for him, at least when her own income in the wine promotion trade enabled her to keep up with her bills. Including some Cal was supposed to pay.

I liked to half-listen as she did that well-known classic, the ex-wife monologue, in her own fashion. I could dream along with her account, filling in the snippiness, the sarcasm, the resentment, the lyric arias, the dramatic verses, the post-marital sex—the things she left out and the things she didn't leave out—when Suki paused, sighed, and apologized for taking up my valuable time.

"You are my valuable time," I said. "Don't you know I'm greedy?"

She cast her eyes down modestly. Okay, then it was all my fault if I let her talk about Cal Crowell and his former missus and their only child.

Cal had two children. Actually, he had three, if he counted Peter, his son by Suki, but he had two kids with his new wife and (jaw jutting) *they were very very happy together*. Chapter 11 couldn't keep an enterprenoor down. An enterprenoor keeps corporate separate from personal. Personally, the new Crowell family was remodeling a house in Burlingame, doing a lot of the work themselves on weekends. Even the kids, a boy and a girl, were remodeling their playhouses. These were non-union kids. There was no role definition in his family; everybody remodeled together. The boy seven, Cal Junior, just seven, was so cute he put talcum powder in his hair. He wanted to show what his father's hair was getting to look like.

First Cal thought it was dust from the remodeling. But then he realized it was the white that followed the blond which had seemed to him at one time to make such a perfect match for Suki. Everybody now knew that striking hair similarities made for a happy marriage no more than dissimilarity might. A farsighted business-technology student like Cal should have thought it through in a logical and cost-effective way, but Suki was such fun—she seemed to be such fun in those days—he didn't.

So Cal, in addition to his kids, had this adolescent child-support item, Peter. And every once in a while, growing white-haired, much on his mind to weigh him down, no longer a match for Suki, it behooved him to get together with her to discuss like competent and mature human beings the questions that came up: money; the direction the boy was taking; payments for doctors or tuition or just general support; the goddamn way the boy was headed; money. Did the therapist really have to be an M.D.? Couldn't she be, like, a school counselor? Did it have to cost so much?

Suki didn't like to nag. She had too much dignity. She liked to keep good relations. She just made demands. And Cal didn't like to argue. He just knew how to remain silent and resist. He was in that minority of lawyers and entrepreneurs who chose to perfect this poorly understood traditional negotiating technique. It was even helpful when a person had to take his company into Chapter 11, due to unforeseeable changes in the money markets.

Neither of them enjoyed the discussions; Cal because he always lost ground in the end, Suki because her gain was a foregone conclusion and therefore no real contest. But since she was both generous and contemptuous, she never won enough. Eventually, out of irritation, a final resolution not arrived at, receding, still out of reach, they would have to schedule another discussion. After all, Peter was still their oldest child.

Suki and Cal made a periodic ritual of meeting for lunch. Sometimes Cal came into downtown San Francisco for business reasons; Bay Area Rapid Transit, the underground, was fairly convenient, and clean, federally subsidized transportation helped to increase the value of the house being remodeled in Burlingame. Suki used to put up her hair in her custody-child-support bun and they would try to find a quiet financial district restaurant, not the Iron Pot or the Poodle Dog, something a little out of the way and peaceful. There were a couple of dark and cozy taverns in some of the alleys between the new skyscrapers—Suki suggested Mario's. She made the trip downtown as a convenience for Cal. She always enjoyed Mario's with the little oil lamp on each table and the tablecloth as thick and white as they used to be in the old days. But it was so confusing for Suki: She pushed him back and forth, she let down her hair suddenly, taking out the pins, forgetting she was not supposed to seduce him, she had to try three or four garages before she could find a place for her BMW. It was also confusing for Cal.

They agreed about lunch not always being the greatest idea.

So Cal would just come to her house after work, maybe visit with Peter a little, maybe the kid liked that, sometimes they do; and then Suki and Cal would have a drink and talk.

Once, maybe a few times, they went to bed. Not the greatest idea, either. But there was no really right greatest idea in this enterprise of being a modern parent. So here was Cal again, remembering that in addition to his two kids at home, at the new house in Burlingame, he had this other boy. Who was two inches taller than Cal. Who was the child of Suki. Who was causing his mother a lot of worry and she wondered if just paying for things here and there was all that Cal intended to do about it, not that she didn't sympathize with Cal's new wife's desire to have Calvin around tipping over buckets of nails when the specialized union workmen were finishing up something in the roof or the wiring. Perhaps he could do some father stuff with Peter, too.

She remembered it like this, with me filling in the gaps for myself:

"Work going well?"

"It's okay." He didn't inquire whether she meant his Chapter 11 legal activities or the remodeling.

She was making nice, pouring a little Oil of Language over their meeting. "You doing redwood shingles?"

"Oh, come on, Suki. Can I have a cup of coffee, instant'll do?"

"You know I only serve good coffee. I do instant nothing. How about espresso? I make cappucino, too." She couldn't resist: "You're *not* doing redwood shingles?"

"Skylights," he said, "with yellow-tinted glass, well not really glass, it's a transparent plastic, epoxy sealant, and they cant it at an angle to catch the north light—"

"Because you need a little sunshine in your life, don't you, Cal? Does she really call you Cal-*vin?*"

He was breathing shallowly. "I drove over here today. Usually I don't take the car. I came to talk with you about Peter. I'm here."

She touched his wrist. "I'm sorry, I'm sorry. I must really still like you so I want to climb on top and prove—I'm sorry, Cal."

She could win by disarming herself if she didn't win by destroying her antagonist. She preferred to be accommodating, but of course she knew what was important.

"I'm here, Suki—I need to know what you want."

"Peter," Suki said. "He's running with some rowdy rich kids. The poor ones aren't any better. Rowdy's not the word. Well, forget the word. I mean he's, I'm sure he's doing a little grass—okay, so what? He's hard to handle. He doesn't have a clue what he plans for the future. He doesn't plan anything. I mean I'm his mother, but you're his dad."

"It's been hard to take hold."

"You shouldn't have stepped aside."

"I didn't. You . . ."

"Okay, I made it unpleasant for you. I admit, I agree. I'm sorry. But long after it should have stopped embarrassing you, what I did, if there was a man in my life—"

"Embarrassing!"

"Okay, then. You should have stopped being jealous. Our marriage was over."

"A matter of opinion. I agree that in the end your opinion turned out to be correct."

"So you should have worked harder on your only son."

"Now I have two other kids. I work hard. I enjoy them. I don't have to work hard on them. I work hard on my job and on the remodeling. Sheila and I work hard on it together. I know how to work hard when I can, Suki."

"Toughie. You weren't a toughie when I knew you." A little wrist action again. He flinched as if it hurt, that stroking of his wrist in the odd way she had.

"So let's get to business."

"Peter's not business."

"It's not necessary to criticize how I express myself, Susan. I'm here for a reason. Let's get to the reason."

"I'm worried about him."

"He's an adolescent. That's their main occupation—to worry parents."

"You're not worried, then?"

"What's his problem?"

"I worry about his driving. About motorcycles. About what chemicals he's using. About his friends. About girls."

"At least he's straight."

"That's an assumption."

"Look who's talking like a lawyer." But he was puzzled and troubled. "He's not?"

"He's a free person. He can do anything he wants, as long as he's decent. And me too, Cal, so what I'm doing is worrying and asking if you can take hold a little."

"Of what? Take hold of what? A handful of water?"

"He's your son. There's some blood and bone in there, not just water."

"But just try to take hold of it. For years you thought he was produced by partheno—what do they call it—genesis, Suki alone all by yourself, didn't need me except for the checks—"

"Which usually came late."

"Which came. So now you want me to *take hold*. And I'd like to know of what? What kid? I barely know him. I can look at the color of his eyes and think maybe he's mine. But a lot of people seem to have that color of eyes."

"He's *yours*."

"I'm only explaining how you made me feel."

"Do you have any feelings you can claim as your own? Coming just from you, Cal?"

"Look, that's wrong of me. I shouldn't say that. I have a problem dealing with you. I'm sorry."

This time she did not touch his wrist. It was an experiment, watching him float by his own strength. "It takes a big man to admit he was wrong, Cal. So something has made you a big man, and whatever it was, I congratulate her."

"My wife likes me."

"Sheila."

"She does. My kids do, too. It's not the life I planned with you when we were very young. But it works fine. The family works fine and the house will, too, soon as we finish." He laughed. "Building the house together helps a lot. I can't tell you what nailing shingles does for a man when a kid he likes a lot is standing there and handing them up to him and saying, 'Here it is, Dad.' "

"Can you answer him with tacks in your mouth?"

"I wear the nails in a little bag on my belt, dear." He waited for her to ask what else he carried in a little bag on his belt. She did not ask. "So can we get back to business now?"

There was a hard revving motor sound on the street. Suki tilted her head and said, "He never comes home in the afternoon if he's not already here sleeping."

"It's Peter?"

"He'll know we're talking about him."

Cal looked about. "Do you want me to hide?"

"People don't have to hide in this house. That's not our style. Wouldn't it be funny to have the former husband hiding from the son?"

They stopped while Peter thrashed through the door, swinging something that bumped the wall—a duffel bag—and then Suki said, "Careful!"

Peter stared at his father. "Hey, man, you two together again? That'd be a kick. Am I in the way here? Listen, I got to grab a quick shower, so while the water's running, you'll know I can't hear you, whatever you're doing."

"We're talking, son, that's—"

Peter shook his shoulders as if the word *son* brought him a sudden chill. "Makes no difference to me what you're doing. Hey, seeya, Dad!"

"I'll be here when you come out of the bath."

Mom and Dad stared at each other. For a moment they felt the ancient complicity. Suki patted her husband's hand. This was for her sake as well as his. "All by himself he's a home entertainment center," she said. "I should put our Peter on tape for when I'm bored, but of course—"

"You never are," said Cal.

"I never am. Bored is not my problem."

There fell upon the room that silence familiar to Suki, during which she stared speculatively, alertly, and sideways at the man, deciding what she wanted to do about him at this time. If she wanted to bed him, they might be obliged to enjoy merely a quick adolescent non-bed wrestle while her son was taking one of his long teenage showers which included the massaging scrape with a pile of towels. She used to like to dry Peter's back, rub him glowing and grinning, tickle him a little, a lot; but she had decided it wasn't such a good idea—about three or four months ago she had decided that. Peter had the bad habit of using every towel in the bathroom. Although he was a big boy, this was wasteful. Afterward someone has to stick them in the Bendix; often mothers have this job.

Cal was staring at her.

A quickie, standing up, or leaning and shivering against the wall, with the father of the boy— it would have to be that, or arrange something for later, when the impulse would probably pass. Suki knew the impulse was light and fleeting, one of those unexpected alertnesses that came over her.

Cal stared.

Suki sighed. "I'm grown up." It was a suspicion she had. She put off the pleasure indefinitely, shrugging, lightly darting forward to rub her nose like an eskimo belle against her former husband's nose. "I don't do that so much anymore," she said to him. "Isn't that good? It's not just you. If I did with anyone anymore, I might with you."

"Thanks," said Cal. He was trying to imagine it was only her assumption that he, a happily married man and father, was waiting for his former wife's invitation to part her pale rosy thighs and lift and unzip and press panting and moaning and flinging himself heedlessly into her. It would be an act of useless revenge and desire and childish hope. Nostalgia was not his sort of thing, really. She could only assume something stupid like that about him, that he might be capable of pressing her against the wall and fumbling at his pants and letting them fall around his ankles for an instant of thrusting and mumbling (Suki would giggle at his haste), because she knew him through and through.

In general, he was grateful for her new, lying, sensible character in life.

Suki was smiling and jittering and singing very softly, sweetly, almost as if it were an anthem, the song that had been a big hit in California a little before they met, and Cal had bought her a record of it by—was it the Four Tops? no, the Eberle Brothers—"Runaround Sue." Neither of them remembered whether Sue stopped running around by the end of the song, or ran around forever, but both of them remembered having fun with the song; Cal, because it was sad and true; Suki, because it was true, although no one called her Sue anymore since she discovered her real automobile (BMW) and her real name.

"Do you still have it?" he asked.

"I haven't lost it," she said indignantly.

"The record, I mean."

"I remember, Cal! No. I think it got mislaid when one of us left the other and there was so much moving around."

They could hear Peter knocking over containers in the bathroom. When bathroom containers used to be glass, they used to break. So many things had improved since Cal and Suki were children. Products and goods had adjusted to the traditional phenomenon of people misbehaving in the bathroom yet not wanting to cut their feet.

"It's my fault. I would have kept it if I could," Suki said.

"That's all right, I'm—"

"You're what?"

He blurted out, "I'm very happy with my wife."

"And your kids, you're very happy with them, too," said Suki, touching his hand like the star she was, wielding one of the many in her repertory of touches, this stroke the consoling one of pure palship she used for her gay friends—not that she meant it in that way or that Cal would take it in that way. It's just that certain gentle touches are like others. There was no way he could identify the brush of her fingertips as that identical brush with which Suki consoled Hossein, Brian, or Dennis for the chagrins nature and history had thrown in their paths.

There was a Peter noise from the bathroom.

"Open the door, who can hear you with the door shut?" Suki called.

The door came open and a billow of steam emerged, followed by Peter wrapped in two towels. "I said: you finished out there?"

"Finished with what?"

"Finished what you're usually doing, Mom—"

Cal thought it might be time to move along, take the forty-minute drive back to his wife and children, skip the office this afternoon, though he had not properly finished the business that had brought him here into the dangers of seeing Suki. He would have liked to enjoy a friendly farewell with his nearly grown son, discuss school, girls, athletics, a few brief remarks, whatever came up, but under the circumstances he was not sure how to manage it.

"—with your boyfriend visitors," Peter said.

Suki was smiling. That's all there was—smile. She knew she couldn't get blood from a stone or from someone whose blood had all seeped out. She smiled upon her former husband as if he were a fact of nature that could not be reformed, deserved no contempt, just lay there inert in the world. The same smile served for her son because she was only beginning to wake up to the storm. The first thing was to survey the damage, try for control, even admire the trouble on its way. It was her all-purpose Storm Central smile.

Looking at her bright face, Cal might have thought someone had uttered a kindness, a flattery about him. But he also thought he should leave at once, and did, nodding to his former wife and forgetting or not figuring out how to say good-bye to his son.

"Bye, Dad."

Maybe just a "Bye, son," would do.

Suki managed to stir him whenever he saw her, no matter how firmly he changed his life, putting far away that terrain of earthquake and eruption.

With a precise hemorrhoidal waddle, Cal strolled out toward his blue Renault-American Motors Le Car. Suki wondered that her husband should have become so solemn, so swamped. He used to be only two years older than she was.

"Frank!" she asked. "Have you been listening to me? Did I put you to sleep with this awful stuff?"

"I've been listening."

"You've been dreaming your own version of it. Don't you believe what I say?"

"I also believe what you don't say."

"You've been making it into your own dream, like you do, Frank! To your detriment, don't you think?"

"Maybe."

"Frank, tell me something," she said, leaning forward, aglow with amusement and intelligence. "In your version, are you Cal? Or Suki? Or maybe Peter? And why don't you try just being Frank?"

EIGHT

The laughing dick called, but he wasn't laughing. "Alfonso—remember?"

"Sure thing. We talked about fingerprinting, didn't we? Suki's birthday." I wasn't going to say, You used to be the two-hundred-fifty-pound and high-I.Q. black detective, aren't you still? If so, people tend not to forget.

He paused. "I'm the schwartzer," he said.

He wasn't laughing by phone. This easy, hefty, roll-through-life fellow had his own trade on his mind, with me mixed into the business. "I'd prefer to have a little talk," he said. "You could come down to Central Station, but that's so formal—the interruptions and all. Or we could meet in a place, you know, a bar, a nice joint. So why don't I just drive on over to your house and you'll make me a cuppa instant is all I require?"

149

Which was what had been on his mind all along. He wanted to talk and he wanted to see my place and he wanted to look us over. He didn't want me to be too nervous, but he didn't mind if I were a little. People might tend to flutter a bit at his approach. It's natural when a detective has this trombone-solo voice and a fleshy swiftness, which he had. It wouldn't be traffic tickets. It wouldn't be shoplifting, since I hadn't done any noticeable shoplifting since I was a kid. What would it be?

Like any fine upstanding citizen, I felt guilty and angry. I was sure I had done something and I was indignant. And I played the game he was playing. "Sure, love to see you, Alfonso," I said.

Maybe he had me on that interstate heavy truck deal—the time I hijacked a Tonka from the Weinstein Kids' Gift Shop when I was eleven years old. If so, I'd just confess, cop a plea, and strive to pick up the scattered shards of my life.

But it was serious.

He rolled in with that fat, smart, high-on-the-qualifying-exam grin on his face, but no audible chuckles. The sound was turned off. He looked about, checking, as if he were trying for the polite place to put his coat. He wasn't wearing a coat; this was Berkeley.

The sun through my stained-glass windows made lizard stripes on the walls, patterns dating from the Aquarian age. A fellow who had been around, like Alfonso, might have assumed a Telegraph Avenue stained-glass girlfriend back in my graduate student days. He would have assumed wrong; the house was part of a long-desanctified rectory, unblessed in a prudent political and real estate maneuver by the Episcopal diocese. After a 1971 escalation in the nonnegotiable demand industry, they decided to use the chapel funds for a Black Panther breakfast-and-custom-tailoring program. But Alfonso probably knew his Berkeley history and remembered all that. Or didn't; Bay Area political hassles weren't his specialty. He had a job to do. I made mountain coffee, eggshells and ground beans. Old graduate-student habits die hard.

Some of the books on my shelves had bleached bindings from the steady rainbow sunlight. Alfonso seemed to notice that, too—he carried I.Q. slopping over in that big skull and wasn't required to devote everything to law enforcement and investigation.

Alfonso's look: This guy isn't normal. This is not your normal straight-arrow non-tenured adjunct professor of journalism.

Now how did he get off looking at me like that, with his cop's fat grin? There was no malice in it, but there was calculation. There was threat. As I poured the coffee ("Black, no sugar, that's cool," he said), I heard my heart thumping and blessed my healthy metabolism for not giving me shaking hands. Not yet. I didn't hold still to verify. Alfonso was watching me intently. A few more visits like this one and I'd have my Parkinson's disease. Lizard colors were shifting and glowing on the walls. I tried to see life through Alfonso's eyes. When a vehicle passed on the street, it was reflected in reflections; the sunlight swelled and the rainbow colors blurred, fuzzed, refocused. If I were Alfonso, I'd say it was pretty; but I wasn't Alfonso, and Alfonso was oppressed by the tidings he had to bring me because we had met socially, friendly, just nice folks, and he hoped to do his job as gracefully as possible for a man who was a colleague in the general arena of San Francisco hanging out; and he was sighing, still grinning, no chuckles, but the sighs were so heavy they began to blow over into the category of yawns.

"The boy say," he began.

And the sound was turned off.

I waited a while and then asked, "The boys say?"

"The *boy*," he said. "The boy say you—"

I heard a shriller Frank Curtis, as if my voice box were constricted in Alfonso's grip. "What me? What boy?"

"Peter."

"Oh, shit. What does he say?"

"You used to play with him."

"I've known him for years. Still do."

Sighs and heavings of the heavy dinner muscle, a cotton edge of T-shirt appearing beneath the separated buttons of twill or gabardine or whatever that practical institutional fabric was. "I mean *play* with him. We have no other evidence. And of course he's about eighteen now, so the alleged offenses occurred when he was a minor, but if he appears at a hearing the way he looks, trying to grow a mustache—"

"*What?*" I was saying like a duck, what-what-what.

I was dizzy. I was weak in the joints. I wanted to throw up. I wanted to give myself the benefit of the doubt; I wouldn't throw up.

The cop sighed. "You spent nights in his house."

"In his *mother's* house."

Alfonso said, "Shum." The machinery was working. Like a true advanced-training cop, he said, "Evidently." It came out *evidentally.* "I think I know that. But you understand there's been all this stuff about molest, *this* molest, *that* molest, even fathers, mothers, boyfriends, we even got a complaint of a molest happened a girl-friend—"

"I can't believe this."

A bad case of the mutual sighs. I was hyper-ventilating and he was swelling out his chest and letting go and swelling out again. "This kid is definitely not an animal," Alfonso said. "He fits into the human bracket. Gives input, takes output. He's proximately in the bracket. In any case, the boy is almost eighteen. The alleged per-petrator was a close personal friend of the mother. Is. Of course, in my community that's often the case. But we're not dealing here with my community," he said, frowning in a way that made him look more black—it was the lips, the pout—and then added: "What I hate most is these kind of cases, even though there's not no danger to me personally, the types are never wild or violent, that's probably their trouble."

I said nothing. Let him ramble. I was not wild or violent—did that make me suspicious?

"Without other corroborating evidence, I doubt it'll hold up. But it's what he's telling his psychological counselor."

"He believes him?"

"Could he identify intimate moles, I mean little tricks of the skin or hair, you know? He says he can."

"You believe him?"

"Not necessarily. Says you have a dark spot on the underneath side of your, well, for purposes of identification, cock. I mean, is that true?" I was silent. "I mean, you'd have to get pretty close to notice a thing like that."

"Alfonso, you believe him."

"The trouble in my business is almost everybody's a perpetrator, including the ones get off. I'm not necessarily convinced, but she is."

"Who *she?*"

"His therapist. She asked us to check it out. The kid wasn't looking for legal action, not at first, he was just gassing off. Something to make the hour worth Suki's money—sort of like a special added offer. Maybe his dad, what's his name, Mr. Crowell there, pays medical bills, I don't know—"

"Jesus Christ!"

"It's the big idea these days, they call it the biblical transgression, one of them anyway, incest, only I guess you're not the father and Peter's not the daughter. You're only the mother's plaything, but—"

The word made my legs jump. Alfonso shrugged and extended his purplish palms. Plaything—he was sorry.

"It's the best they've got. Therapist say the kid tells her the truth 'cause she can always tell. She didn't mention she's a miracle person for seeing right through to the bottom of everything, but I spose that come with the office. Dr. Kowalski, she call it Kowalska, thinks it has something to do with his little problems here and there and everywhere and you just happened along to take advantage. Since she doesn't know you, she doesn't know your reasons. It's the best she could think of, being a miracle person and all."

"With Peter's help she thought of it."

"Yep. With the boy's help," said the detective investigator from the City and County of San Francisco. "Ska, ska, *ska*, she corrected me a dozen times."

The coffee was boiling away. Both of us had gotten distracted by other matters. I put it in mugs, it was very strong and bitter now, and we warmed ourselves, wrapping our hands around the matched pottery Suki had given me for my birthday two years ago.

"Statute of limitations doesn't apply here, I looked it up," Alfonso said. "Also the kid's age and all, he's kind of a plausible they call it witness. That's a word of art. There's also the possibility of civil action, lawsuit, damages, get himself some greedy contingency lawyer, hear about your job, you own this place, which don't involve the criminal code directly, of course—but you see my problem here, don't you?"

"*Your* problem."

"Since it's come up."

It was time to sip a little coffee and we did so. We did so to give me time to think. I thought I could hear Alfonso humming under his breath because he had talked more than he liked, going uphill with me, and the fan over his motor snapped on. Nice of him to consider it his problem, too.

"I mentioned something," he added uncomfortably.

"You sure did. Shouldn't I have a lawyer for this talk?"

"Aw, come on, Frank . . . That little mole he said you have?"

"It's a scar. Yes, I do. Maybe he watched me with Suki. A kid might do that for his mother."

Could she have told him?

"Maybe he—" They've got zoom lenses on the home market these days. They've got close focus. The Germans and the Japanese have done marvelous things about getting equipment into small spaces. A genius can make documentaries, catch spies in the act, maybe doesn't even have to be a genius. A talented operator could work the knobs and adjustments, come in close with no interference while his subject happens to be a fanatic about his own business . . . But I didn't want to drift into nightmares while Alfonso's red-rimmed eyes were following me, taking note of my moves, not letting go. "Maybe," I said, "he saw me coming out of the shower . . . I want a lawyer, Alfonso."

"Aw, come on. Hey, man, a *scar?* Who's biting around here?"

"Where I had a mole removed. By a doctor. Who sutured it. Because a mole there, when the skin is stretched, tends to get irritated if there's friction—"

"Gotcha, gotcha, ooh, that hurts." Alfonso had empathy, or maybe he just saw himself with a stand-up mole that could get scraped against another person on a weekend or holiday.

"I can give you the name of the doctor. Not a bite. It was strictly a medical procedure, including lab tests. My doctor sent me to a dermatologist and the skin man sent me to a scalpel man."

"Ooo-weee," said Alfonso, "enough, enough, have a little mercy, man. . . . Thanks."

That was because I took up my end of the conversation with a moment of silence. He was thanking *me* for not making *him* uncomfortable. I would have appreciated an opportunity to thank him for the same thing.

"Okay, terrific," he said. "How would he know about that? Peter, how would he know?" For a cop, Alfonso had a live, clean, moneyed, entertained look; the sighs were compassionate ones, plus maybe a little extra gut. His cheeks were fat and friendly and would be pink (looked almost purple) except for his ancestry in the African aristocracy. His rump was like his cheeks. This was a nice, happy, bright guy who was frequently rendered temporarily uncomfortable because of his job. But someone has to be the dick in this town. And these days it doesn't always have to be the Irish or Italian kid. "I mean, life in the fast lane and all that, but how," he asked, "*why* does he have to know about the mole or the scar or whatever, hell I'm not going to personally look, on the underside of your I'm sure very attractive and frequently studied, uh?"

"I realize that," I said. It wasn't an answer. I should have thought about Peter and me and not about Alfonso. I should have come up with an answer. I didn't like any of the answers that occurred to me. The one I was sure of, although I am sometimes absentminded, the way professors get, was that I had not stuck this thing anyplace near, in, or about Suki's son. An event like that would not slip my memory.

I took a chance about how Peter must have known about my little scar. His mother told him. The way she rattled, how she kept no secrets—that was the best stupid explanation.

"You know how he knows?" I said. "I don't like to think about it."

"Me neither. Pal, we better think about it anyway."

Detective Alfonso had been trained for a lim-
ited repertory of emotional expressions when he
wasn't laughing. A lot of it involved breathing,
lungs, thorax, chest cavity. He slid like a trom-
bone between sigh and groan. "Does she believe
this?" I asked.

"I don't know."

"If she's been told, she must have an opinion."
Alfonso showed his pink palms. "She's in a—"

"What?"

"Dignant. She's in a dignant. Sometimes I
don't know about what she thinks, you know
that too, Frank? I mean you found that out? I
mean personally, none of my business, that part
of it—" Heavy exhalations, mouth breathing, si-
nus blockages usually well hidden in the chuckling person who was now tirelessly sighing.
"She says a peculiar thing. She says it's not her
problem."

"Now it's *mine* goddammit?"

"What she means, pal, is this may sound peculiar. She don't think it's her problem if her lover
or ex-lover or sometimes lover, whatever, keeps
himself busy sucking the . . . or vice versa or
whatever of her one and only beloved son. She
thinks it's their problem if it gets to be a problem. She wants to keep her mind on the big picture. That's the way I read it. I mean Suki is
different, like we both know."

What, I wondered, did this have to do with
straightening out a sickening misunderstanding
that happened to fit into the current popular

crime enthusiasm replacing white-collar fiscal malfeasance with white-collar corruption of children? What did this have to do with a clear issue for the police and me and psychiatrists and Peter and goddammit libel attorneys, if they weren't careful?

Not thinking. Not working my head in a good direct line.

I didn't like how slowly things were moving.

"I prefer to straighten this out," I said.

"Isn't that what we're doing?" Alfonso asked. "If possible?"

"Passes on her problems so she never really knows them. Passes them to Peter, to me, to some new man, to anybody. Even you got passed a problem."

"You worrying about Suki," Alfonso said shrewdly, "that so nice of you. But Frank, ask me, under the circumstances"—and now the wheezing sighs broke forward into his jolly chuckles and station house emphysemic wheezing laughter—"ax me maybe even if Suki got it coming to her, even so—"

"Yes?"

He was saying Hahahahaheh.

"Maybe, maybe you should have a little straighten-out talk with Peter before everybody round here gets in a mess a trouble. This is unofficial, pal, I don't care what you do so much, but I hate mess. This could get to be one we don't bring it to a halt."

While Alfonso drooped his surprisingly thick-lashed eye lids, as if the discussion was making him sleepy, I thought of Suki in her house filled with framed photos of Suki in ski togs, Suki at Lake Tahoe in simple white frock, Suki leaning against mountain to hold it up, Suki waving from a Mercedes SL-280—a different man in each performance, not even cropped out when she moved on to the next man. "What goes around," Alfonso was saying, "comes around."

"Pardon?"

"It's an expression among Mah People, a little folkways," he said, "maybe you heard already," and the eyes blinked shut to end this interlude. When they opened he had another subject for me: "Why spend so much time alone with Peter?"

"Don't. Who said I did?"

"He does, my man."

"Suki used to run off to work and leave me for breakfast."

"For his breakfast or yours?"

"Don't be funny."

"I don't think it is—do *you?*"

I signed *no* in dumb language.

"What I hear, to my ears, is you're upset. It's not necessarily proof of guilt. That's what I see to my eyes also—you're sweaty."

"Is that what you smell to your nose, too?"

"It don't necessarily mean you're a molest. You ever have any contact personally with molest?"

"I think I've been molested by adult women. Does that count?"

Alfonso beamed. He was content to think of me as non-criminal. A criminal subject is fortunate when the investigating detective knows the accusation is possibly a crock of shit. "That Suki sure do molest persons a lot. She a great little perpetrator all by itself. But it ain't a federal, state, or local offense, is it?"

I wondered if I should tell Alfonso how Peter tried to seduce me. I trusted him, but I was still protecting Suki; I even wanted to protect Peter; maybe I didn't know how deep I would sink myself when we got into this black hole. I wanted to distract myself from thinking about it, too.

Besides, I was sure Alfonso's red-rimmed staring and his sighs and his sudden fat grins when he looked away and talked about his cop's life and career, changing the subject as he did, when he wasn't really all that interested in telling me how he became a detective—it wasn't essential to tell me—meant that he knew about Peter. He was urging his attention to roll elsewhere. He might even have been giving me a little credit for not wanting to heave all this up against Suki and her son.

He might also have been taking away some of the credit because he thought I still had ideas about Suki and me holding hands together on the beach in the sunset. A sex scandal with her son might tend to take away some of the romance.

Alfonso was noticing that I had fallen silent. Thinking was always a bad sign in an alleged perpetrator. Alfonso's breathing was heavy and juicy, almost asthmatic, but his grin was merely patient and maybe the breathing sounds were just there to fill the space. Sweat was coming through his shirt at the belly. He nodded encouragingly.

"Hey, Alfonso?" I asked.

"Brother, you may proceed."

He intended not to make it easy. He went along with my reluctance to get into areas of more trouble; we were in the area of embarrassment already. He deeply preferred to find a way out that left his friends unbroken.

"Look, Alfonso, you brought something up—"

"We're trained, brother. We learn to pick up the dust. We gossip a little this way and that, we cough—" Actually, what he did was sigh. "We scrape around for clues. Sometimes it's not just your little sex felony, it's life and death or your major fraud."

"I'll bet you passed your detective exam with flying colors."

"Color," he said, drawling a little. The eyes looked shrewd and yellow and red-rimmed, and I could see how, with a little twist of his parental supervision, maybe a few beatings by his uncles, he could have grown up to be one mean station house cop, slamming around the drunks, the druggies, and the alleged perpetrators who, everyone happened to know, were actual culprits.

"Color, color has nothing to do with it, man. I took no avail of the minority quota. The department can take that minority quota and shove it up their ass. I ain't no different from anybody else except better. I won without my black points, finished second citywide, could've been first, probably misspelled a shitty traffic reg."

"Congratulations, Alfonso."

"I been in grade long enough the thrill's done wore off. And you sure you didn't get yourself dirty in a little kid, son of the lady who maybe fucked you over one too many times?"

I wasn't a thinking person just now. If I had thought, I would have taken care about what to do next. Instead, I climbed into my little unreliable Fiat, wearing my hiking boots in case I wanted to kick somebody hard, and drove across the Bay toward Suki's house in the Cow Hollow annex to Pacific Heights. People don't sing about the view from the Bay Bridge as they do about the Golden Gate; the name gives the other bridge all the attention. But the jagged ramparts of downtown San Fran are pretty from here, especially if you're in a frame to appreciate water and city and a long cabled stretch of bridge with an occasional battleship passing beneath. A person admires the medieval mortgage ramparts of downtown a little less if he is the losing side in someone's game of Dungeons and Dragons.

If I'd have thought about my problem instead

of just letting it wash over me, I might have
done this more carefully.

I didn't care which Crowell I saw; they were
both to blame. I'd have it out with Peter or Suki,
whoever turned up. I wanted to run it down and
squash it. I would wait till someone came home.

No one was home. I parked pointing downhill, front tire squashed against the curb. I
waited.

I wondered if this was bad for the tire. I
thought of leaving because no one was home.

I waited.

Peter drove up on a Vespa I didn't know he
owned—maybe he didn't own it—with a person
in shaved head, black boots, stoned eyes, orange
plastic shirt. The person was clutching his waist
from behind. He dismounted and the skinhead
waited to let Peter help him off a Vespa back
saddle—maybe bad knees from crash dancing,
maybe just a matter of etiquette. "Hi," said Peter, as if he expected me. "You know Harry?"

"Now how would I know Harry?"

"Everybody knows Harry, don't they,
Harry?"

In addition to bad knees, Harry had a slow
tongue. It curled slightly in his opened mouth,
and it had a milky, grainy texture as he considered answering Peter's question. The question
gave him difficulties because of its complexity
(consider all the people in the world; how could
they all know Harry?). Or perhaps the swiftness
of the brain encamped behind that outcropping

of tongue recognized that no answer was truly required.

"I want to talk to you, Peter."

"Sure thing. Out here or inside? The garden's nice."

"Alone."

"Oh, Harry doesn't care. He's not jealous. He won't even listen, will you, Harry?"

Finally Harry took utterance. "Don't wanna be call Harry no more. My name is . . ." He thought about it. He didn't come up with anything suitable. "Well, you call me Harry today, but pretty soon gonna get my new name, it won't be call Harry."

"Come on inside, y'all," said Peter. "My mom left some brownies in the freezer. We thaw 'em, they're good as new. They come from Humboldt County brownies."

Harry, who had a sweet tooth, trudged behind Peter. He wasn't wanted. Maybe I wasn't wanted either, but I was trudging third in line up the walk and stairs.

Perhaps it was better to have a witness than not to have a witness to this conversation. I was not sure if Harry, future something-else, maybe Fred, was the witness and impartial observer I required. The look on Peter's face was so smooth, so teenage calm and unblemished by doubt, that it seemed he had been expecting me. So I didn't meet his wide happy gaze. "I thought you might come around," he said.

"I've been talking to Alfonso."

"Which one is that?"

"The black guy. The detective. Why did you say what you said?"

"I didn't say it to him, man. It was my shrink. You got to say something for the money your mom pays."

"You had to say that?"

"I caught her sleeping—Dr. Kowalska. I don't like people nod off on me."

"So you—"

"Shit, I was trying to remember my dreams, but I couldn't. Maybe that was one of my dreams. So then she got all waked up and made me, made the phone call herself, and then . . . Are you sure it's not the truth, man?"

I had no comment.

"I mean, how would I know so much about you? I mean, you want me to say I watched you fucking my mom? That's *embarrassing*, man."

"It's not embarrassing to say you and I . . . ?"

He was smiling happily. His lips were pulpy and red. They melted all over his face. He worked them soft. "I think I'm just a poor misunderstood child."

"Stop fooling around, Peter. You're not a child anymore. This has consequences."

"I don't fool around. I play hard. I don't mind results. Right. I'm not a poor misunderstood used-to-be-child anymore. I got my own stuff and I'm serious, man, serious stone serious. Harry, listen to this." He put his arm on the skinhead's bony shoulder. "I don't have to be rational, do I? So I'm not always rational."

His happiness was so smooth and slick he could chew on it like gum.

"Me neither," said Harry.

"Frank, this wouldn't be any fun if I didn't like you. You're terrific, Frank. Mom thinks so too, least she did as long as she usually does. Terrific isn't that long-lasting."

He watched me whistling my breath in and out in a Japanese ritual of murder. In rage the body takes over. My eyes felt swollen. I concentrated on not speaking.

"I mean, what is an actor if you think he's not being himself, Frank? That's just bullshit. When you know he's throwing something off—you see it's him and not him—that's stuff."

"You like lying."

"I mean, if Mom was a virgin, but she had me anyway—that's be great. To be Jesus, man. Or she fucked everybody she likes, like she does— no, she only fucks the ones she likes, but she likes everybody, such as you—but she wasn't just a whore. I mean, like she was a loving good mother. That's be fun too, man."

"Wanna *do* something," Harry said.

"Lots of things can be fun," Peter said.

"You said we was gonna *do* something," Harry said.

This was no fun for Harry or me. It would have been a change in the discussion to punch the boy out. But some small prudence seemed to be working behind my sudden asthma and I only stared and wheezed with a breathing that was cousin to Alfonso's sighs, and then luck and irregular household routines gave us the clack-clack of Suki's bright high heels. She was hurrying.

"Hiya, you guys. Hey, the whole team is here."

"This is Harry, he's my friend."

"I don't know you, do I, Harry? Which one are you?"

Harry looked at Peter as if the world had gone seriously astray in the solar system. And everyone knows the universe is spinning out of control, so it was a drag this afternoon, the whole deal. Harry's head needed a shave; there was five o'clock shadow. "Goin' back to my place. It doan look like nothin's happenin' today."

"Suit yourself," Peter said. The kid could be an executive; he had crispness resources, like Suki.

"How'm gonna get there? Who's gonna take me on the back of their wheels?"

"Shit, man," said Peter; but he was a responsible lad. "And leave Frank here alone with my mom? Okay, I'll do it."

Harry relaxed. He rubbed a hand on his scalp prickles. Maybe the day could be rescued. "Buy me a sangwich?" he asked. "We pass Wendy's on the way. I got this coupon, you buy the one, we get the freebie."

* * *

"I've got to talk with you, Suki."

"I love talking to a well-informed person like you, Frank, but today I've got to shower, wax, take care of some personal matters—"

"This is personal."

"Before the evening. Personally I've got an early engagement. It's prior, Frank. It'll have to keep."

I stared. "This is about Peter."

Distraction and discomfort made her frown. *Don't spoil things.* Her frown went further: Don't *you* spoil things, Frank, don't insist, since you do want to be my good friend.

"So if it's Peter," she said, "then won't it keep? I mean, I see him every day at least once or twice, you see him a whole lot, we can talk all the time—"

"Suki," I said.

The wrongest thing to do with Suki was to insist. This was a place of danger and suppressed rage. "Is that why you were here, to visit my son?" And then she was sorry she had fallen into the trap of asking a question, which might just provoke an answer and prolong an unnecessary chat. "Not that I mind, you two should be good friends by now—"

"He's making funny noises. Worse than that."

"Oh, dear. Oh, dear. Didn't you at his age?"

She looked frightened. Now she had to hear me. There was panic and anger in her darting glances, making sure everything was still where it was supposed to be—furniture, flowers, the walls of her house. She almost had to hear me. "Out, Frank, *out.* I love you a whole lot, but out now. The meter's on late." She made a little mouth. "Kissy? We'll talk very soon, won't we? I can tell you have a good story on your mind, so give me a kiss and scamper, okay? Call me."

NINE

Under ideal circumstances, tossing and turning
is not the best exercise for getting to sleep. Inner
turmoil and hyperventilation fail to qualify as
aerobic sports, even in this part of the century
and northern California. I was unable to choose
my emotions. I curled into misery, fret, and leg
cramps. I lay awake in my retired refectory, my
cottage in the Berkeley hills, redwood shingles,
attractive butcher construction, sagging godly
desanctified porch—my persistent non-tenured
assistant prof style, even though I had made adjunct associate—and then I lay uneasily asleep.

Alfonso had put thoughts in my mind.

Peter had put thoughts in his.

Not all thinking is admirable; some of it is
merely rotten opinion. I was almost ready to
think Suki and all her works were finally too
much for me. This fear had come to sever my

sleep in the past, and often, but I had not yet accepted my decision as final. It was none of my business, really—it was only my career, future, and life.

A rhythmic chanting on the leaf-strewn street outside awakened me from non-sleep sometime after two A.M. *"Fuck you, Frank Curtis. Frank Curtis, fuck you."*

It had been the kind of sleep where a person is sure he is not sleeping. I had even been trying to figure out what kind of a shrink Dr. Kowalska must be to accept the word of Peter and inquire after evidence such as the mole on my. . . . It took me a moment to figure out that, yes, I had fallen asleep at last, my legs and arms were heavy; and yes, I was now awake, my legs and arms were twitching; and yes, this peculiar singing chant outside was not a dream leftover. It was what had interrupted whatever dream I had been dreaming.

"Frank Curtis! Fuck you. Fuck you, Frank Curtis."

I had felt chilled and depressed at bedtime and was wearing pajamas. That was a plus. During the late sixties and seventies, most of the houses and cottages on Julia Morgan Street had replaced the old Berkeley glass doors with iron grillwork or at least tough wood, but I had not done so. That was a minus. I was proud of the fact that my cottage had once been a neighborhood chapel, the Episcopal Congregational Unitarian Fellowship, a center of ecumenical faith, and thought its holy rationality, its former good works, including the Panther breakfast program, plus its eccentric tangle of garden and murky overgrowth, its charm, would cause the local break-and-entry psychotics to bend a knee and move on, brother; please go elsewhere, brother. That sentiment was now a clear minus.

A monotonous picket was intoning: "Fuck you, Frank Curtis."

I peeked through the window and saw nothing, not even a shadow. This was unremarkable, given the deciduous trees and the non-deciduous ones here in verdant, formerly low-rent, middle-upper Berkeley. A person with my caller's message to deliver by repeated shout would probably not be standing in the glow of streetlamp. He wasn't. Perhaps he was not proud of his job.

"Frank Curtis! Hey!"

I listened carefully, checking back through associations and resonances. Debris from the real world had come to torment me in the night. I tried to place his voice. I imagined him crashing through the glass door.

"Frank Curtis! Fuck you!"

Without putting on any lights—but I can go to the bathroom by the street glow suffusing my cottage—I looked around for a useful tool for this occasion. No club, no gun of course, and a knife was impractical. I wasn't skilled at night combat. Goddammit, only a tennis racket. I should have called the cops, the 911 line, but they would only say, "What? He's yelling *what?*

He a friend of yours?" and take their good old public-servant time about not showing up.

I waited with the tennis racket, crouching, legs spread, ready for a forehand drive at the head that would come pushing through my shattered front door. The voice continued its chant outside. I thought I saw a shadow—branches shifting in the easy nighttime breeze. Nobody visible. That voice, those words.

I got tired of waiting. I crawled back into bed, still listening—the voice growing hoarse—with my arms around my Don Budge wooden racket which I still used as a spare when the new fiberglass one was being restrung. I was bored with the human noise like a car alarm outside.

"Frank Curtis, Fuck you. Fuck you. Frank Curtis. . . ."

When I opened my eyes, the sun was spilling through the window and a dog was barking someplace and my arms were tenderly encircling an old wooden tennis racket I had used in high school. Funny things put a fellow to sleep. I lay there a while, not even going to pee, trying to remember exactly what had happened during the night.

No, it wasn't a dream. I was not playing night singles in the queen-sized bed I had inherited from the last Episcopalian out of the rectory.

I went to my front door and looked outside, still armed with my tennis equipment. A chalked message was scrawled in mirror writing on the walk, in case I hadn't heard the messenger. I didn't have to bother getting a mirror to read it. In due course, after I checked my class-and-appointment schedule for the day, I'd have to take time to scrub it off. It would be the neighborly thing to do. Otherwise some kid would come down the street, just innocently happening to carry a mirror, and read the message and fall off his skateboard.

I wondered if Peter knew something good for scrubbing chalk off stone. I hoped it wasn't crayon. It was nice that it wasn't spray paint. I knew the voice had not been Peter's, I tried to remember the voice of his friend, Harry.

It could have been any friend. It could even have been a non-friend. It could have been a discontented student of mine. But I could not avoid thinking about Peter.

Before my appointment with an M.A. candidate who was working on reporting the social interactions of a group of Alzheimer's patients, an invigorating topic, not suitable as a Sunday feature in the Country Living section next to the tofu roundup, I called Alfonso to say, "Just checking in. Any news? A funny thing happened to me last night and don't say why didn't you call the police . . ."

There were rainbow shadows on the wall where the sunlight burned through the stained-glass part of the windows. When I moved, the rainbows moved, too, and I said to myself, Let there be light, as Alfonso was saying: "I might could of driven over and found your visitor, 'cept I would of been sleeping if I would of been home, only I wasn't there last night. You know the definition of a bachelor? Come home from a different direction every morning."

"I told you that, Alfonso."

" 'Deed you did. See how I like to learn?"

Alfonso was willing to be helpful. He just wasn't sure I deserved a whole lot of help.

At my office in Dwinelle Hall I waited for the young woman who was doing the Alzheimer's project. She may have been one of the few of my students who didn't want to be Woodward, Bernstein, Hunter S. Thompson, or Gloria Steinhem, nor to go into public relations with Bechtel or one of the new phone companies, nor to raise the consciousness of America about AIDS or U.S. imperialism or the environment. She had an old-fashioned idea about being a reporter. I thought she had the proper concerned and nosy attitude about things.

"I've got a little personal problem," I told her, "but I didn't want to cancel our appointment—"

"You could have, if you could have reached me. Do you want me to go now?"

"No, no, I want to tell you it's good work. I think you have a chance at a magazine, maybe one of the popular science magazines. But you should talk with someone about the genetic engineering approaches. Why don't you see Ron Cape at Cetus? Down in Emeryville? At least a sidebar about any research they have on electrical stimulation of the brain."

"The neurons," she said rather morosely, "it just gets soggy in there. Nothing passes through."

"You've been living with this a while. You should feel good about the work."

"Fifteen percent of people over sixty," she said.

"I like the part about that brain disease the cannibals get. I hadn't heard of that. The slow-acting virus. Could you call New York and check with the Rockefeller Institute, get some quotes, how closely related the viruses are?"

"If . . ." she began.

"Do you know somebody with a Wats line? You should make some calls."

"*If* it's a virus," she said. "My father isn't senile, it turns out, he's turning into a vegetable—"

I stared at her. "I'm sorry," I said. "I thought this was just a project."

"It is a project," she said. "One thing I'm hearing now is maybe there is an element of contagion, or a greater likelihood in certain families, so funny thing, every time I forget a point . . ."

I repeated that it was excellent work. I told her I would write some letters for her when she finished. I told her it was worth doing as well as she could, and not only for credit in the course. I repeated that I wanted to see a sidebar about the genetic engineering aspects, or maybe it could be integrated into the text. I told her I was impressed with how she had kept her personal grief out of the story. "You're a professional," I said.

She brightened. It occurred to her that she might not have Alzheimer's disease yet, or that a good word from her instructor could counteract the virus. We have that power over students— need it. She pulled her ski jacket around her shoulders and picked up the Xerox copy with my notes. "I can see you're bothered about something, Mr. Curtis. May I see you again next week?"

Next week, I told her, I hoped to be bothered less about something. With the typical concentration on business of the serious student, she hadn't asked why I came to my office for our appointment with a battered old wooden tennis racket. I would have answered that it was to remind me of something, although I didn't think I'd forget.

She left my office with the world looking better, at least temporarily, and I envied my student. I wanted to straighten out my part of the world, too, even if it would only stay straight temporarily. I telephoned Peter Crowell.

"Do you have skinhead friends who like to come to Berkeley and sing on empty streets during the night?"

"Wah? Wuh?"

"Did I wake you up? Peter, it's Frank."

"Little nap," he said. "Didn't get to bed last night."

"It's Frank on the phone."

"I hear you," he said. "Hey, it's Frank, isn't it?"

"Did you send your friend to get monotonous at me last night?"

"What you talking about? Man, what you talking to me about?"

"Yelling about Professor Curtis on the street. Could get himself in trouble."

"That's degenerate, man, what you say, if I believe I understand you. You encourage that kind of degenerate, man?" He paused. He waited to see if I would interrupt. "Hey, I'm waking up about now. Exactly what the dude say to you? I mean, you got a job and all, at the college, don't you? Couldn't you get in trouble that way?"

The dude was thinking. Maybe he knew that adjunct non-tenure at the University of California wasn't as secure and tenured as it used to be, especially if you mix in a little teenage overage male or female—makes no difference—child abuse. He possibly knew I was thinking, too. I would go on denying, of course. But it's hard to refuse a no-conscience kid; a person might as well be dealing with an ordinary psychopath. Here was Peter, no record, good address, nice mother, bad character, ex-father a respectable Chapter 11 entrepreneur—a funny case. Who would not be suspicious of a drag-ass unmarried professor in one of the soft crafts when faced

with the sworn word of a smooth-skinned youth
of whom he had taken erotic advantage (alleged)
under the guise of courting the mother? The
mother's skin had always reminded me of raw
silk, a duskiness and toughness, but I wasn't sure
a judge or jury would credit my desires about
Suki.

"Why me, Peter? We always got along. Why
are you doing this? What's special about me?"

"You know how the winter's over because you
left your scarf on the bus? Well, that's how you
know you had your last free ride on my mom."

"I get part of it, what you're saying. But I
don't get it."

He was fully awake and entertained. He had a
whole program laid out. "You don't see her
again. You try Mary Hand and Her Five Quick
Fingers or some other kid's mom, understand?
Or maybe you tried me."

"I guess that's a theory."

"Or FCA."

"Eff-see-ay?"

"Felony child abuse. That's not a theory."

"You're no child, Peter."

"Continuing over the years . . . My shrink
says it's probably why I'm like I am. I suppose
you don't mind."

"Why are you doing this?"

"Maybe it's true. Maybe you did me a whole
lot of harm. I have a job in mind for myself,
Frank—somebody got to pay attention. Maybe it
should be you."

"What about your mother?"

"Don't you see? Aren't you involved? Isn't it working, Frank?"

Rock climbing or hang-gliding might have been a better hobby for me as I entered middle age, which I sometimes called early middle age. Finding a project. Getting ahead in the world or at the university. Instead, I was talking to him on the telephone and holding the wooden Don Budge racket and wishing to break it over someone's head. Instead, I would consult with Suki. And I noticed the kid had a counselor, a therapist, a shrink, since he didn't have a father he could confide in regularly.

I had best be methodical about this.

"I happened to be seeing Alfonso the other day," I remarked cautiously without mentioning that he also happened to be seeing me with questions concerning a possible charge of teenage molesting, "and we were talking about Peter—"

"Peter?" Suki asked with her big-eyed startled-doe look. It took in the information I was offering; it took note of the room with all her nice things; it took pleasure and reassurance in familiar comforts.

"Peter," I said.

"Well, that's interesting. You must be sure to tell me. Are you a little tired this afternoon—something on your mind?"

"I guess."

So she set out to ease my troubled spirit in one

of Suki's ways, chattering sweetly and confidentially while she poured tea in little flowered cups; added cream or lemon, whichever I liked; nodded at the saucer with thin slices of lemon, all I wanted; handed over a plate of goodies; remembered I preferred nine-grain toast; took back the sweets; went for the bread and toaster and little pots of butter, jam, honey; and all the while she was frowning and smiling and sharing her own distractions in order to let me know she liked me, trusted me, treasured me—"You realize, don't you, Frank, there's as much sugar in this tart nice little marmalade, try it, as there is in these cookies?"

"Yes, I know."

"I'm worried about him, Frank. He's having a crisis the way everybody does at his age. You know, first there's the pre-adolescent thing, then the adolescent crisis, that's a bad one for sure, and then there's the post. The *post*-adolescent never ends, does it?"

"What's he up to?"

"God didn't fine-tune the animal in us, did he? We don't think of that when we think how nice to have a little baby of our own, just because we're so young and the sap is strong. I'm concerned, I'm upset, Frank, just like a mother."

"What's he up to? What do you think?"

"Who knows? Mischief, I'm sure."

Mischief. "You're worried, Suki, I can tell you really are."

"So give me the answer, please."

"That's what I'm asking you."

"I'm a mother, I'm his mother, understood, grant that, but it's his problem. I've got my own."

"Alfonso," I began. I knew Suki didn't want to hear certain things from me. I knew there were rules in her friendship. I knew it was time for me to start violating the rules. "Alfonso talked to me."

She took tea, her hands fluttered, she looked for help to the rug, the walls, the frog on her desk. "You said?"

"I said Alfonso was talking to me."

"That Alfonso really is kind of cute, I always thought, but a *cop?*"

"He's a detective."

"I always liked big strong men, but a *detective?*" She frowned and shook her head and shoulders with a graceful little shiver. With an effort she brought herself around. "It doesn't seem to matter if your kid is in trouble, does it?"

And then the look of panic returned to her face, the eyes slipped away from mine, she sought a reassurance, a normal distraction. She took a deep breath; breathing is a normal distraction and pleasure; often the air is tasty. She reached into herself and found an enduring subject. She had the strength for it. I could always trust her to be Suki.

Cups clattered, a spoon went into a saucer, she remembered something I would surely want to hear about. These were matters we could share, couldn't we? How a person gets through the days, nights, and years in alert expectation of something not yet discovered but festive in the evening just ahead. She touched her hair and the electricity passing between her fingers and the shimmering helmet caused a storm if there was a man nearby. Often, good luck, there was.

"You make your luck, Suki."

"Don't give me too much credit. I just put myself in the way. Of course, I don't really do that anymore—only when a person is sort of upset, like when I first met you—"

"The Spaghetti Factory."

"A holiday it was—someone sent me an invitation—I was feeling lonely—"

She told me about the guys she used to meet at MacArthur Park when she was getting over her marriage or a setback in the public relations trade. Of course, she didn't really do that anymore. Or the holiday blues, for old times' sake. Sometimes it was really kind of funny for a person to take a silly chance, like for example. . . . She did an imitation of a good old Mill Valley boy in the leathers and the straw hat:

"Hey, ma'am, you like to have a affair? Twooden take too much a yer tom—bout fi minit. We could jes run upstairs to your place, how bout it?"

I waited till she finished her story. Her eyes were rolling with the amusement of it. She was really too busy to hear about her son's troubles, my troubles, our troubles. She would not enjoy an interruption in the serious progress of her life. We could come back to Peter in due course, when she gathered her strength. With all the silence within her funny gossip she was asking me to wait, to be patient, to help her pull her joys around her shoulders.

"What's the name of his therapist?"

"Oh, Frank!"

"Tell me the name."

"Kowalski," she said. "Diana Kowal*ska*, it is. Don't you think it's kind of neat how even the doctors are women these days?" She frowned. She looked puzzled. Since I insisted, she gave me my way in the choice of conversation. "His father won't even contribute penny one to the cost. Thinks the kid should talk to him instead. But the kid doesn't *want* to talk to his father, so I pay for it and I pick the therapist, isn't that right?"

I waited a moment. She waited, too. I wondered if Suki might ask why I wanted Dr. Kowalska's name and phone number, but she didn't like to meddle in these matters. Probably it was something between me and Dr. K. That was my business, I was a big boy, she wouldn't pry. Probably I'd tell her if I wanted to.

Instead, Suki told me about her friend who referred to her jazzercise class as "Arabic dancing. I think that's darling, don't you, Frank?"

Right. A friend who didn't listen closely. Who couldn't stand to.

* * *

I planned to tape my telephone conversation
with Dr. Diana Kowalska, and would have done
so, except that it's illegal if you don't inform the
other party. I didn't want to upset the doctor. It
would be illegal if she found out about it. So I
decided to record the conversation anyway, just
for my own use and study, for educational purposes only, and trust myself not to mention it to
anyone. I thought I could trust me.

FRANK CURTIS: I need to talk with you about
   Peter Crowell, Doctor.
DR. KOWALSKA: Peter?
CURTIS: Your patient.
KOWALSKA: My patient?
CURTIS: Peter Crowell, your *patient*, Doctor.
KOWALSKA: My patient Peter Crowell?
CURTIS: He's mentioned my name to you.
   Frank Curtis. I'm a friend of his mother's.
   I'm a friend of Suki's. Peter's mother. I
   teach at Berkeley.
KOWALSKA: I'm sorry I can't release that in-
   formation.
CURTIS: I know what my name is and where
   I teach, you don't have to release it. I
   haven't asked anything yet. Has Peter
   spoken of me?
KOWALSKA: [silence]
CURTIS: I'm sure you recall my name from
   something he's said, assertions, Doctor.
KOWALSKA: I'm sorry, it's forty-five seconds

to ten. I have another patient due in, let's
see, forty-five seconds.

CURTIS: [accelerating] I'm having some difficulty with Peter and. . . .

KOWALSKA: I'm sorry, Mr. Crowell is my patient and I can't discuss our conversations
with you. However, if you would like to
make an appointment for personal therapy—

CURTIS: [inappropriately] Fuck off.

Conclusion of non-taped telephone conversation. The non-tape ends here. Dr. Kowalska
fucked off promptly.

The family friend thought there was nothing
more to be lost if he enjoyed another little talk
with Peter. There is a difference between psychopath and psychotic; the boy had a plan. He
was not psychotic. He had an idea about himself,
wheeled vehicles, knew about motors, moved
people from here to there. He had a certain anger. He was equipped to survive in the world
that he had found—unless something could stop
the kind of survival he was equipped for. He
wasn't going to put any brakes on himself.

So if I could shame him, which is hard to do
with a healthy young psychopath, or make him
see his action as counterproductive even if it
wasn't clear to me what he wanted to produce,
or if I could get back to the easy breakfast affability between him and his mother's lover—well, I

wanted to try. It was worth another effort. I didn't need complication, annoyance, or disaster. Didn't he used to like me? Weren't those nice times behind our separate boxes of Kellogg products? Me with my Super K, him with his Rice Krispies? Me reading the news, him the sports? Peter and I always got along at breakfast. Wasn't that the way things should remain around the Crowell family on Filbert Street?

Best not to meet him at home. Doping kids enjoy sweets, as I recalled, they get these terrific appetites, and I like coffee in public places. I asked him to come to the Just Desserts down in the Marina, across the street from the mother Safeway, the flagship of the Safeway fleet, with its mosaic tile and its singles shopping cart jockys, meeting each other near the tofu celebration, the organic vitamins exhibit, the gormay cheese extravaganza. Joggers visited Just Desserts for their carbo rush; the women from the slimming & aerobic salon next door, in headbands, designer tights, and sweat-resistant makeup, came to Just Desserts to network together after working out, sharing determinations not to have the carrot cake; and Peter and I met to discuss the little problem he had. A little problem that somehow we both had.

"Peter," I said, "how can I help you?"

"You the social worker around here?"

"How can I help you avoid making a mess of things where I'm involved, Peter?"

Wouldn't that be nice of me? I managed to sound smug about saving my own comfort.

He plowed into his apple crisp crumb pie. He had asked for it with coffee ice cream. Methodically he attacked the rusty pie with his fork, the ice cream with his spoon, working two-handed, and it sure looked good. I watched him work and admired the commitment and passion of youth.

He finished his sugar rush, his pleasure in apple fragments and his Bud's premium jacoca or jamoca or espresso. He used a paper napkin to scrub his teeth. He too was mortal. He recognized the problem. And he explained himself once more to the thickheaded friend of his mother:

"I'd like to get me some secrets sell to the Russians like those two hunks did, you saw the movie, I could, too." He stopped to consider. "You can't just decide, though. It's not that easy. Getting the right top-secret job in the government is a lot of work."

"You'd like to try a line of work you found in a movie."

"What I don't understand is what's the difference between treason and spying. I mean, I guess I can't see myself really getting into it—all the photocopying, man. That's not supposed to be good for your glands. I don't want to do X-rays or any of that. Personally I'm more a non-linear heavy-metal type." He was still dreamily imagining his triumphs in the treason game. "At this early stage in blast-off I'm not ready to go linear yet. Not at this point in time. Video is *real*, though—hey, you follow MTV, Frank?"

I thought maybe I should check with my doctor about continuing this conversation. I should check with my lawyer, and then my accountant, and then with Alfonso, until I found someone who told me not to continue.

I let it continue. Reggae was chugging from the speakers, so low it was all bass and beat. Just Desserts was supposed to have baroque music, but the folks who worked there preferred a little baroque reggae in the afternoon. I let it take me along. Today I had more pressing matters than to complain about the music to management.

"You want a dessert?" I asked.

He looked around, slightly tempted. He blew on his palm, sampled his breath. "Thanks. No, think this'll do, especially since I just finished cleaning my teeth."

His generation, they had fluoride from the start. Maybe they didn't get cavities, no matter what they ate. Peter sighed and relaxed, temporarily nourished, and thought he should get back to business. "If you *do* do it, you know, maybe at your place if you don't want to go to Mom's and my place, then we could have some munchies, relax, I won't tell people you did it. But if you don't, then I will. See how nice 'n easy that is, Frank?"

Stubbornly, stupidly, I insisted on locating myself. "This is crazy, Peter."

Straight ahead, past the Marina, there were
sailboats on the bay. Nearer, on the green, there
were runners, kite-fliers, mothers with babies,
picnickers, Frisbee players, couples earnestly
flirting, thinkers earnestly dictating into Note-a-
matic recorders while performing their medi-
cally prescribed hikes. People were breathing
the sea air. And here where I sat at a cafe table in
San Francisco was Frank Curtis, discussing having sex with the son of the woman he had sometimes thought he loved.

It would all fly away in a moment if he only
said the right words. I could say them if I knew
them. It was about me. I was that person. The
right gesture would blow it all away.

"Crazy? Hey, it's not crazy. Get in touch,
okay? Maybe it's like treason, people don't think
it's any fun, but they don't know, they don't
wanna try it. They're wrong. You tell me,
Frank."

"What else is on your mind?"

He liked that question. It meant I was involved; he had taken me partway. "How about
we make a deal?" He was gazing at me with a
smile like Suki's, deeply delighted with himself,
teeth showing clean, no apple crumb crisp, no
espresso moka jamoca smear, a good use of cal-
cium, a healthy California metabolism.

"What's your deal?" I asked.

He was grinning and meeting my eyes without any hesitation. "I'll come," he said, "but you
don't have to."

I stared.

"I mean it's up to you. You can do it just like people do, men and women. You can be the man or the girl if you prefer. Makes you feel better, I don't mind you're the man."

Behind us, a wife was talking about hall area rugs with her decorator. At the table just ahead, three women in spandex tights, from the exercise studio next door, were still practicing their carbo loading. Now the reggae was giving me no comfort. Time might help, plus some courageous and forthright stalling. "Hey, Peter, talking like that. Telling lies to me like that. I don't even like your telling lies to other people, but *me?* Hey, Peter, I knew you when you were still just a boy."

"That's the truth."

"Aw, come on. What kind of trouble you want to make for me and—Peter? And you too, for sure."

"For me, you think."

"Pay attention, son."

"You got a better kind, Frank?" He frowned. He meant a better kind of trouble. There was a tuft of eyebrow just above his nose. When I was very close to Suki, I could see where she also grew hairs, and plucked them, leaving only an ant-trail shadow in her delicate skin. The blankness came over Peter's face, that sheet of sulk, the hood that covers kids' heads when they're listening to music while doing their homework and planning the terrific evening ahead. But he was coming back to pay attention to what was going on; he might as well; he was the person in control of it. "Sometimes things get out of hand, don't you know?" he said. "And they shouldn't. My mother still runs around like a babe. So why should I feel so, is that what old people feel like, *stale?*"

"You shouldn't. Hey, no need for that."

"Something's going on. You're looking at it. It's happening now. You got an idea, a couple ideas for me to choose from?"

"I don't know what to tell you, Peter."

He grinned. "Now you're catching on. It's a beginning."

Peter wanted to play Reduction. He chose to reduce the things around him, his mother, me, the world, so he would be bigger. In Reduction, a person has friends like skinheaded Harry, like the howler outside my door, like the creatures with funny hair and elbows at Suki's birthday party. When the world was a reduced readout, like an arcade video game, bold graphics on a screen, not too much complication in the design, a humming and clanging in the mechanism at the proper moment, the world was in his control. Even its violences got turned back into play.

"How do you like your low-rated Fiat?" he asked. "You know, Frank, I don't see anybody I consider a good friend drives an American car. I mean whatever happened to patriotism? Where's the Dodge Darts these days?"

He remembered discussing the rearview mirror on the Dodge Dart when he was still a kid and I was having frequent breakfasts with Suki and him. Even then he knew more about the rearview mirror situation than I did. Suki did good eggs, French toast on weekends, pancakes for a special surprise for me, waffles for Peter sometimes, because kids like waffles. I was moderately important to her for a while. She lay in a supply of bran muffins for me. Peter didn't like them very much, but he was courteous; he said he could see what I saw in them.

"The Dodge Dart was a pretty fair vehicle for its time, so was the Buick Skylark . . ." Peter was talking American folk mumble. He was alone in some other country behind his gold-flecked California eyes. He was taking me on a ramble. He was sure of what he wanted, but he was still thinking things through. "Hey, Frank, one more time. Don't you want to help me be of a whole lot of assistance, else you get in trouble? This might be the last time I'm so kindly." He lowered his voice so that the hall area rug lady would not hear his next idea. "You want some more coffee? You could just go to the counter and get it."

"No thanks."

He sighed. He glanced over his shoulder to see how the hall area rug lady had responded to his whispering. She was discussing the floor pad problem, what a person places under a hall area rug.

"You might as well," he cooed like the sweetest kid imaginable, and I had a sudden memory of Suki's voice when Suki was feeling soft, stretching limber and easy, and oh it was nice then: "You might as well, 'cause everybody's gonna think so anyway, I mean unless I can keep my damn mouth shut, which I sincerely doubt I can—"

"Peter, I've known you since you were fifteen."

"Hasn't everybody?"

"Are you nuts!"

"Isn't everybody, hey? And wouldn't they just love to believe the poor misunderstood youth started to get child-abuse when he was much younger and now he's eighteen and all confused up—"

I headed for the door, past hall area rug people, past aerobic carbo loaders, past newspaper readers—I wanted out.

"What'd I say?" he asked.

His hand was on my arm. He had slid out of his chair and scrambled after me. I let myself be stopped. "Nothing, Peter. You said almost nothing." And waited for him to ask: Aw, stay a while, let's have some fun—*let's have some fun* was what Suki used to say when she wasn't feeling soft and really friendly, yet wanted the right kind of pleasure. She preferred to signal honesty about what she had in mind.

"Can you remember what it was like for me?" Peter asked. "Can you even guess?"

There was such sadness in his voice. The sun outside was filtering down through the droplets, nice clean Golden Gate fog over this hill-and-seaside city, the air all sparkly, as it often is—lucky San Francisco in which this kid was preparing gladly for trouble, entering his griefs and hoping to bear me along with him. The sun was rinsing clean through the fog, as it does. No, I could not imagine what things were like for Peter. Adult abuse tends to wear away at a fellow's empathy. Molest and abuse shade off into each other. Even a fellow's professional vocabulary gets interrupted.

"Prudent family friend ducks out now," I said.

"Wah? What's that? Hey, on the muscle all of a sudden, Frank—why is that? Listen, maybe you never tried it yet, teenage boy—why knock it without trying it one time? How do you know how tight and clean I am? Are you prejudice? Live here in this town and you're still prejudice? People will talk *anyway*, Frank, so why not play the game since you're gonna get the name?"

I didn't think I was too prejudice, but at times I was a little grammar. Suki's son, raised so nicely with everything a boy could ask for, and did ask for, and got, now he liked to try on the street talk he heard when he used his wheels around town; he wanted to see if it fit. It didn't. Words for Peter were like gloves, bags, hats, theme jewelry to Suki, African or Indian or Haitian gleamy stuff—they were accessories, they flashed how she wanted them to flash when she moved.

Peter stood there on Buchanan Street with his hand on my arm. If he had held me, I would have pulled away, but he was only tired and resting, off someplace in the curlicues, dreaming. He was a puzzled pouty kid, waking from his nap, struggling to emerge from a bewitching too-long afternoon sleep. "Hey, Frank?" he asked. "Man take the blame, he might as well—aw, Frank. I mean, you like my mother *sooo* much—"

"It wasn't easy for you, was it."

"Getting easier now. Getting hip to what I can do—fuck anybody, Harry or you and anybody." The gold-flecked eyes had that dreamy, dopey, peaceful California look again. He said, "Frank, you got the words. Man whisper so nice, man got the words—'deed he do, he get so mouthy, don't he, Frank?"

Often I've overheard people saying things in coffeehouses they didn't really need for me to hear. Now I was doing the same thing; Peter and I were doing the same thing. The hand on my arm took a little pinch of muscle. He grinned, I pulled away, he grinned some more. "Hey, man, you know? I got the pictures, man," he said.

TEN

"I must have a talk with you," I said to Suki by telephone; and before she could answer, I said again, "This time I *must*."

Feared, of course, that she would be called away by an emergency whim. An emphatic double positive could easily turn into a negative on Suki's personal word processor. Being her kind of free spirit required a full-time career of saying yes and no when no and yes were expected. She chose her own order for things.

"I always love talking with you, Frank, you're so interesting."

"Okay."

"You always have something to say."

"Okay then, we'll—"

"I hope this won't be just some boring conversation, Frank. You're usually unfailing. Why don't you come over tomorrow evening?"

"How about this afternoon?"

"Oh, dear. This rush doesn't bode the best, does it?" she asked.

There are different ways of being depressed, such as nervous or jittery, charged up for flight, or love depressed, marriage depressed, divorce depressed (that one stays with a person), job depressed, sick at heart because time just rolls along with no magic filling it—this could make a little song—and also it sometimes even happens in America that someone has died or the nation is at peril. Those last suggestions were not usually what caused me to go into a funk, much as I appreciate the nation's being at peril. The path through life which I followed that morning—sleepy, chilled, bleak, and leaning toward hibernation—was to yawn and clobber at the fog in my head. Which didn't clear—a wintry field-based fog it was. Poking did no good. I lay on the couch after breakfast, after three cups of strong coffee meant to yank me into the day, and fell into blackness. Sleep is supposed to be the body's prologue to non-sleep and dealing with the problem. I should have awakened after this morning nap to cold coffee, stubs of raisin toast dating from first breakfast, more orange juice, and eager emergency jitters. Instead I was dreaming one of those peculiar dreams in which a person gives himself up and becomes someone else. I was Peter, walking through sheets of rain, stumbling in the gray of a northern woods, mud slipping down the hill as I slogged up it, rain slanting and hissing—and all the while I was watching the person, Peter, myself, not me. Peter was walking and stumbling and walking again, an infantryman slogging in a war with no visible opposing army. I was not Peter. I was there. I was Peter.

I awakened in a condition of shuddering anxiety. At least in my own dreams I should have the right to be myself. I preferred not to be Suki's son when I slogged backward into sleep in the morning.

The drive across the Bay Bridge from Berkeley was a help. The person who paid the toll, prudent Frank Curtis, plucked the correct change from the little plastic snap-pocket on the dashboard. By the time I got to Filbert Street, Suki's house recently painted for her birthday in sunny yellow and sky-blue, hair and eye colors, with the new ivy just starting over the brick foundations, I had shaken the bad sleep off and was ready for a difficult conversation with a lady who sometimes caused me pleasure and pain; perhaps I had passed the time for her, too. I took a deep breath in the garden: Suki's fresh garden smells.

The metal gate was unlocked; odd. I heard voices. No answer when I rang, so I went in anyway. Suki was shouting, "Why don't you start to grow up?" and Peter yelled, "Why don't you?" and then they saw me.

"Frank! You sure got here fast, wasn't there any traffic? Open the fridge if you're thirsty."

"Is this a bad time for you?"

"No, no, no," Suki said. "Was my voice too loud?"

"It's a bad time for her. You wanna listen to the old lady, Frank? When she has a hard-on, she's braver."

I turned to make my way back the way I had come, but Suki said, "You might as well stay. My son here is asking me for money and I say he could get a job weekends, after school, if he wants to do grown-up things—needs gas and good dope and—"

"Wait and listen, Frank," Peter said. "Get yourself an education, okay?"

Suki was gulping and pulling at her velour workout shirt. I could read the calligraphed word on it: "*Advent.*" She looked skinny and girlish, which was her custom, and distraught, which was not. She opened the refrigerator door, on which Squaw Valley photographs were taped—Suki skiing, a young and pretty Peter skiing, various men standing in the snow, squinting against the glare, skiing with them— and poured me a glass of orange juice and gestured to me to take anything else I wanted. And said: "If you had a kid, you'd know what a problem it is."

Peter grinned like the men in the photos. "Oh, he's had kids, Ma."

"Now what do you mean by that?" I asked. No one seemed to hear me.

"He wants to make trips, buy a new VCR and

equipment, some kind of gear, upgrade his transportation situation, and not have to account—my son's got a lot of demands these days."

"I'm negotiating," said Peter. "Aren't we negotiating right now? We even got a what you call it, arbitrator, isn't that what you're doing, Frank?"

As I turned toward the door, Suki said softly, "Stay. I want you to stay, Frank. Didn't you want to talk anyway? Please."

"I'm sure he did, and listen, too. So listen: Ding-dong the witch is dead," Peter sang. "That's a goddamn fairy tale, man. It ain't true at all."

"Are you being funny? You may be my baby, but you're not a kid anymore. Why don't you start being a man?"

"Like your men, Ma? I'm joining the information economy. You know, serious stuff like airline tickets, dope, and cassettes—whatever. I'm not into capital investment."

"What you seem to like is to take money from me."

"That's not my kind of investment, Mother. What I mean by the information economy, I find out how to talk to you and then I don't have to take. I'm *persuasive*. I make you give."

She asked in a warning voice, "Should you be talking to me like this?"

"Always did hate small business."

"Should you be talking to your mother like this?"

"You won't remember. You'd need ears in your crotch to listen, Ma."

She slapped the boy hard. He was jarred and went pale. Then he didn't move. He was silent for a moment.

"You'll feel bad you did that," he said. "I'm your only son. Even if you got your tubes untied, it's too late now. You won't have another. You're too old. Hey, can I borrow your wheels for something I got to do needs a communication of nice wheels, Ma?"

Suki put her hands together, locked her slim fingers, hurting, and cried, "I've got to get out of here."

Probably she shouldn't have done that. This was her own freshly painted nest on Filbert Street. Another woman would have stayed it through with her son, but Suki had personal ways of dealing with trouble, her solutions to the problems of men. Getting out was a proven weapon in her arsenal. It was her way of taking control, it had always worked well enough, and this time she paused because maybe she shouldn't just get out.

"Then I'll stay a while," said Peter. "Maybe I'll enjoy myself a little visit with our Frank here."

"I want to talk with your mother—"

"But she's leaving, man, don't you see?" He spread his arms in that generous pride that was meant to state: *Hey, that's my ma.*

Suki said, "I've got a temper. I'll be better

about this when I have a chance to cool off. I've got a couple errands to run. I'll be back. Excuse me, Frank, I can't—I'll be back—"

Car keys, purse, no sweater, half a good-bye, and Peter and I were alone in the house as I did not want us to be. How did he work this out so neatly for himself? He was smiling and saying, "Uhthefuck."

"Pardon?"

"What, the, *fuck*, Frank. She have to shop or she just not want to lend me her wheels? 'Sokay, you and me got our business anyway."

The kitchen was still filled with the scent of Suki, a light cologne, that sexy anxiety smell, plus radishes in the sink. She had the French habit of buttering radishes for herself as a treat. I went for the faucet to fill a glass of water—dry mouth—and Peter gestured to the fridge where I was sure there were Perrier and Calistoga and other high-fashion versions of water. He shrugged. I didn't have to accept any invitations if I didn't want to. All he wanted was to make me want to.

"You're a bright person," I said, "got things going for you. I can't figure out why—"

"Why you?" he asked.

"Okay, why me. I never did you any harm, did I?"

"Let that pass."

"Why pick me out to make a lot of trouble which you won't get away with anyhow?"

"That's for me to find out if I won't get away with it."

"Peter, this is dumb. This is not some game just cost you your quarters. Come off it."

Peter had his head cocked for attentively not listening to what I said. He was closely tuned to emitting his own message. "You got a key to the house?" he asked.

"No."

"Used to?"

"Never did. Maybe I knew where you stowed it."

"Above the back door on the ledge. Near the electric meter. So that's the same thing—you have a key to the house."

"What do you want, Peter? What are you asking me?"

"I been living with the secrets I been hearing whispers about. Through the walls, getting whiffs in the bathroom, on the towels."

"There's no secrets then, it sounds like. I'm sure you know all about them."

"Dark, soft, wet, that's what I mean—"

"That's not all the secrets you were wondering about."

"—and bloody, I want lots of that, too."

"Your secrets are not kind, Peter."

"I don't need any of that, *Frank*. C'mere, you know we got a VCR, Mom did, let me show you my cassette. Hey, come on in here."

I expected a bootlegged film; no. I expected an "Amy's Secret Bedroom" or "Joe & Jim Come in

Frisco" tape from the Mitchell Brothers; it wasn't that. I expected something bad and wrong.

"Close the shades, better light definition," he said. "Sit you down and come to the movies, but we don't serve buttered popcorn."

I sat.

"Lights! Camera!"

The Sony flashed some tape readout numbers, a color spectrum, and then there was a shadowy blue scene, bad color, bad light, bad focus, two people in twisted sheets doing some twisting. It was cheap tape and the light was mostly blue, but it was clear who the two people were because one of them had a halo of sudden white where her hair would be a pale summery yellow in real life. That was Suki. The other person was Frank Curtis. I didn't need to watch the sudden rictus on my face that represented pleasure on this historical record. I think I looked away. I said nothing. Let surprises be done.

Peter switched on a lamp. He stared, then shrugged with appreciation at my interesting failure to respond. "Wait," he said. "'Nother movie. Remember the good ol' days, you were a kid, a double feature?"

This time the tape quality was even worse, as if there were an unfocused lens or filter, and the shadows were darker, it was night, the light was bad, and one of the figures on the same bed was Peter. The other was a man. I strained forward because it looked very much like the man with

Suki. I squinted and now I was really staring, holding each detail, waiting for the man to turn so that his face would come clear out of the electronic flicker and haze. It didn't. The couple on the bed finished. The bluish Peter was smiling, haggard, drying his crotch with a pillow and peeking around it at the hidden camera.

"Not me," I said. "That's not me."

"Who says it is, besides the chicken? Only I say it is. I was just a kid, right? But I was there. Taken advantage of by a guy who wanted—God! —both the mother and the boy." He picked a sliced carrot from the water glass, where it had been soaking since last night, bit a sharp crunch, and said, "They're not bad. Don't get so stale like other things left out the night before."

"What's the gain, Peter? What are you asking for?"

"Not bad," he repeated. "So Frank, who's going to believe the other person, chickenhawk says he wasn't there?"

The curl of his mouth was helping him feel the excitement he planned on. It was releasing the right rush into his brain. He was working his lips. He used his body to give him what he wanted, and so what if it was different from what anybody else wanted.

If only the kid were a normal teenager with pimples. Because then I could pick him up by the pimples and throw him through the glass door. But he was a clean, good-looking, almost girlishly good-looking boy with wide shoulders and narrow hips and fluttering lashes like his mother's.

"Peter, c'mere," I said.

"You want to talk to me or what?"

"C'mere."

Maybe he thought I might swing on him. He put his face forward with a little pucker on the lips, his eyes closed, something I remembered about Suki when she was being cute. I used to call it her centerfold face.

If what he was thinking was that I might swing on him, he was a boy-prophet in his own time.

Now his nose was bleeding, his cheek was abraded, and he was still talking kindly, calmly, happily. "A picture of this, too, Frank. Every little bit helps."

ELEVEN

My hand hurt. My heart hurt. My feelings hurt.

I was running from my lopsided old Fiat toward my cottage and lair, in which no one awaited me, in which nothing much awaited me but the spectrum of the rainbow as the sun made its way across the stained glass, as it used to in vestry days.

Once I was lucky to fall into a teaching job when the scramble of freelancing had tuckered me out. Once I was lucky to use my gloom where it belonged, in academic life, where it just made me look serious. Once I had been fortunate enough to find this desanctified chapel in the Berkeley hills where I could spend mornings or evenings with a red-pencil at student papers while the birds twittered outside; smoke a joint now and then, review the marriages of my friends and colleagues and be glad I had avoided

their fates, occasionally find the flicker of infatu-
ation making me stay out late and have breakfast
with a stranger—mostly I found myself alone,
enjoying the middle of a depressed middle age.
Well, in this vale of confusion, no good luck
seems to last forever.

The raccoons had gotten into the trash again.
It was a sign of distraction when I neglected to
strap down the can.

If it didn't rain soon, I might see the deer flit-
ting nervously down from the hills, looking for
damp and green. I didn't mind about the deer; I
liked them; my garden could always use a closer
trim. I could do without the cute, skunk-faced,
untidy raccoons.

Sometimes, in the dry months of early fall, I
would step up the walk toward my cottage in
Berkeley and hear the sharp crack and splinter
of a leaf underfoot. It was like the autumn leaves
clattering into dust in any other normal part of
the world; not across the bay in San Francisco,
however, where the dry burning of the sun
never quite finishes off that verdant all-year
springtime dampness. In San Francisco, in Pacific Heights, stepped-on leaves merely bend.

My hand was swelling in a glove of lymph and
furry flesh. How do people who regularly hit
other people deal with their injuries? Do they
consider them a mere detail, the cost of doing
business?

I held my hurt hand and fumbled with the
lock. A person can't nurse a swollen hand and

open a sticky door at the same time. I thought
ouch and used mushy fingers and a shoulder; it
was open; and then I stopped a moment, half in
and half out. A milkweed seed came sifting like
air gauze down the draft from the roof. Next
winter, if the shingles hadn't repaired themselves, I would have to think about fixing the
leak. A man shouldn't live with a pan in his bedroom to catch the rain drippings—not two win-
ters in succession. Alfonso certainly wouldn't.
That came close to misdemeanor personal negli-
gence.

I wondered if I would turn into an old prof
who received anonymous notes about leaving his
fly unzipped. Not for a few years, I hoped. I had
always thought my wife, when I found her,
might not object to reminding me about such
things in the morning; the rest of the day could
be up to me. I didn't mean to abdicate responsibility.

The milkweed was still in the air. Nice breeze
up here. I hurried inside, filled the sink with water, put in the plug, dumped a tray of ice cubes
into it. This was the plan that I had developed as
I drove back across the Bay Bridge from Suki's
house. Somehow ache and anxiety manage to
take precedence over other matters—bone and
flesh pain, I mean. I had long ago noticed, for
example, how as vulgar and trivial a matter as
traveler's diarrhea seemed to cancel out meta-
physical speculation or aesthetic appreciation of
a cathedral or a museum. A person just sits there

oinking like a pig and praying like a true be-
liever for things to get better. Even if he has lost
his religion in childhood and now thinks himself
a man, secure in a wise skepticism, there are no
atheists by the dawn's early light over a foreign
toilet.

I wondered if I'd broken something in my
hand, a knuckle, ripped a tendon, jammed a
joint. I dreaded the wait in the Oakland Kaiser
Hospital for a yawning Third World doctor to
look at my hand, marvel at the stupidity of
Americans, suggest an X-ray, send me down the
hall to another corner of transplanted Third
World medical care. More likely, in the grand
tradition of brawling, the swollen bone bruise
would just go away by itself.

I stood at the sink, looking to practice a wise
skepticism, or if that didn't work, a mature se-
renity. That didn't work either. My hand
throbbed and my heart plunked and thumped. I
stared at the pot straight ahead, hung from a
nail, and noticed a crust of tomato soup in it.
The last time I had heated a can of Campbell's
tomato soup was before I had become a star of
hidden video. In those days I used to drop a raw
egg into the soup, cooling the simmering salty
tomato paste and cooking the egg—a dual effi-
ciency which also buffered the salt—and my life
had been boring, lonely, and peaceful, as it was
not now. I stared at the line of tomato crust and
longed for the good old days. Neatness counts;
cleanliness is a part of neatness. Someday, if oxi-

dation didn't do the job, I might need to take a Brillo pad to that pot.

My sudden gusts of housecleaning would have raised suspicion from coast to coast if anyone had known about them. But from coast to coast and sea to shining sea, my intimate habits were unknown to the women I had never married, the sons and daughters I had never sired. How advantageous that I had finally stopped brooding about the matter.

Another matter didn't seem to be going away. Peter had shown me something, he had sent me somewhere, revealed a lie. Lies can be almost as important as truth to a man who is living out the endless California childhood. The furious sincerity of Peter's deceit invaded my routines. Like anyone unjustly and wildly accused of crime or sin, I replied with enraged protest, denial, and indignation, I knew I was entirely innocent, and wondered if I might have done it.

Well, if not like anyone unjustly accused, like some. Like Frank Curtis when the deed flashed against an eroded fantasy deep within the stupid soul of the man.

I was innocent.

I swear I did not commit the violation.

I confess my freedom from guilt.

I wanted the pain to stop.

I stood at the kitchen sink in my converted chapel, vestry house, the Frank Curtis Memorial Redwood Cottage, which was leaning aslant on the backs of the termites who gnawed at it too slowly to wreck the foundations in my lifetime, if I didn't live too long. I looked at my hand again and plunged into a sink in which I had put cold water and emptied a tray of ice cubes. I couldn't make a fist. The goddamn hand was swelling and cramped at the knuckles, too much jammed in there. Fear and anger were being converted into throbbing pain for storage in the fist I could not make. I was pretty sure cold was supposed to do the trick, not hot, but I didn't have enough experience in punching people out to be sure. It was like the Heimlich maneuver; better if a person does it right.

It got uncomfortable standing at the sink, but the right hand felt better in the basin with its gently clicking ice. My feet were sweaty. I tried unlacing my boots and removing them with my left hand, while keeping my right hand in the sink. This was a mess. When I finally managed it, water was splashed all around. I had undipped my icy swollen hand, there were wet spots on my socks, I was miserable. This was a nice distraction from the odd distant terror I felt. Physical discomfort can be a help.

I began to dislike the line of tomato crust on the facing pot.

Peter had no right to heave this confusion into my life. Let him stir himself into any wasteful distraction that caught his fancy, let him sit sneering from a motorized bicycle if he liked, but I was a grown person, an adult with an exceptionally cozy job in an advanced educational system. All I had to do was not do anything out-landish, coast on my way, cultivate my appetites if I chose, not let them get in the way of meeting my classes or reading my students' attempts at journalism—company reports, publicity, a copy-writer's cubicle would be the fate for most of them. Not mine. I was a professor of higher things in the information economy, but after a while retirement would take it all out of my hands.

Peter had no rights in my life. He had the right to make trouble for himself, but not for me. I was intended to settle reasonably into a routine of riskless unfulfilled longing for his mother, basking without burning in her light.

But what if Peter had hold of a truth?

Surely I never wanted to embrace that bony boy—*never*. Of course I was not interested in sex with the son of the woman I craved. I knew no such temptations. Out of the question. Idiotic. And yet I wondered if my stunned queasiness, these peculiar waves of nausea, meant something more than merely No.

I decided to put it to the test in scientific fash-ion. I was not going to be thrown off the road by a mere teenager without knowing where I wanted to stand. If I was going to be accused, I wanted to be sure I was innocent. Or be sure I was guilty, in case it had to come down to lying. Guilty or innocent, I wasn't going to be a mere victim, run over by a United Parcel truck be-cause I didn't know where I was.

So what I should do was go to Telegraph Avenue in Berkeley or Polk in San Francisco, to Castro or the Tenderloin, buy me a kid, feel foolish, let him laugh at me, let him do me half-naked, pants hobbled down to my ankles, feel dumb, pay him, feel dumber . . . I could hear Alfonso telling me, "Hey, man, I thought this wasn't your scene. Ain't you spose tell the truth to ol' Alfonso, buddy? Don't you have a real stupid side to you, Frank-o?"

Yup. Deed I do.

Maybe Peter was a boy agent of the Attitude Police, the Do It Squad. ("Hey, you're spose to look at me, old guy, you know, like you really care . . .")

Why me? Maybe this happened because Peter liked me most. Because Suki liked me some. Because I was a target. Because I was wanted. (Optimist with swollen hand in sink of ice and water thinks crazy thoughts of hope and tries to figure out what could be good about them.)

I had dreams like any normal person. The ice cubes were clunking around the sink as I stood there ungainly, half-asleep and uncomfortable, aching, wondering, and wasting the valuable time of the universe by failing to take care of important matters. I was being done not by a boy but by a sinkful of ice cubes.

Instead of merely letting things run over me and then trying to get my hand to stop hurting, I should move on to business. Someplace there were remedies—Dr. Kowalska (no), Suki (how

217

could she help?), Peter (enough of that), or some good friend, expert, and counselor in these matters. Alfonso. Friend, expert, counselor, and if I were lucky, which I didn't seem to be, protector.

I dried my hand and used a numb finger to punch the buttons.

"Hello, Alfonso, sure glad you're answering your phone. Yeah, because you're smart is why you recognize my voice. No, I'm not talking with a lawyer, but I might need a doctor. No, what I'm calling—can we get together again on the same basis? . . . Really appreciate that."

When I hung up, I wondered if I was doing the right thing. He had said everybody always really appreciated the things a person does for them, but he wasn't all that sure what white folks meant by that there statement. Sometimes he had noticed folks weren't all that sincere.

Alfonso liked to get his digs in. Maybe it kept him awake.

I drove back across the Bay Bridge to the address at Hyde and Ellis that Alfonso had given for our meeting. It wasn't exactly an address; it was a place in the Tenderloin, a bar called Lezboise, he said. When I got there, the flickering sign said: "Les Boys," yellow and orange and a profoundly murky purple and a jukebox pumped waves of basses, drums, large horns out into the street, all of it Wurlitzered down to the primary pulsations. There were also words, *Unh Unh Unh Bay-bee one more time Unh Unh.*

I stood at the curb and wondered what would happen to my Fiat parked there with its vinyl sunroof just asking for a razor or a knife and a helping hand in the radio and the glove compartment. Up and down the street there was plenty of company, clumps of six-foot-high girls who were not girls, tight jeans and cutoffs, a bent-can food emporium and a barber bargain for educational purposes and other bars like Les Boys. V.J. Tavern. Bottom of the Mark. Coffee Cal's, "Open All Nite, Christmas Every Day—Hot Microwave Sandwiches. Tacos to Go or Stay."

There were men like me, looking for some sort of entertainment in life, an answer to the unclear questions, and there were the southeast Asian kids playing with bike wheels and mothers who seemed to have arrived in San Francisco by sampan; space people crashing and beached boat people. At a storefront entrance, a line had formed, "Aid to the Disabled" outpatients waiting for a coupon or a lab result. Upstairs, above the businesses on Ellis, rooms and apartments were available by the month, week, day, hour. I could see a tie-dyed purple swastika through a curtain where a man stood with bulging crotch in whitened blue jeans, no shirt, a copy of *Swedish Girls*. He was also watching the street as if he planned to do something on it from his second-story window, just awaiting his opportunity for maximum pleasure.

Maybe Alfonso had to come on duty down

here today. Or maybe he just wanted me to be on duty down here because of some idea he had.

The hard dust blowing in the street had been baked during the long day, and now was leaving the pavement in late afternoon swirls of wind and fog in search of water so that it could fulfill its destiny as mucus. I guess San Francisco streets are supposed to be clean compared with New York or Bangkok. Alfonso, bulky and grinning, stood like a barker, filling the door of Les Boys, beckoning to me. "Hey, fella, come on in, got your hands in your pockets already, you're eligible."

"Alfonso, what the devil, is this your office now?"

He rested his heavy paw on my shoulder. "You think this here's a toilet? This here ain't a toilet, fella—a cesspool, maybe—not a toilet."

"I thought I wanted to talk with you, but you got something in mind."

"Tell you what, Frank-o—let you know 'bout pretty soon." He stood there in the street, unsmiling, taking my measure in the flat late sunlight before we entered into a cool cave of winds, smelling of ripe brew, disinfectant, ashtrays. "This here's where the kid might be headed. This is gonna be his style. This is what we got to deal with, if we can and I don't know if we can —what you thinking?"

I felt better around Alfonso. I said: "I wonder if Suki was worth it."

"Leave us all wondering, don't it? Be doubtful

in some cases, don't you think, 'less you getting in deep, ah, devotion."

"Right."

"In deep devoted that there barbecue pig shit, Frank-o."

I intended to tell him about Peter's video. I expected to ask for advice and counsel. I hoped to inquire if forgery by video happened to be something in the detective's experience. Instead, I was explaining that I cared about Suki and therefore didn't just want to run away, preferred to see her and me through a little rough spot in our friendship.

"Okay, okay, you got something else to say, you better say it."

Alfonso was impatient with me and I was impatient with myself. I was afraid to take the next step if I didn't have to. If I told him what Peter was doing, what I thought he had done with his video equipment, it would be the end for Suki and me. Alfonso would have to go looking officially. The trouble that came down would bury this fragile friendship. But if Peter got it into his own head to knock it off, finish the game, he could save himself, he could save Suki and me, everyone could try for an average life. I could imagine the young man coming to wonder in a few years, *Hey, I was crazy, wasn't I? Shows what happens when you give a boy expensive toys.* . . . But once I sent Alfonso looking for tapes, we would be racing downhill too fast to stop.

I held the news about Peter's video games for

some other time, some other neighborhood. This didn't seem like the correct moment for video discussion. I said: "I liked her, Alfonso."

"*Liked* her. Oh, fella."

"I like her."

"*Like* her. Ooo-weee."

"That's what I mean. That's all I'm going to say just now."

He moved his beer around on the table, making wet paintings and watching how very slowly, in this humidity, the artwork disappeared. He moved his bulk around, too. The leather kids and the shrouded hoods knew he was a cop; two men conferring by the light of the Wurlitzer, one showing something he didn't show, the other showing money he did show, moved into the gents' to complete their transaction. Alfonso moved his lips in a way he had, like a complex shifting of gears, going into another language, practicing, playing, but he didn't speak yet.

"What?" I asked.

"Who speaks of love mostly has sad eyes," Alfonso remarked, grinning, "but down here, man, they get the sad eyes without speaking above or about love. They talk about clap, AIDS, crabs, being busted, trying not be busted, county farm, getting off their habit, getting a better habit, getting Aid to the Totally or Partially, and they manage to do that without much jerking themselves up about love. They get sad eyes anyway, man."

"Doesn't surprise me," I said.

"So if Peter comes down, looking for his sad eyes which he hasn't earned yet, you won't be too surprise, will you?"

"No."

"So you can hope he get his sad eyes. Maybe he live long enough and get them. You can hope that, man, since you be so fond of Mom over there in Pacific Heights."

"Cow Hollow."

"You talking to a spade, man. All that territory kind of look alike to me."

I could feel the bass from the jukebox vibrating the linoleum at my feet, the fiberboard under my butt. There were rainbow waterfall colors fading higher and lower, then lower and higher, above the bar, some kind of beer advertisement. I wondered if this territory looked like other territories to Alfonso, and that's why we were here, or if he was testing me in some way, seeing if I could make myself at home in a gray-wolf Tenderloin bar at an hour of the day when the old hunting wolves hadn't come in yet to sniff out their chickens.

With his eyes little and red rimmed, squinted and intent on me, Alfonso was watching me take in the place. I hoped he would approve that it was new to me. I wanted a little credit for that. "You asking yourself something," he said.

"Right, I am."

"I didn't imply you a perp. I might of *said* it, but I didn't *imply* it."

I wasn't going to ask him to spell out and explain perpetrator. I was going to let him know I could follow his twists and turns. In fact, his pet worm might now turn: "You ever heard of delire verbal, Alfonso?"

"Sir?"

"Verbal delirium. People who stand in public places and just talk. Or other people like to switch their chatter around because maybe they're not so sure who they are, they want to try things on. Peter is like that. They need to have some speed circuits in their brains, a kind of smarts. Peter is sure like that."

"You say. I ain't. I got other reasons for what I do—a few laughs, f'rinstance. Know who I am, man. . . . Maybe I just remember I was a kid and like to play—kids'll do that. I won't say you're wrong about me just 'cause you full a shit."

"Thank you, Alfonso."

His haw haw haw startled the bartender, who looked up from the rinsing of glasses, saw it was only the big cop laughing and clapping me on the back, went back to his profession. On the bar, while he worked, he studied an Aryanman comic book.

"Okay, now you got a little back at me, man, should be proceed."

"Can we stipulate I'm not even a former perp?"

Both Alfonso and I liked my getting a little even with him. It made for a fairer game.

He leaned forward, opened his eyes wide, practically touched his large flat nose to mine, blinked winsomely, and whispered: "Let's you and me stipulate together." He touched my nose with his finger. "Or that be you and I, Perfess?"

"I think I need your help," I said. "I have no special reason to think you might want to, help I mean, if you have the time or inclination to do such a thing. But I need it."

He sat back. The actorish grinning and laughing and wrinkling and sweating seemed to tune itself out. He had won so many times by playing games that he had to make a decision now, call time-out, before he could stop. "Uh-huh," he said. "Know what you saying. Yuh."

And stared while the men in the Les Boys tavern padded around in their running shoes as if they were wearing slippers, some of them limping as they walked, hurt by morning stiffness. The thump of gay disco music screened one conversation from the next. "Let me tell you 'bout other people problems," Alfonso said, "then you can lay out yours. I had this kid stabbed his buddy in the back. He said that's what the poleese claim, but what do they know? It was self-defense. His buddy, not his buddy anymore, burned him in a little deal, was running at him backwards, they'll do that, just to stimulate your weak emotions."

"He expect anyone to believe him?"

"He expeck serve twenty-two months with good behavior 'cause the buddy didn't quite die,

that's all he expeck, plus give me pose when I
hear him. Shit, man, that boy ain't very smart,
the perps usually ain't. 'Nother fruit beat up his
buddy 'cause he spose say, *vroom vroom vroom*,
like a Hondo motorcycle when he sit on him,
hold his thumbs, but the buddy thought he was a
BMW, didn't want to be no Hondo, so they
couldn't do it right—unfulfilling, y'know?—and
he rob him. This perp rob the other guy 'cause
he wouldn't go no *vroom vroom* . . ."

"Hey, Alfonso. How do I get Peter off my
case?"

Alfonso was squinting at a black-and-white
hand-lettered sign above the bar: "Unbridled
Saddle." He put his index finger through the
looped thumb and index of his other hand. "In
case you tired," he said, "it really pick you up,
they say. One of them native Tenderloin home
remedy, they get it from the little people, them
Viets they got around here. . . . Tension span."

"What?"

"I was answering that there question you ask
'bout Peter. Tension span. A-*tention* span. Most
likely he just move on up to other thing. Most
likely he proceed. Big problem is—you main
problem, how I see it—is Suki."

"I'm not worried about that. But there's more
to it about Peter."

"You might not be worry, Frank-o, but you be
sad. You might not be legally liable, but you take
on some fret there."

"Hey, Alfonso, do you really insist on that

black talk? I know you play around with every goddamn kind of jive you like, but when you do that, running through your routines, I never know if you're putting me on or what."

"That's what I doin', *what*. Can't I have a little fun? Okay, now listen to me."

He wanted me to get clear about what I was messing with. He wanted me to understand the kid was as dangerous to himself as he was to me. He wanted me to know my liability was more than legal. He had a large sense of the problem. He wanted me to know that being in love with Suki involved more than merely dreaming about her. He said in plain English: "You ready to suffer? You ready to sacrifice that comfort of yours?"

"I'm not so comfortable."

"You ready to give up your dreamy blues, man? That's the question. That's what I'm saying here on this occasion. That kid is centerfold material in *Horror* magazine. This case is mental, but that don't help you much. He special, so are you ready for the game of Lie and Consequence?"

"I like her, Alfonso. He's her kid, so since I like her—"

"You on the wrong side of the street, man. You in the wrong army."

"I'm doing the best I can. I'm following my feelings this time."

"So what make you feel you should join this

army? What you think you really gonna get on this side of the street?"

"I like her a lot."

"Oh, kid. You about the age of sonny-boy there, you know what I say?"

"Okay. Okay. So probably nothing will come of it."

He blew his breath out as if it were stale and unpleasant to him. He stared at me with his eyes red and bulging in that face full of dark shiny mounds. "Nothing comes of nothing, man, as usual. That's your dreamy blues again. Hey, what I'd druther, I'd druther you open your face to what Peter is dragging around with him, behind that Pacific Heights stuff, that squeaky-clean Frisco stuff, and what you gonna get from that crunchy little mouse you put her in your mouth, 'tween your teeth, you bite down."

"What?"

He didn't say anything. His breathing was noisy. Perhaps I had already answered his questions and he didn't choose to answer mine. I had lost my leverage.

He relented. He wouldn't leave me dangling. "Oh, you crunch, she's good, she really crunches good, make a nice little crunch there. You a boy in love, man. You like that mouse too much for your health—you get worse'n hickies all over your face and mind . . ." He waited. I didn't speak. "Come on, you wanna say me something more about Peter?"

I didn't answer.

"I mean, I could be your better buddy if you let me. I don't think you can wait this one out like you do most of your life." He listened some more. He twisted a finger in his ear. He shook his head. He looked at me as if I were the stupidest mark he ever saw. "And you *know* I'm a nice guy, don't you, Frank-o?"

"You are," I said.

"And you stubborn, man."

He waited some more although now he understood it was useless. I was a hopeless case, he could just go on easing his pleasant way through life, I could just go on being stupid. To each his own. He said: "Okay, okay, so now you take a walk around, I got some calls to make on the pay phone here, Downtown want me to call them, you come back after a while. Hey, I be here, child."

He meant it. He waved me away. He opened his hand, which was filled with quarters. I thought he was saying, though I couldn't hear him: "Pay an extra nickel, for your convenience."

I stood out on Ellis Street, watching the hookers on stilt-like shoes, slapping each other's hands; at this corner the men with torn net stockings used to be men but now, with the aid of hormone shots, they were halfway elsewhere. A boy on a skateboard, with a T-shirt that said "San Antonio, Heart & Ribs of Texas," twisted in his dance of speed, swirled himself around the little clutch of transsexuals at the corner. "Ooo-weee, taste some my warm pasta salad?" one cried after the boy. His purse jerked with his laughter. "You sho carry a lot of mouth," another said to his friend, and the friend answered, "All of it user-friendly." "At room temperature!" "Ooo-weee!"

I had a queasiness in my stomach. The message I was sending myself was: Mistake not to accept Alfonso's offer to help. In California a person is supposed to tell his troubles and the nice other person is supposed to listen and then everything gets to be fine. But I didn't follow the rules that worked for so many happy people. Maybe I was still thinking, Officer of the Law, stranger, big guy, black man, laughs all the time and I don't know how much he is laughing at me . . . when I should have been thinking, Friend.

If this came to be public and some clever reporter like one of my ambitious students—

I still hoped Peter, as smart as his mother, would decide that no trouble is better than trouble.

Puzzles, if they're games, are designed to be solved; messes just get sloppier. Whatever Alfonso had in mind, sending me out onto the street like that, I didn't need to learn what he wanted me to learn. Not necessarily. Not unless I wanted to. Although I was surely eligible for some learning.

He had that fistful of quarters for the telephone. I'd better give him a little more time. A person really did have to call in, a person engaged in his line of work. I hoped this wasn't just another way of pushing me around.

There was a tropical rum smell on the street, sweetish, bacterial, mixed with spoiled food and the sudden heat of a laundry surging through a basement window at ankle level. This was the American Third World of dropout and wasted, keeping up the traditions of the city. Grit was blowing. The men on stilts dabbed at their noses and eyes.

When I returned, Alfonso was looking into his beer in that dreamy way a man has of easing back into things. He seemed to be at peace with the world and his telephone calls. A couple of quarters lay in a wet spot where the mug was being moved around the pitted tabletop. "Message on your machine," he said. "Ought to call Suki."

"How do you know what messages I have on my machine?"

"Both of us play God, fella, we better be lucky, 'cause neither one of us sure ain't your typical hometown deity."

"How the hell you know what messages come onto my machine?"

"Just lucky, I guess."

TWELVE

I'm not prepared to suggest what my strong points are, but mechanical aptitude isn't one of them. I was crouched in a spit-smelling telephone booth at the corner of Ellis and Hyde, fumbling with electronic signals to my beeperless answering machine, which I seldom called from outside, while a skinny black speed freak, in a dress and under a wig, pointed to his wrist and pursed his lips and dramatically mimed the fact that he had a very, very, *very* important telephone call I was keeping him from making. His eyes widened and batted. Not that he wanted to trouble me, but this was his office.

I got through to my Phonemate. Suki's voice on the tape had an edge of panic to it: "Call me, Frank, I need you to call me."

I started to put in two more dimes when the speed freak rapped sharply on the booth with a high-heeled shoe he had removed from his purse for this purpose. "Mister, one call allowed per person, don't you think that's more than fair?"

"Fuck off," I said.

"Oooh, a cop, you talk like a real cute officer." But he teetered away on his spikes, deciding to find a more congenial telephone booth for his important business.

I leaned against the glass and faced the half-open broken door, ready to block any visitors in my booth, and dialed Suki.

"He's moved out," she said. "He's run away. I don't know what he means by this."

"Peter's gone?"

"That's all you can say, Frank?"

"No wait, listen—"

"No letter. No word. Gone with my Visa card —now you understand?"

"Suki, I'm stupid like anybody when I'm trying to think. I'm thinking. Wait."

I was also taking note of something else: *She called me. Suki turned to me.*

"Okay, I've stopped being so stupid now. Listen Suki, *wait.* Just wait till I get there."

The skinny black speed freak in his party dress raised a finger as I hurried by. He was making a sizzling sound that meant, Ooh, hot. He had made his call already, or perhaps he had just been making my acquaintance in the office and his call wasn't so pressing.

* * *

I entered the room filled with flowers and Suki did not see me. She was sitting, hands primly folded in her lap, looking at a white place on the wall—a place where there was no print, no painting, no bookshelf, no poster, a mere space of white; no television screen, either—and she was staring into the space with a look of such white longing, such dreaming distance, that I drew my breath sharply with astonishment. This was not the Suki I knew and didn't know. It was a mother in despair. She heard me come in.

"Caught," she said. She grinned and busily undid the quiet in which I had found her. "Caught," she said, "gone to Alpha."

"Jesus, Suki, why are you apologizing?"

"I just didn't know you were there, but I'm glad to see you—hey, here, come put your arms around me, fella."

The pale cool blue reflected at me as I kissed her. She did not close her eyes, but it was not a tender stare. It was to drive me back where I belonged, make me forget what I had just seen.

"What's happening, Suki?"

"Just a second. No rush." She put my arms back around her. "Do this first, take care of this chilly person."

I hugged her. I could feel a suppressed ticking in her body, the throbbing of heartbeat, the blood and organ shiftings through flesh, a machinery of distress. There was caught breath and grief in the interior of this geology. Within me, as I listened, there was pride that I could even for a moment ease her turmoil, though I know men cannot control the power of earthquakes. I kept my arms around her until she suddenly let go, signaled I could let her go.

"Dr. Kowalska says I should just wait. It's like taking hostages she said. Let him get tired. She says he's not really a minor anymore—Frank, he's my boy!—and she says he's like a survivalist, he wants to prove something to himself—"

"I guess he does. Maybe to you, too."

"Are you being funny again, Frank?"

"Am I ever funny? I don't think so. To me, too—" She looked bewildered. "Prove something to me, too."

This was not the time to tell her about the videotapes. I decided I would not tell her now, although I didn't know when the proper time might be. Judgment doesn't always bring the right decisions anyway. I decided to wait with the help not of judgment but of her saying, "The things that go away are the things I love. My little boy. And things—a person—that hasn't come to me yet."

"Okay," I said, moved more than I wanted to be.

"You're a good man, Frank. Maybe I should stop waiting at my age, stop hunting."

"Hunters don't like to stop hunting."

"I'm still a woman, whatever you think. I don't want to do this forever, do what I keep on doing, since before Peter was born and while he was a beautiful little boy and now."

It was not the time to tell her about the video-tapes and then she was speaking of her own search and it became the time. Perhaps it was not intelligence working in me, or lack of intelligence either, but merely impatience. I told her.

She was calm. She asked if the man in the video with Peter looked like me. Somewhat, I said. She asked if the man with her looked like me. It was me, I said. She smiled a little. She was a little pleased at Peter's skill with machinery. She thought it had been inherited from her, but maybe also from Cal, the father, a little.

She wondered what to do next.

I said I didn't know.

She said Dr. Kowalska said to wait, to give him time.

I said she had told me that.

She wondered if the information I had just given her changed that plan.

I said I didn't know why it should.

She fell silent for a while. Without asking if this was what I wanted, she poured iced tea from a pitcher. She was right not to ask because I didn't know what I wanted. We sat facing each other with iced tea in frosted glasses. She moved once again to get fresh lime, she squeezed it for both of us, and then she sat facing me again. Just now she was not waiting for me or Dr. Kowalska or even Peter to make the next move. She was waiting for her own next thought.

Head tilted, lips pressed together in what might be a smile, might be something else, shy and unamused, she was studying me. She was sitting in a wicker chair with wicker arms and she hammered the arms lightly. Little speculative taps of the fists was all they were. She was practicing a new way of looking at me. I might have thought she would be angry and bewildered in general about the idea that I could be the seducer of her son, but instead I was the occasion in particular of making her consider if some man was. Whatever I might predict about Suki was not what Suki did. Her son had disappeared and suddenly she was vexed with me. "I mean, just out of curiosity, Frank," she said, "I mean, just saying for oh, sensuality if you want to call it by a long word, I mean the pleasure of it, people do that, trying a new thing—not Peter, of course, but some other time—other boy—I mean trying a new thing or sort of taking the offering of joy someone freely offers, Frank, just exploring, whatever was right at the time—"

"Are you embarrassed to ask me, Suki?"

"No. Did you ever go with a man? Or a—?"

"Boy? The answer is—"

"Don't tell me! Don't fib! Don't tell me because in general, for curiosity or inquiry or just for, I mean you don't have to tell me if you don't want to, not that it makes any difference—" Her little mouth was open and damp, her little teeth were gleaming, her long sentence was not completed. Her question could be answered.

"I've probably had fantasies or dreams I don't remember. I had buddies when I was a kid. The answer is no."

She looked disappointed. "I wouldn't have judged you, except maybe you were braver than you seem to be."

"And about Peter? How would you feel?"

"I just want him to be happy. I just want him to grow up like a real man. I don't care what he does in or out of bed. I don't care what anybody . . . I don't want him to do it in an alley, I want him to respect himself, Frank—that's what I want."

"But you'd also kind of like it if I had another side to me."

"Frank, maybe you don't know about children. I'd like to do things I don't want to see Peter doing. I'd like you to be—take risks—but I don't want Peter . . . oh, yes, dear, I'm scared for him. Where the devil is he? Thing about you, maybe it's your trouble—I know you're not crazy, you could be crazier—is Peter's my son and I'm not so sure about him."

She was confused. She cared. It seemed that way. She didn't know what to do. From what she was saying, I couldn't make out more than I made out and it was enough. It was especially enough because she looked worn, older, frightened, and like the mother of a teenage boy who was in trouble and bringing others with him. There was a parchment frailty in the translucent bluish skin under her eyes.

"Maybe we should just try to find him," I said. "Don't you have the idea he's in the Tenderloin?"

"Maybe we should. Dr. Kowalska's not his mother."

"That's right."

She stared at me, she picked at the wicker arms of the chair, and a new idea seemed to come to her. Neither of us had thought of it before now. "Maybe I should ask Cal," she said. She seemed to be looking at me for approval. I nodded.

She reached for the telephone above the kitchen counter and I left the room. I didn't want to hear this conversation. I stood looking into the back garden and the space in the open garage where Peter's bicycle with the motor attached used to sit. There were grease rags and an open tool kit. An old bicycle wheel hung from a nail on the wall of the garage, next to a shelf on which Suki had put potted plants. Suki had prettified her garage with ferns and the sprouted tendrils from the cores of pineapples. She had taken a Saturday afternoon to make her garage pretty; it was the sort of adventure she might invent for herself.

She was smiling when I returned. The parchment at her eyes was crinkling. "He says he has his own problems. He says the boy is a man now, it's not so unusual to be on your own at his age. He says he's all tied up with his own family —I know that. He was very courteous about wishing me well in all my endeavors and he didn't hear a word I was saying. In the nicest possible fashion he doesn't care if his son . . ."

I believed Peter was Cal's son, but for his own reasons Cal didn't seem certain. Do I look like anybody you know? he had once asked Suki, and she had answered, Peter, and he had said: One thing used to be true about you when you were my wife. You used to tell the truth.

The conversation had puzzled her. She thought she always told the truth, as much of it as was helpful; and when I laughed at the qualification, she had asked, "Is there a better way, Frank?"

It was not a matter to be discussed with her today.

"Frank, I can't just sit here, no matter what Dr. Kowalska says. Are we being held hostage?"

"Maybe he'll telephone."

"Is that what we do? We wait? Is that what's right?"

"Let's talk."

"It helped when you held me. Hold me, Frank—"

I did so.

"—as if you love me, Frank."

I did so. Someone needed me.

She started to laugh in her peculiar low, throaty, giggling way. "Are you conscious?" she asked.

"What?"

"Of what you're doing?"

"What?"

"Don't force the key into the lock."

I was frightened by what I was doing. I felt stupid.

"The door is open, you don't have to push so," she whispered, and pulled me down over her on the kitchen floor with the door open, leading toward the sunny yard and the open garage where I had noticed the smear and marks of bicycle tires and oil. The floor was hardwood; we were not very practical; I saw white kitchen utensils all about us, and then gave up to seeing nothing.

Later she said: "I had a mother who thought life was about shopping. Even as a girl, I knew she was wrong. It's about breakfast, picnics, trips, espresso, horses standing in a field . . . this."

"What?" I was thinking about the lonely horses standing in the field.

"Especially this," she said, "there's a muck and mire here. I think a poet said that."

Silence. I couldn't compete with a poet.

"I think the poets like to do this. It's not about things. Are you a poet, Frank, what you're doing, or do you just like me?"

I couldn't compete with a poet or a mother who believed in shopping.

She sighed. "Sometimes you don't know what to say. You're not a poet. Or you should say: Maybe I just like trouble. But you don't. So just slide in and let's be sweet to each other.

Oh, I had already slid in. Oh, I could be a poet maybe, or a finder of trouble, but not the sort of trouble she meant.

"When everything is over," she said, "some things remain."

She knew how I wanted to possess her, be a poet with her, rescue her son, have a child, and could not. I was wanting foolishness and disaster. Love is not supposed to be a joke about vanity.

"Why am I here?" Suki asked. "Why me, why you, why us? You're supposed to be smart, you're certified smart by the university, tell me."

"That question," I said. "I'm not smart. When we're in trouble we ask that question. I ask it a lot when I'm alone." She was looking at me with great thoroughness. "I'm alone a lot, like all bachelors, come home in the morning and find four kinds of peanut butter in the refrigerator for breakfast—"

She didn't ask: *Come home in the morning?* Said: "I thought not," meaning: I knew you wouldn't be able to tell me what I need to know.

Why was she here and why was I? I had nothing useful to say. Repeating her question wouldn't help.

"There are no survivors," she said, "and we're not included on the list of the survivors."

"There's not even a list, Suki."

"Pity." She was brisk again, and remembering to toss the helmet of hair for what it was worth —putting a lot of sunlight on the words, maybe.

"Used to think there was a list. Used to go to church. Used to be a stupid little girl. Then I thought if somebody held me as if I were the only one, the only one ever, as if he loved me—listen to how dumb I was, Frank! That would be enough!"

"Inside that's what we all are. We pretend to grow up. We're still banging on the high chair for Mommy to bring us something sweet."

"Care about ourselves," she said.

"That's a fact."

She was silent a moment. She was troubled and ashamed and her eyes were large and perplexed. "There's something different, Frank, and it's scary. I'd rather die than—I'm just going through the motions with everything else—I'd rather die than anything happened to him."

She put her hand on her mouth as if she had just said something obscene, blasphemous, forbidden. I too was shocked. There could be something more important for Suki than being held as if someone loved someone.

"Let's go find him. To hell with Dr. Kowalska. Can you wait any longer?"

"I can't," she said.

THIRTEEN

I thought I knew where he'd be. Alfonso had given me a suggestion, and among the skinheads, punks, transvestites, speed freaks, alkies, hookers, the souls of the Tenderloin, seemed to be the place to find him. "Not that this isn't a very American residential area," I explained to Suki. "It's sort of a Welcome Wagon to Southeast Asia. There are lots of nice fresh-faced kids from Cambodia digging in the garbage cans."

She was silent as we parked, I said a silent good-bye to my Fiat, and we headed up Taylor toward the taxi dispatcher's office. The drivers and the woman who worked the phones kept an eye on the street. There may have been lots of nice east Asian orphans out there, but there was also the dark churn from the city's diseased butt-end. Next door to the taxi dispatcher's, a Chinese diner served breakfast all day, twenty-four-hour-a-day breakfast, no MSG, breakfast of whatever a person desired in the Chinese food line. We waited for the proprietor to collect three dollars and twenty-four cents for an afternoon breakfast for one. He wondered what we were waiting for.

No, he didn't recognize anybody from my description. He didn't see nothing. He spoke only menu English. Since there was no way I could get through to him with a description of Peter that used the available language, sweet and sour, pork fried rice, oyster beef, double-happiness fish gill soup, I decided to move on to the cab dispatcher. As we paused at the door of the New Canton to look at the headline on piled copies of a free newspaper—"Great Masses of the People of the Tenderloin Protest Ramada Inn Imperialist Hegemony"—Suki took my arm and held me. The Chinese proprietor was saying to a cabbie at the counter, "Fuckin' dicks walk in 'speck me get my place fired, askin' stupid questions about some fuckin' runaway."

On the sidewalk Suki said, "He didn't even care if we heard him."

"He wanted us to hear him," I said.

"I told him I was the mother."

"He doesn't believe in motherhood, Suki. Maybe he hasn't had that experience."

"But I *said*—"

"He's got his own problems."

Same results at the taxi dispatcher. The gum-chewer who stared at us through Coke-bottle lenses was more forthcoming with her talk, but not more helpful. She kept an open mike. "Couple corner Fillmore and Sacramento, red house, ring the bell . . . No, I see a lot of kids on the street outside, some o' them gooks 'bout yay high to a cockroach . . . Need cab to Oakland airport, anyone in Richmond . . . How the fuck would I know him? Sorry for my French . . . Brian, you in the Richmond, come in Brian . . . Yeah, Oakland airport, they sound white . . . No, I was talking with some goofs in off the street, they're not French . . . Say, mister and missus, he the kind of kid you talking about comes in to chat with taxi dispatchers?"

I repeated the description.

"Listen, I got a job to do, fuck off, will you? No, not you, Brian, I got some foreign guests here in the office . . ."

On the street, Suki asked me if she looked like a policewoman. I said no, not to worry about that, but she looked like an outsider to these insiders and they don't prefer people who come poking around because that's what cops do. "I'll bet they like Alfonso," she said.

"Oh, bet they just love him."

"You don't think they do, Frank?"

It was an odd, exhilarating feeling to be in control with Suki, at least a little bit, steering for us both. It was not an experience I had managed earlier in our friendship. I could admire how she kept the lid on her fear and panic, how she looked inappropriately bright and clean and wrong for this place, eyes blue and shining, how persistent she was in being Suki, herself, even as she was also a frightened mother looking for her son. I liked some of it, but I could take a pass on other parts of it.

The street here was a stretch of rolling desert asphalt, melted, then fissured in the sun under truck tires. This was not Pacific Heights down here; the city officials' limousines didn't send street repair signals up through channels into official brains. A boy on a skateboard, which seemed to be the preferred local transport for young joyriders and purse snatchers, twirled around us, playing solo games, skillfully doing his wheelies up and down and across the sidewalk, making a whirring asphalt hum, then cement music, and helping the turns with mouth English. His orange Mohawk was fixed with glue; not a breeze disturbed it. "Hey, mister, gimme the kiss of life," he said.

"Pardon?"

"Let's go for it, hey?"

"Slide off, kid, before I lose my precarious balance."

He liked that. He grinned. "Okay, then gimme a dollar, wouldn't that be right, mister?"

Suki got interested; she wasn't frightened by his zooms and swoops around us on Ellis Street. "What did he ask for?"

"The kiss of life, hey, I can see you do good blow jobs, too, ma'am. So why'ncha just look inna your purse a second, I need a dollar for now, something I need to pick up at the store, hey! Don't like your competition roun' here—"

He saw me getting ready for him. Although he wore knee pads, elbow pads, and was surely quicker on his feet than I was, he didn't want to risk cracking his hair. He shot down the street with a screech like that of a Mercury bike messenger. "You didn't ask if he knows Peter," Suki said.

"No, I didn't."

"I guess you didn't think it was worthwhile," she said.

I told her I was looking for a certain bar. I didn't mention it was the one Alfonso had taken me to. I wondered if there were eyes watching behind the T-shirts and Jockey shorts drying on lines at the windows of the second-floor rooms above Drang Hao Foodstuffs, Adult Books & Cassettes, the "Do Not Disturb Private Residence Dog Okay But Watch Out for Tenant" sign. The movie down the street was playing, *The Best Little Warehouse in the West*, plus *Men Who Work Forklifts*. A tall black transvestite in a red wig—maybe it was the same person I had seen in a blond wig not so long ago—said, "Hey, I'm hot, ain't you col', need be warm a little?" When we walked by, he called after Suki, "Hey, lady, dropped your hook."

Suki was holding my arm very tightly and not speaking. This was different from making love. The sensations I was feeling were painful and shameful. The pressure of her arm was sweet. I

248

was sure it was not an exercise. She held my arm, and that pressure on my shoulder, that heat, the furnace of need, was coming from a place she did not often use. If she had used it, I had not known it.

"Right here someplace," I said, "I know it's right here."

She wasn't scared of what she was seeing. She was frightened for Peter. I wondered if this heat came from a different furnace.

Suddenly we turned a corner and I saw the sign in yellow and orange and purple, and could hear the jukebox working its deep rock-and-roll throb, thoroughly working the lower registers. Les Boys; how could I have forgotten? I didn't stop to think if we would be welcome without Alfonso. Suki held my arm as we entered, and then let go. She didn't ask what we were doing here, but I gave her an answer: "We might be thirsty at this point."

"Are we, Frank?"

The way everyone looked at us was economical. No one turned full and stared; they didn't waste the endangered resource of their attention, but we had their careful notice. It may not have been benevolent concern. No one came to take a drink order. Perhaps the waiters were all doing their morning fix at this hour.

I told Suki I would get us something. First she said a glass of white wine and then gave me a little smile, finding the idea funny, and corrected it to beer. "Don't ask for light," she said, "just anything from the faucet."

At the bar I asked for two drafts, and the bartender said, "Bud or Heineken?" and I said, "Heineken," and this was a conversation that was not very interesting to either of us. The bartender had gone through it more often than I had, so he was even more flat-faced about it. I put a few dollars on the bar. He shoved the glasses toward me and said, "Phone for you."

I took the glasses, said thanks, and started to move back to Suki.

"I said phone for you, mister."

It hadn't registered the first time. He looped up the extension cord and clanged the phone down on the bar. I felt like a juggler for a moment, panicked, with two glasses of beer in my hands. I set them down, not spilling very much, satisfied with myself for that, and picked up the telephone. "Whom are you calling?" I asked.

"Hoom? *Hoom?*" And a thick sugary rumble of laughter washed through the wires. "Hoom am I calling?"

"Alfonso," I said.

"Listen, brother, you takin' care of things?"

"How'd you know I was here?"

"Everybody got to have a job these days, man, got to work or go on the welfare. I prefer to work, welfare being so chintzy since the Great Society got offed."

"Why should I be followed?"

"Man, you think I bother to put a tail on you?

Oh, man, hoom! That's beautiful. Hoom am I calling!"

"You just want to laugh at me, Alfonso? I guess that's better'n threatening."

He stopped abruptly. He turned it off. I could never tell, so abrupt were his shifts from amusement to other states, how much of his serious play was just an act. It occurred to me that he had this dangerous ability to flash from one mood to another like someone else I knew, Suki's son, Peter.

"Okay, man," he was saying. "Don't get in no trouble, okay? I don't want you to think I know where you been or where you going, I ain't what you call it am-knee-sent, you be so stupid I can't tell what you might do. All I know is where you be right now."

"Okay, thanks."

"Don't want us to get your hoom in a sling, does we?"

"This where I be, Alfonso."

I think he said good-bye. But he was all choked up and I'm not sure if chuckles were the sign-off I deserved. I meant to ask him if I practiced could we play Amos and Andy at the Policemen's Fresh Air Fund Benefit.

I carried the glasses back to Suki. She took a sip, licked her lips, and said, "You know, if you sip beer like wine, it's more like a beverage." She shrugged, waited a second, and then said, "I didn't know you get messages here."

"Alfonso wanted to say hello."

"Alfonso?" She sniffed the beer. It was hard for her to get out of the habit of treating it like wine, though she seemed adjustable in other ways. "You told him we're okay? This is the kind of neighborhood a person feels safe almost any hour of the day or night, like Beirut? It's more like Halloween all year round, I guess." She put the glass down hard. "Frank, what good is this? How do you think we can find him in this city or this part of the city?"

"Let's wait a while. Maybe he'll find us."

"He's not looking."

"If he knows where we are, and knows we're not running around crazy, making trouble for him . . ."

She didn't see any alternative, either. We would sit there together, making a pastime of drinking draft beer as if it were white wine, and waiting. Because we didn't see any good other way just then.

Tropical mites swam in the air. They must have known it was supposed to be California. My eyes had gotten used to the spectrums of fluorescence—tubes and jukebox and beer signs lit the place for business. There were no live cockroaches, but in a corner there was a small gathering of dry, gray, dead ones. Someone used a broom but not a pan, or perhaps only sweeping into the corner was his job, not scraping them up.

Suki suddenly spoke again. "We're a mismatch. Anybody can see that."

I must have looked startled and disappointed. "I don't mean *us*, dear." She lay her hand on mine. "I mean us and this place, that's a severe mismatch, in my opinion. *Here*. Okay, feel better?"

I didn't have the time to feel better. A boy with a shaved head covered with pale astro-stubble, a no-sleeve undershirt, an ant-trail of amateur tattoos on his arms, poked his head through the door and stood looking at us. He didn't seem startled and he seemed to have more tattoos than I remembered, all up and down his arm and on the shoulder, also a fish on his cheek. "Hey, isn't that—?" I said.

"Harry!" said Suki, and jumped up. It was the kid I'd seen on the back of Peter's bike.

We were both heading for the door of the bar and the bartender was saying, "Can't bring no minors in here," and I was grabbing Harry by his arm, which had only his electric primary colors and a nail-studded leather wristband to keep him warm in the Tenderloin damp. We didn't have a chance to ask where Peter was. Peter was standing next to him, saying, "Fergeddit, Frank. Fergeddit, Mom."

"Forget *what?*" cried Suki. "What's going on?"

Harry said, "Jeez, Peter, this is weird to the max. We have to go through this shit *again?*"

Peter turned to Harry, and at the same moment moved out of range of Suki, as if she might imprison him in her arms—she was stretching toward him—and he was moving as light and easy and graceful as she moved. "Aw, Harry," he was saying in a voice of supplication, the kind of cajoling teenage intimacy that is reserved for non-family, "why don't you, aw, come on, why don't you just fergeddit, Harry—" There was need and craving and an awful risk in his face. The boy wanted something, wanted it badly, sought a way to fill his vacancy, and I felt a pain of sorrow for him, as if I were the father he needed and didn't have, the lover he needed and didn't have, and therefore I could do nothing but watch him suffer; and I could see Suki's face shrunken and pale and stricken with grief for her child who was appealing to Harry, begging Harry with his tan fringe of stubble on a shaven head, mouth bloated with disdain and his own lack and need—nothing but healthy nourished American bodies here, shrunken, deprived, lonely souls, all yearning and fragile—"Aw, Harry."

Peter looked from Harry to his mother, and then back to Harry again, saying, "Stand near me to proteck me from that cunt?"

Both Suki and I were moving on him at that moment. As I flung myself forward I noticed the nobbled spikes in the leather wristbands that both Harry and Peter were wearing. I was thinking it was important to aim for something particular, the pendulous lips of Harry, not simply to express a flailing out in the general area of a person. I was unpracticed in this matter. I punched at Harry, thinking *lips*, thinking *get*

blood, this is important, and he was swinging his
arms in an odd, looping, backhand gesture, trying to scrape me with the wrist spikes, and Suki
was flailing at her son—no, Harry was trying
not to scrape me but to impale me with his
wrists, tack me to the leather—and now I didn't
mind hurting myself if I could also hurt him.
One of Suki's shoes flew off. I got a glimpse of
Suki's foot being scraped and filthied against the
sidewalk, and she was not screaming like a
woman but there was an enraged purring coming from her, a low growling from the cave. I
had not thought it necessary to destroy Harry;
perhaps I merely wanted to drive him off, get rid
of him, perhaps I wanted merely to kill him; but
he was reaching into the loose Japanese pants he
was wearing and came out of fabric with a
stump of something—then it seemed to leap and
flash forward—a switchblade. "Shit no!" Peter
screamed, and kicked Harry's hand, sending the
knife sliding into the street, as I punched the
kid, missing his mouth, feeling a bunched yielding and wet of nose, as if I had hit a mouse with
my fist. He also made a squeaking noise.

Then both Peter and Harry were running.

Suki and I were standing there, gasping. She
bent, leaning her hands on her thighs, and I saw
her mouth open. Nothing came out.

I was bleeding where the wrist spikes had cut
through my jacket.

We were alone with our thoughts as the clattering sounds of running diminished and died.

A Vietnamese boy with his mother, their shopping bags filled with dumpster harvest, came toward us with flat blank expressions on their faces and separated to walk around us as if we were natural objects, rocks, trees, nothing much useful to them on the Ellis Street trail. The boy stopped, bent down to pick up Suki's shoe, looked back at her and straightened up again, leaving the shoe where it lay.

"Goddamn, Goddamn," I was wheezing, trying to get my breath. It made no sense. It also made no sense that we could fight them off and away, as if they were misbehaving children. They wanted it, they wanted to be beaten, and yet Harry had gone for his knife. And Peter had stopped him from using it.

An old Falcon, the kind of automobile a person generally sees with police department stickers on the windshield, ordering it to be moved or else it will be impounded, slid to the curb in front of a fire hydrant. The driver's door opened and a hefty, smiling black guy came toward us, shaking his head and saying, "What a person gets into when he takes up my line of work, which was all that's 'vailable to a person from the ill-behaved sector of the economy."

"Thanks for the company, Alfonso," Suki said. "Now you can pick up my shoe."

I picked up Suki's shoe and asked him, "Aren't you a little late?"

"Seems like you people be keeping track of my job better'n Central Station," he said. "I guess I won't run you in on suspicion of assault and battery on yourself. I think we got to work out something institutional, don't you, Suki? Come on, get in, I don't want you wandering around anymore." Suki held his arm and put on the shoe; she had already retrieved her purse; we climbed into the Falcon. Suki got in front with Alfonso. He was saying, "This is a problem I never had quite like this. I want you both"—he half-turned and looked at me, too—"I want you both to know I'd sure like to figure something out if I could."

He was patting her hand, and then held it a moment, looking at the red welts and swelling where she had punched her son. She had delicate skin. Suki was lean and quick and a tennis player, but she didn't normally do much with herself in the karate or boxing lines.

The bartender stood in the doorway, grinning at us. "Hey, Alfonso, they wanna nother couple beers for sipping purposes?" he called. He was happy, at least temporarily—he was diverted. A few solitary drinkers in the Ellis Street afternoon could be brought together by a sporting event. There was laughter from this audience while the bartender served as fight commentator. "Hey, Alfonso, I'll spring for it if you promise to just *sip* it."

FOURTEEN

Alfonso drove very slowly, coming to a full stop at all the stop signs; looking both ways, right, left, then right and left again, then easing forward into the intersections. Suki and I were watching him handle the loose-shifting Falcon, thinking how a black man must have it in mind to obey the rules as if he doesn't want to get pulled over. I wondered how he would manage it if a cop he didn't know pulled him over. Or perhaps he was driving so solemnly for another reason, not talking, giving us the chance to recover. Suki and I were also silent.

Then, at Suki's house, she straightened her shoulders back, shook off her shoes, excused herself a moment. She didn't go to wash or be alone; she splashed a little water on her face, that was all. She also returned with a bottle of white wine and three glasses. Alfonso set his glass down and waited to hear us out, although listening didn't really seem to be his job. Maybe he wasn't drinking because he was supposed to be on duty.

His muzzle was turned up. His eyes were half-hidden, like those of a clever swamp rat that didn't want to jump until it knew which way the flow was running. When he wanted to go slow and wait, he went slow and waited. We sat at the kitchen counter, Alfonso overflowing the high stool—heavy loose flesh there around the sleek muscle—and Suki said: "He didn't like to kiss me after he was a baby. When he was a baby, he used to like to suck my arm, my neck. I used to get monkey bites all over, everyplace his mouth was. He was jealous, like some kind of lover."

"Did you nurse him?" I asked.

"What kind of a question is that? That's rude, none of your business. I was just a kid myself, I wanted to keep my figure, I wasn't sure I was going to stay with Cal, and since it turned out I didn't—that's a stupid rude question, Frank."

"Now, now, folks," said Alfonso. "Here we are, all excited, no sense getting worked up. You know what I read a kiss is?"

"No, what is a kiss?" Suki gave him her attention. I knew her style. Partly this was not giving *me* her attention.

"I got this nearly complete recall of interesting things I read my off hours, due to lots of time waiting around for something or other to happen. A kiss," said Alfonso, rolling his eyes, his cheeks gleaming, basking a little, "a kiss is a pleasant moist attention to certain neural trails. Now why don't you two fine folks just pay some pleasant moist attention to your neurals?"

"How do you ever get police business done?" I asked.

"This is San Francisco, man," Alfonso said. "You got to wander 'round a little. You look for your chance and you don't blow it. If you're not having a little ramble, you ain't in touch with ree-ality."

Suki sat there, stricken. "What about my kid? What can I do? Where's Peter now?"

Alfonso gave her his attention without his buffoonish smiling. It was hard to distract her today. "Let me tell you something, Suki. We could pick him up on assault 'cause of what just happen. You want to prosecute your son? You ain't even hurt. Bet he hurt more'n you hurt. We could maybe almost get him as a runaway, but his age, juvie so crowded, I doubt we could hold him. He run away again and where are you. We could wait around for him to come back—"

"Can't do that, Alfonso!"

"We got to list our options here. We got to try to figure out your son. He almost complicated as—" And the detective was tactful. He did not want to say Peter was as complicated as Suki, or as simple in a complicated way as his mother, or anything that would push Suki to where she seemed headed, the tears that would not help at all. "I'm gonna leave you here at home, Suki, maybe he call, besides that you take a little pill, get yourself some sleep, maybe you try call the doctor again—no, Ski-Ska she won't tell you nothing—then I drive Frank back to his car he left on Ellis, if his luck be good, if it still there. Okay?"

Suki nodded. She turned to me, her eyes red-lidded. She understood that Alfonso wanted to have a few words alone with me and she expected me to let her know what he said. She didn't know what else to do. She was exhausted. Alfonso was probably right. She didn't keep tranquilizers in the house; he didn't know that, but he was right about almost everything else.

Did she want someone or both of us to stay here with her?

No, she didn't need to be tucked in by anyone. She wanted a soak, a long hot soak, and then she wanted a rest, if she could manage it.

Alfonso waited in the unmarked Falcon outside while I talked with her at the door. "I'm sorry," she said. "Thank you."

"For what? My problem too."

"My son is a *problem*. Funny word for a son. Thank you," she repeated, and then made an odd gesture. She put out her arm and we shook hands, and then she shut the door.

As I walked back to the SFPD Falcon, I wondered why she had winced. Of course. Her hand was swollen; she had hurt her knuckles. Problem was a correct inadequate word.

Alfonso headed back to the Tenderloin, still driving in that slow, deliberate, rule-abiding

Herbert Gold

way that he may have reserved for unmarked cars. "We got a few minutes to talk, if we got anything to say—how about you, Frank?"

"Not much," I said.

"Well, we put our heads together now, sometime two heads be better than three. Which one of us know a piece of Peter? Maybe you and me might could try fitting the pieces together."

"What I know doesn't fit," I said. "Can't figure out if he likes me or hates me."

Alfonso grinned. "Maybe neither. Maybe he *loves* you."

"Thanks a lot."

"In the nicest possible way I say that."

"You always do."

"Okay, you mind? I been giving this kid some thought. I don't mean that social work stuff, his father no father, blah blah blah, I got some other idea—like he might be crazy but he ain't what they call neurotic. Get my drift?"

"Tell me."

Alfonso was a reader. He was a bachelor. He had had a wife or two, kids someplace, maybe nearly grown by now, in Brooklyn or Los Angeles or both places. He lived alone with the music going and he played a lot and he thought about things. When he got home, the radio was still playing, because he liked company. Now he enjoyed telling me his thoughts about Peter as we drove through San Francisco, stopping very carefully at every stop sign, since this was not an official black-and-white and he didn't want to be

262

hassled with this Falcon clunker and one of the new boys on the force asking himself why some fat black dude was driving through Pacific Heights and down Russian Hill and on his way to business in the baddest part of town. Alfonso was taking his time, turning me into audience for a couple of his theories.

"No nausea capability," he said.

"What? You got a son his age, too?"

"Listen what I say. The kid ain't got no nausea glands in his conscience, not even no polyps. You hear what I say, I'm not paying too much attention the physiology of the bod. The organism interest me, see what I mean—he don't get sick to his stomach when he think of things make you and me and maybe even Suki sick to our stomach. Let's give you another example. You know that funny smile people get on their face, they say they don't sign petitions, they don't give their name or vote or anything? They so proud they not involved, but also they scared advantage might be taken? I mean that's another angle on the thing. All by a person's lonesome through life."

"I'll bet he's lonely," I said.

"You got no takers, man."

"Makes other people lonely, too."

"You don't like risks, do you, Frank-o? You got yourself some safe bets there."

"Makes a tape of people, tells people they're doing things they didn't do, works up a whole lot of riot about things—"

Alfonso pounded the steering wheel. "Those are mere details," he said, chortling and wheezing. He was one of those drivers who could look everywhere while steering and not lose sight of the road. I've always thought such carelessness was an illusion and people who were really distracted eventually took punishment, but maybe not. "Let me run this by you some more, see if you understand me. Spose you could put it in better University of California at Berkeley main campus language for you-self, but that don't make no never-mind, do it?"

"Alfonso, why do you keep slipping into that Amos and Andy routine?"

"Love it! Raised on it! We had a radio in the house! Hear me now: I was talkin' 'bout *nausea capacity*. You prefer I say capability? You see the problem: Even he lose his own life by some accident or design or some friend or enemy lose it for him or he plan it by himself, it do not make him go *unnnh* in the gut with the idea. I mean he only get dizzy when he want to, got a good time in store. I mean some people so bad they smile sweetly at anybody's pain, I see that more'n you suspect in my line of work. But this boy, he smile so sweetly at his *own*."

"His own?"

"Own *pain*, man. Boy don't care, you can't predict him so good. Uh-oh."

"What's that?"

Alfonso was easing the Falcon to a stop in front of the fire hydrant at Ellis and Taylor. He was shaking his head. He rubbed his chins. He seemed profoundly disappointed. "Here's your car," he said. "Them meter people not doing their job. I only see one citation blowing under you windshield wiper. Time you been gone, this part of town, you should get two, three minimum, maybe you be tow."

"Thanks a lot."

"Man, you so lucky in life, got yourself a nice lady like Suki, got yourself"—there he went again—"nice stepson, I mean son-in-outlaw, young Peter there, now you don't even have to go find your yellow Fiat with the sunroof all slit by somebody knife, dig it out of the tow yard, pay eighty-five dollar—man, you belong to the lucky race!"

"Shit, Alfonso, I think we're friends, but sometimes I doubt it when you're running for comic on summer replacement time."

"Not me, man," said Alfonso. "In my present job I got tenure."

Just when I began to know the people down here, new populations migrated to the territory. A patriarch with an amplified voice instrument, loudspeakers on both sides of him, and his family lined up to present rapt Nancy Reagan faces to his lecture, Tricia Nixon faces, David Eisenhower faces, plus his own face presented raptly to himself, red and swollen with angry belief, was delivering a lecture about his oldest and best friend, Gawd, or as he was known to this hoarse peddler of truth, Dear-Gawd-a-mighty, who will preserve us from our daily sins, our sometimes thrice daily sins, if we're underage hoodlums, countless sinnings under dear-Gawd-a-mighty's vengeful sky, the muggings, rapings, blasphemings, and yes, the skateboardings, too, for if dear-Gawd-a-mighty's will had wanted us to ride on skateboards instead of Buick Skylarks with Tennessee license plates, he would have put wings on our feet, but he didn't, he only put wings on the shoulder blades of his angels, and us he gave used car lots plus no money down, plus he asks us to drink his own pure water, not that poison Florida water, or that sinful French water causes all kinds of French diseases and occupations, cause Man when he procreates is spose to look his lawfully welded spouse in the eye and tell her what he is doing this to her for . . . I'm quoting from memory. He was speaking to us from deep in this vale of tears and bad conduct, his thoughts amplified by equipment.

It was hard news to me that fluoridation came from south Florida, where all the Cubans, dope peddlers, and dentists were, speaking their native Hebrew.

Alfonso and I got out of the Falcon together. The preacher seemed to recognize cop, he was streetwise enough; he didn't mention the colored folks of Florida in his indictment. He turned down the volume on his mike. Electricity was divine, but it also tended to violate the laws against preaching the Word in public immoral places. Alfonso grinned at the reverend and made a gesture of encouragement, rolling his open hands, showing beefy palms. The preacher felt encouraged. A sudden flare of optimism lit up his lantern face. "This nation can be saved from the Apocalypse in our time! Our sins can be redeemed! Oh, it is coming, my brothren, but this country can survive the flood, the fire, the moral fiber from Colombia and Peru!"

I turned down the amplification on my own attention, noticing that Alfonso had left the door open, the unmarked Falcon now marked a little more with a dent as the door swung against the fire hydrant, inviting someone to run up and grab inside for the radio (there was none, just stumps of ripped wires) or the trash at the pedals, the Styrofoam cups and fast-food napkins. Alfonso had a compassionate reason for walking me toward my Fiat. He plucked the ticket from under the windshield wiper and stuffed it into his pocket. "One more thing not s'prise you 'tall," he said. "That boy a menace. He is unpredictable. He got all sorts of stuff in him we didn't grow up with, machinery and shit, not caring for what we care for and shit. A menace we don't really know to who, Frank. Like you say, to hoom."

"We managed to have all this long conversation about Peter without talking about his mother."

Alfonso grinned. "You think so? Look like that, what we been doing, does it?"

"How is that?"

"Well, my buddy, we know what is *really* be dangerous, don't we? I mean, person wanna be a victim, just walkin' round dreamin', askin' for it, pretty hard to stop him. Fall asleep in Lezboise, say, wallet stickin' out of his pocket—or go up to a place with some sweet thing got her hand already in his jeans but he don't look at her too close, just for an example—well, might could pose some riskiss, couldn't it? I mean there is different ways, but he choosin', this hypotheoretical person. He just askin' to be a mark, don't you know?"

"You're saying Suki's a lot of trouble. I can't believe you think I haven't figured that out for myself."

He made a little snort of wide-lipped disapproval. He was merely judging the quality of my attention to this vale of tears and bad conduct. He wasn't going to argue with anybody; that was not Alfonso's way. "Frank-o," he said, "that only be one old cop'pinion, y'understand, no legal force or weight, and you don't even have to hear me or answer right if you don't want to, that be your legal privilege, entirely up to you. I see when a man gone on his own way his dick swingin' out like a dog in heat without no wisdom in him at all."

"That's your view of me, Alfonso?"

"You enjoy now, won't you?"

He cocked an ear to the street preacher, who had gotten back onto sin, fluoridation, dope, communism, and bank credit. He too was trying to do too much, an over-achiever in the Apocalypse-avoidance line. Alfonso shrugged, sighed, and started the Falcon. He was smiling when he spoke to me, but as soon as he stopped, without waiting to get out of my sight, a mask of fatigue fit over his face—fatigue and gloom and no fun at all. As he turned into traffic, he lifted one arm to wave good-bye because he knew I was still watching him, waiting, sure he was clear about most things, not sure I could learn what he would have preferred to teach me.

Down here, Alfonso could drive with any damn carelessness he liked, and with that swamp rat look of sleepy alertness on his face. Some places, though, he had to be careful and look careful.

He wasn't sure I had learned the lessons he had grown up with; lessons I needed to learn about Peter, about Suki, and about myself.

FIFTEEN

I rested at the geological bottom of Nob Hill. I was left on Ellis by Alfonso with no instructions. We weren't getting much clarity around here.

There was heat at the places on my cheek and hands where I had been scraped by steel and leather wristlets. Blood was going that way, leading the heat, spreading a harsh flush, carrying away infection like jungle ants; there were welts; I wouldn't know for a while if this would get worse or if my fever was a speeded healing. This time I wasn't going to fool around with ice cubes in the sink. My remedies so far didn't seem to cure the bad news.

I had read the newspapers and written for some. I had dealt with random bad news that happened to other people, to whole populations and nations. Random bad news that happened to me was something new. I looked up and down the street, and felt like a wary animal. A town-and-campus body had been cast out into an unaccustomed world of jungle travel without even leaving home. All I did was cross the Bay from Berkeley into San Francisco, where previously most of my damage had come from high-tech bachelor sociability.

I suspected my bad news, recent and to come, was not just random.

But San Francisco was really a city like other cities, and therefore Suki might be a woman like other women. Her son was not a boy like others. I had spent years trying to keep the secret that I was just like other men, only slower, which was my word for dumber. Now I could feel my tides betraying me, blood rising to the challenge of bruises fading off into sting, a few punctures, a speckle of future scabs on my neck and face. I was even less a beauty than usual, and getting ready to go someplace—back to Berkeley? back to Suki? to Kaiser Hospital, playing safe with some tetanus shots?—and I was avoiding looking at myself in the rearview mirror, when I caught a flash of flying individual alongside. A kid on a skateboard swooped across the street and did little jiggling wheelies near the driver's door. A diesel Busvan truck was roaring by, so he waited, killing a few seconds with another wheelie.

When the noise stopped, the skateboard rider stood grinning into the Fiat with his lips parted.

Harry held the rim of my vinyl sunroof, which I had opened as I usually did. "Hey, man!" he said. "Peter ain't mad. He really needs to talk to you now, really really. He really does, it's weird. *Really.*"

"What about?"

"Hey, you don't mess in my business, I don't mess in yours."

And he started a little whirling flight away, but then turned abruptly, spinning, and said, "Hey, wanna folly me? Down here on Eddy, you just folly me."

In the Hong Kong traffic of the Tenderloin, a skateboard moved faster than an automobile; low wheels gave better control for both purse-snatching and locomotion. Harry led me around the little knot of Christian exhortation, past the newsstand and Uhuru Likkers where the temporarily prosperous went shopping, along the street with the Xang Hsu Herbal Supplies, the Adult Artists Video shop, and a couple of storefronts with curtains where people had taken up the business of living. The transvestites patrolling the sidewalks looked as tall as Watusis with their spiked heels and purses which could be used as missiles when necessary. One opened his bag and raised it to show Harry something, but Harry was concentrating on his task with me and the Watusi said, "Don't come asking next time you need something, skate-boy."

There was a family feeling to these streets which did not necessarily make me feel at home.

Harry stopped and did little Here We Are wheelies in front of a sign that said "Video Investigations Highest Quality Integrity Equipment & Results." He coasted up and down a ramp, sidewalk to street, sliding sideways, sidewalk to street again. The ramp had been put there by the city for wheelchairs but also served nicely for skateboard scouts and guides. A blue madras bedspread, like that of a gypsy fortune-telling mitt shop, blocked the Highest Quality Integrity Equipment & Results storefront window. The wares inside were not being displayed. One corner of the madras had been pulled, fly-specks etched against the dark, and beyond the plate glass I could see a low table with an electric hot plate and a coffeepot. The bedspread had been pulled because there was someone pulling it and watching me. The enthusiastic whirr of skateboard on sidewalk was announcing our arrival. The scout was proud of having brought me safely home.

I stood at the door. It was glass, but an iron-work grille protected it. There was a bell with exposed wires, and another madras bedspread over the door glass, which was filmy with accumulated breath, grease, and dust. My shadow and melted features were reflected against it. The image was fuzzy. I considered inviting myself not to ring or buzz but to think about coming back another day.

I rang; it buzzed.

"Hey, you!" cried the skateboarder, dancing a

little, bobbing up and down, enjoying earth's gravity and his ability to deal with it. "I'm Skum! Say thank you! What make you think I'm my brother Harry? Next time you see me, say Hi, Skum, how ya doin'?"

The door was rattling, and with that focused vision of the animal in risk, knowing it is suddenly quarry, I could see the splinters of the warped wood, a new little bunch of toothpicks each time the door was pushed open or shut. Skum was gone. A slow and wary old man with an aluminum walker was climbing up the sidewalk ramp, leaning on his device, trying for breath, maybe wishing he didn't have so much emphysema. Peter was pressing the latch to open the iron grille. The man with his hands on the upper level of his aluminum structure sighed. He wanted something to happen to make his outing worthwhile and all that was happening was that Peter was opening the iron grill-work gate.

"Hey, Frank, get in here, that street's not safe," Peter said. "Look at the space monster."

The old man lifted the walker in a sliding motion, took a step forward, lifted it again. I wondered what it felt like to have no reply for someone who called him a space monster. When he had only been smoking ten, twenty, maybe even twenty-five years, he would have had a reply. A few steps away, when he realized no one was coming after him, he stopped again, stubbornly watching.

Peter was saying, "I ever get to be your age, Frank, by that time you'll be so old you're using one of those, hey, those things—not a wheel anyplace on it—a watchamacallit. A walkerman they call it."

"Good thinking ahead," I said. I stepped inside. I didn't like his shutting the grille again, that clang, shutting the door again, the light from the street filtered through blue madras, a dead and dusty light. "And then a little later you'll be using one too," I said. "So what?"

The music was coming from a speaker in another room. It was whining synthesizer music, the outer-space soundtrack from a movie I didn't know, squeaks and long stretching high notes that would have been pretty close to voice if a voice were something made of microchips, transformers, and alternating current, in the throats of eighteen-inch-high creatures.

"I won't be alive," Peter said. "So I won't."

He looked calm about this. I decided it might be a joke or a sample of teenage philosophy. But I also decided to express another opinion, speaking for myself, personally. "I'll have a hip operation. I'll be alive. I don't plan on using a walker. I might be old, though. I plan to get old, Peter."

"Man, what I say, don't have to wait to see that one, man. You *are* old."

"We sure do talk a lot." Since I was supposed to be the mature adult around here, I wasn't going to argue the point about my age. I tried crinkling my eyes; encouraged my mouth to perform

a mature and kindly smiling move. "How about
this, Peter? Considering all your movie and tech-
nical skills, your energy, always had that kind of
talent, you've got a lot on the ball, maybe instead
of messing around with your mother and me,
maybe you should think about college. How
about that? Maybe a film and TV program
would fit your interests." I paused and tried to
give it a proper twist. Peter liked twists. "Use
some of that trouble productively, if I may make
a suggestion from self-interest."

"Don't," he said. "Your conversation is above
me, Frank."

"Good boy. Breeding tells. Trained to thrust
and parry. *Great*, Peter."

"Are you putting me down? 'Cause that's
what it feels like."

"You are really Mr. Junior Congeniality. Why
should I get mad at you? Take me on a joyride to
the movies as the alleged star. Put me in a place
where I have to break up a fight between you
and your mother. Send various creeps around to
my house in the middle of the night to wake me
up and threaten—"

"Only one. Only one creep."

"You're Mr. Congeniality in your age group,
Peter."

"Sure feels like you're putting me down, taking advantage of a younger person—what the
fuck's he want?"

There was a whirring buzzing metal and sidewalk sound outside, a skateboard doing wheelies,

and then a banging on the grille, the structure shaking and rattling, and the skateboarder yelling, "Hey! Open up!" and Peter saying, "Fuck off, I'm busy, come back tonight," and me thinking this young man was altogether out of the competition, a veritable maestro of congeniality. I studied him while he opened the glass door but not the iron grillwork gate, repeating to the skateboard messenger that he should go away and come back again some other day, minimum tonight. Young as he was, Peter already showed what happens when they lose their boyish good looks, which happens to boys even in California, as if somehow they cross the Nevada line and settle in Elko or Minden or Tonopah at age thirty or forty or fifty, depending on the care they take, the destiny and character they find for themselves. Early in this potential schedule, despite leanness, lankiness, dewiness—all the good stuff he took from his mother and father—Peter already looked worn at the edges, his mouth pissed off. If things went right maybe the knocks could still cause him to start using his head; he had the native synapses for it; but mostly he was just wary and grasping for salvations, portents, omens, straws, and a helping hand from willing or unwilling others. The kid was tough before he should be tough, wounded without adequate preparation for learning from his hurts. He was a taker without knowing what he should be taking. He wanted to be justified. He wanted his own way. If he couldn't get his own way, he wanted justification. And yet, pissed off as he was now, there was still the softness of a child around his mouth, a purplish pout, the gimme look of a spoiled kid.

He locked the door again and took note that I was watching him, thinking about him, working him over in my head, and he was perfectly willing to give me time for this; he kind of liked the attention, he kind of liked it a whole lot; he just preened a little, turning the latch, and then turning himself, grinning, leaning, stretching, yawning, trying out his whole repertory of moves, playing the tape of himself in his own head, letting me be the camera, wishing he could have it all for posterity, make copies for his summer home and his yacht and his winter home . . .

"Hey, Frank? Done now?"

I said nothing.

"What you think I'm selling?" he asked. "Stuff?"

I thought: Sure is possible, girls or boys or grass or blow. Or information. But as a cautious person, not quite a father substitute, I only remarked: "Trouble, that's what you're offering."

"How much?"

"Trouble for your mother, for me, probably for the authorities if you don't cool off. Mostly for yourself. Can you just cool off for a while?"

"Not when I'm hot, mister."

"You're making a statement. You've made your statement. Wouldn't you like to back away for a while?"

"Refer to my previous comment listed above."

"I know you're smart. I know you've got a lot of aptitude, what you did with motors, for example—"

"That was when I was young."

"Two years ago, wasn't it? And what you do with video—"

"Oooh, sarcastic."

"I'm just commenting. You've got what you need to go on okay and—"

"Oh, shit, never stop lecturing, do you? I know you're a teacher. I got that figured out already. So I'll stop some things if you'll stop teaching—is that a compromise, okay?"

"What's your idea of a compromise?"

"You heard of Safe Sex? Where you don't get disease? That's compromise—things like watching your VCR, using your imagination, safe stuff like that where you don't get Aids. I mean, you're the teacher, man, you should know. But maybe you don't teach Safe Sex. But you sure look like a gray wolf, hang out at the White Swallow Tavern, buy your stuff at Hard On Leathers, Polk Street. Personally, I'm broader in my scope."

"I'm sure you are. You have more to say to me?"

"Yes." But he fell silent. He was making chewing motions with his mouth, not speaking. He was thinking and chewing, though there was nothing in his mouth. He swallowed. Then he opened the empty, chewing mouth to show me there was nothing in it—opened it wide. Like a child asking for the spoon, he showed me his anxious hunger, though the gold-flecked eyes showed no desire at all, or showed the desire for nothing at all. His appetite lay elsewhere.

I didn't like looking at these eyes and this mouth. The tie-dyed German eagle on the wall was no great pleasure either. Underneath it, someone had stencilled, with a child's stencil set, the words "FRISCO SKINHEADS FOR-EVER," and carefully painted over the K: "FRISCO SKINHEADS FOREVER."

These were busy lads down here. At the back wall there was a VCR and a garage-sale bookcase filled with tapes. I walked over and examined them; a few movies, mostly homemade with scribbled notations: "Skateboard Riders"; "Bike Dykes"; "Who's Afraid?" Peter was still making his chewing motions, but now he had popped something into his mouth and was swallowing it. Something to wake him up, I imagined. I didn't need anything to wake me up. I picked up a tape that said "Frank Curtis Rides Again" on it and asked, "You made copies? Who's the actor plays Frank Curtis?"

"Oh, man, trade secrets. You think we tell things like that?"

"Tell me, Peter."

"Gimme a break, man. Oh, are you fulla questions and no answers."

I whirled on him and shouted: "Peter! What answer do you want from me!"

"More questions," he said, "one more question."

I grabbed him by the shoulder, and it occurred to me that there might be a hidden camera here too, but that didn't stop me from shaking his shoulder—only an instant—because then he pulled away and fell against a table, opened the drawer, and came out with something, saying, "Don't touch now, man. You can touch sometimes but not now." What he came out with was a long kitchen knife that had been sharpened so many times it was merely a shiny, thin, crooked rope of steel.

There are things you can do against some weapons, I remembered from the army. All you can do against a knife is run. Since the door was locked, and the grille latched outside, I did not have the time for that option. U.S. Army basic training didn't mention talk as another option.

There was a rattle at the door behind him, leading deeper into the building. This door was also locked; the person behind it didn't want to unlock; he rattled the door like an animal in a kennel, trying to get attention. The voice came through muffled. "Hey, Pete? You making too much noise. Can't concentrate."

We weren't making that much noise.

"You make noise, Pete, I come out to get you. Someone hear you—" I heard the rest of the sentence in my head, although he didn't say it: *They come in here. Neither way, Pete, we don't want that.*

"Is that some kind of a lab in there?" I asked.

"Christ, you never stop, do you, Frank?"

But his voice was lowered. He also lowered the knife. He didn't put it down, but pointed it downward, as if it were detumescing, losing its gleam and charm for him. He glanced at it with academic interest and disapproval. "I spose," he said, "you think I should go to school . . . kind of like Stanford or East Los Angeles Community."

Trying to keep my eyes from the knife, I asked, "Why?" It was a pleasant surprise not to hear a quaver in my voice. I didn't feel as talkative as usual.

" 'Cause Stanfoo got those richen pretty boysngirls. East L.A. got that great L.A. dope. Everyplace got something recommend it."

"Does that mean you'd like to go to school?"

"You mean: do I want some rich boysngirls and good dope? Maybe yes. Do I want some video and motor training? I got the background. I spose I know what I need, but shit, I'm like everybody, can always use a little more."

I looked away from the knife. I could manage to laugh and I did. "This is America, isn't it?"

"No, Frank, you got that wrong. This is my territory—San Francisco." He grinned. "This is Suki's boy talking to Suki's man, one of them. This is Suki's man which humped Suki's boy's mother." The knife was turned upward again and the person in the locked back room was silent. The gleam was bright on the blade. The gray light of the street seeped through the madras bedspread that covered the window. I could see shadows moving outside and the shadows could see nothing in the darkening room.

I believed I had to think of something to do. He was preparing himself to use the knife; he was making ready; it seemed to be rising in his fist of its own will.

Outside, an automobile drove up very rapidly and screeched to a stop. It was double-parked and it blocked more of the daylight through blue madras and the room grew darker. A car door slammed and someone was rattling the grill, a deep voice saying, "Hey! Peter! You there, Peter, open up!"

Peter was grinning. He liked the fear he saw. His face seemed stripped of flesh and gleaming like the blade.

"Peter!" said the man outside. "I have to break this if you don't open!"

The fear that so entertained Peter was on my face. My stomach was sick, I wanted to lurch away, it was bitter in my mouth, if I moved he would dart forward with the knife.

"Peter!" shouted the deep voice outside, and the ironwork was shaking and clattering.

Peter raised the knife to let me see the ragged point of it. Someone had gone to a lot of trouble, inaccurately sharpening and narrowing.

"*Peter!*"

He reached in the drawer again and pulled out a videocassette in its black box. He threw it at me. I let it hit me; I flinched a little; I tried not to move. He shivered a little. He was transmitting within for instructions about what he wanted to do next. There was one more summons he had awarded himself, but he hesitated. He listened to the rattling at the grille and he only had a moment. He held the knife with both hands, raised it as far as he could, and plunged it into his right eye.

He fell with a long exhaling sigh and a thin trickle of bleeding. There was not very much blood, there was no cry and only a soft crumpling sound. The blade was sharpened at the point like a pick.

Alfonso was still shaking the grille when I let him in. He was an impatient police officer, working his routines, shouting, "Where is he?"

He saw him then before I could try to answer, and understood there was no hurry anymore, only business to take care of. "Let me have that cassette," he said. "We don't want that floating around, do we?"

SIXTEEN

On another forever-springtime day in San Francisco, a Saturday afternoon, Suki gathered her friends around her. Just as at her birthday parties, her friends honored their duty and pleasure to be with her. They also needed to give and take comfort; they had heard about sorrow; Suki needed comfort most, more than anyone, and they understood about that, too.

Small child, small pain. Suki remembered the old saying. It was a part of life. Large child, large pain. She was trying to understand what could not be understood. Learning to forget was a part of the process of remembering. It was her duty to celebrate a history the only way possible, by closing ranks. She accepted her duty to help everybody, and herself, through the stubborn and clotted procedures.

She didn't know what to do, she knew she

didn't know what to do, but she would do her best. Call it healing. She looked to her normal procedures and ceremonies. She would go on being Suki as best she could.

Through the front windows of the house I glimpsed Nella, Sherrie, and Watkins, the law professor from Davis; Alfonso would be there for sure; I expected Jerry Whiner and the Greek caterers and perhaps some new former lovers of Suki. I couldn't know everyone. When I looked into the house, filled with flowers once more, flowers from her garden and flowers that people had brought and sent, I didn't see any of Peter's friends. I didn't expect any.

Suki's back was toward me, her shoulder blades sharp against a dark sheath dress. She had lost weight. The dress may have been black, but with her pale skin beneath it, and the light off all the bright flowers, fabrics, shining plates, prints on the wall, it seemed blue. She hadn't noticed me yet. Perhaps she was less alert today. I wasn't ready to see her yet.

I slipped around the house, into the garden, and then to the garage, and there was Peter's bike, the motor wired to it, and his skateboard, his VCR, the video equipment. There were boxes with clothes and shoes. I recognized his running shoes, blue Adidas. Suki had lettered a piece of cardboard and stood it up against the neat mound of goods and machinery: "Huckleberry House Pickup."

She had given thought to the matter. She had

moved his things out promptly. Anyone would agree this was wise. Huckleberry House was a refuge for runaways and abandoned children. No doubt she had intended for his things to be cleaned away before this afternoon, but the worthy institution had missed its appointment for the pickup; the arts of soliciting and collecting donations are not always the most developed skills of rehabilitation institutions. Staring into the garage, I was in a peculiar floating state of mind: dreamy it would be called, if I were a kid; stunned and deadened at my age. My arms and legs were heavy, the joints clogged. A party was not what I needed.

I remembered that some items among Peter's toys should not go to Huckleberry House for the distraction of the runaway teens and their counselors. I stood above the neat piles—lacrosse stick, tennis racket, a bundle of instruction manuals, a sleeping bag, jeans and T-shirts in garment bags. I didn't like to move things but I did. There were no black Sony tape boxes for the VCR. Suki had thought of everything. I didn't know what other tapes there might be.

A squadron of hummingbirds seemed to be suspended in the slanting sunlight above the garage door. I could see the marks of the screws where a basket for basketball practice had been removed. The hummingbirds wheeled in formation and disappeared into the garden. I took a breath and entered the house through the kitchen, where the Greek caterers were busy with platters and bowls and the trimming of things at the sink. One pretty Afro-Swedish Greek girl was already rinsing out wineglasses; Suki hated plastic, wouldn't use it. Another Afro-Swedish Greek was cutting the beards off carrots. Suki didn't allow the packaged and trimmed supermarket carrots; she took care with details, although just once I had seen baby carrots in a plastic sack in her kitchen, already shiny and scrubbed and pinkish, but that was an experiment. Suki kept an open mind—tried to. The caterer sisters were talking with that easy intimacy of close family, murmuring almost like lovers: Where's the celery salt? . . . for *carrots?* . . . Anything goes good with one thing goes good with another—this is California . . . This is *northern* California. . . . Did you listen to me? . . . use the sea salt it goes good. . . .

"You're a disgrace to your people," I said, and one of the lovely bright dark-eyed sisters looked up sharply. "Oh, hi Frank! Sad occasion, hey?"

"Here's the celery salt, dope," said her sister. "Keep on your toes, I don't care if it is."

I wasn't sure if she meant California or Sad Occasion. Today was not a day to collect information.

Suki saw me, her pale blue gaze registered me, she did not seem to need to greet me. She was busy with other guests, many duties and detailed supervisions; I was familiar with the house and could take care of myself. She was smiling and chatting with a woman who, I realized, must be

Cal's wife. She had a heaviness in the breast, the upper arm, and the butt that marked her as an outsider in this group, among Suki's friends, as surely as would a chador. Not that archaic forms of flesh were alien to Suki, but they were exotic and unexpected. She tried to judge people by their grace and character, and it just happened that the people with the grace and the character generally took strict care of their bodies, healthy foods, aerobic exercise, attentive to the messages of their senses. But surely even an Iranian Shiite in a musky chador might have an interesting story to tell and Suki was always ready to listen, especially in her hostess mode. Her former husband's wife's upper arms were not her concern on this occasion. Her concern was to make welcome.

Cal was holding his wife's hand; he was also gripping their daughter by the wrist, a little girl with round eyes, bit sleeves, buttoned mouth. Cal was protected. She wouldn't try to escape. His son, the one who helped him so much when he filled his mouth with nails during house repair, was standing alongside in a Young Man's Fancy outfit, gray trousers, navy jacket, gold buttons, bravely putting up with his parents' social obligations—worse than a mouthful of roofing tacks. He had never seen much of his older half-brother and couldn't be expected to know the rules. He felt something might be expected of him. This thought made him shy.

"Oh, Frank," said Suki, "this is Cal, you know Cal, and his wife, uh, and Chuck? Charles?"

Chuck ducked his head modestly. He was flattered. His father's wife-in-law had remembered his name, even if his mother's name had slipped her mind for the moment.

"How do you do?" I asked both the wife and the son, and released myself without waiting for the full answer.

Hossein Farassian and his lover were at peace with each other today, perhaps out of respect for the occasion. They also wore matching navy blue blazers with gold buttons, just like little Freddie—Chuck it was—but Hossein was wearing a black mourning ribbon around his arm. His lover had cut a piece of the ribbon for his own lapel. Hossein said to me, "I thought that boy was the Standard of Excellence, but what do I know about America? A tragedy, a significant tragedy, a beautiful young man."

Hossein's friend was nodding. He didn't want to say the wrong thing, but a warm and sympathetic nod of the head, tucking the jaw in, is never out of place. He had learned from the spitting episode at Suki's birthday party—perhaps he had been instructed later—that spitting at a person's lover at a party, even outside in the garden, not exactly in public, is almost always out of place. Hossein wished his lover to achieve a certain standard of excellence in behavior that could hold them together through the inevitable jealousy episodes of a significant relationship.

"Everyone knows my country has made a tragic turn," Hossein said, the voice caramel with solemnity, "and I am the first to agree—if I told you, you might not believe the madness, sir, the madness!—but do people realize that America also has problems? I sincerely hope so."

Alfonso navigated through the room like a heavy watchman in his Responsible Negro Leader public manner. He put his arm on my shoulder, but spoke to Hossein. "You buy that sport coat here?" he asked. "The both of them?"

"Paris," Hossein said, "the English Navy Gentleman Shoppe at St.-Germain-des-Près. It's the Standard of Excellence in weekend dress. With the dollar where it is on the Paris Bourse, nobody can afford not to."

"I can, brother," said Alfonso, grinning. "I might could name a bunch can sure afford not to shove off to Paris for their weekend fly. Bet even Frank-o here knows a few, don't you, pal?"

Hossein's friend slid alongside and whispered confidentially into my ear, "I just had a litter." I was astonished at this miracle. I glanced across the room toward the feline Iranian, but his friend continued, "In this her time of need, wouldn't Suki like a kitten? I can spare a really cute one."

"I don't think that'll be necessary, but thanks."

He stared accusingly, wondering what gave me the right to make decisions of the heart for Suki.

"I suppose you could ask her," I said.

"Everybody needs somebody to care for," he said, "and you wouldn't believe how a kitten gives to a person, just gives and *gives*." And then hissed: "Two weeks old, and already gives more than that butch son of hers ever did."

"Better not ask her," I said. "She's got a lot to take care of already."

Alfonso's close, red-rimmed stare said, *Hey, man, handle it, catch you later.* He moved stately and slow on his rounds, beaming, and turned once to fit his index finger to his nose in a gesture of looking at me, counting on me, we'd get together real soon.

Hossein's friend was tugging with his fingers at the torn piece of black ribbon in his lapel. It was a double-ply ribbon. Not only did it show grief about Peter, but also, to any discerning eye, it demonstrated that the significant relationship between Hossein and him had only been deepened by the unfortunate garden episode of some months ago. People who go through a prolonged spitting thing with each other wouldn't share the same ribbon.

I hadn't seen Sherrie, the flight attendant therapist, the former stewardess specializing in flight attendant problems—sexism, molestation, public image, roommates and, of course, the Triple-A's, anomie, alcoholism, anorexia—since Suki's birthday party. She was still slim and girlish, keeping up with her clients, "so they can identify, it's called transference in the field. Isn't it terrible what . . . ?" she asked, her eyes stark behind the perma-tattooed lashes as she looked searchingly into my face, agreeing with what she had just almost said.

"You're remarkable," I said. "Someone who looks like you." Her hair was a little lighter than it used to be, and like Suki, she could pass as she moved for little older than a girl. Almost, anyway; small bones; the blurring of swift gestures. Her hair was lighter, her makeup darker, but she was still the Sherrie I had met years ago, skinny and eager and a survivor of her beloved dad's normal male psychopathic behavior.

"No, Frank," she said, "I feel I should avow to you individually, really one-on-one, especially since this tragedy . . ." She shrugged; we both knew; why dwell on it? "I used to get younger every year. Now time has passed, so I stay the same. I tell my clients that's all a person can hope for. It's an ethical. You have to accept the pluses—seniority unless Pan Am goes broke, for instance, and then you can kiss your seniority g'bye."

"No change in you that I notice."

"A sense of reality is important. My clients have got to learn to face reality, it's vital to access your pain—so go for it! Not that a little mellowing out and careful accessorizing of your outfits won't work major miracles, that too. Attitude definitely counts. And speaking of attitude, Frank, I want you to know how wonderful you are—Suki gave me a hint—how you—your capacity for innate—"

She was chasing the thought with both hands. She caught a passing tray of food, just in the nick of time, before the pressure went on to organize her condolences. It's always hard to tell a person he's wonderful when you have doubts. It was easier to lift away the teeniest egg roll anyone had ever seen: "Hardly even looks like one," she said. "I'll eat it anyway." She popped it into her mouth. "Even tastes small," she said.

"Probably a wonderful egg roll," I said, keeping the theme alive.

She smiled gratefully. I had taken her off the hypocrisy hook. She smiled her little-girl tomboy smile and I did notice a difference. She must have had her teeth smallified; they were such buds now, a definite reminiscence of youth. "So aren't you going to have one?"

I knew her for a former smoker, today an ardent gum-brusher, but this looked different to me—her teeth, her mouth—seriously remodeled.

"—how you took charge here, Frank, like I want to say, did your best in a trying role, so many men would not. I have to get this out. Don't blush and shift like that from foot to foot. I told Suki you were a gem in a carload, she has *got* to treasure you beyond price—"

"Thanks, Sherrie." I tried one of the miniature egg rolls. I reached for it as if it would save my life. I wondered if the time of sushi had passed.

"Hey, good, isn't it?" Sherrie inquired. "And so are *you*, Frank, and don't you forget it."

Wirt Olmstead, the collagist and Breatharian, was busy not eating around Jerry Whiner, the screenwriter from Mill Valley. He was telling Jerry about how irresponsible nutrition had made (lowered his voice) Peter overnourished. Too much sugar, protein, carbohydrates, fat, and fiber; not enough chlorophyll and meditation. Vitamins and minerals weren't worth shit. Those so-called trace elements do nothing but clog the pineal gland. Ever hear of a dandelion or a cactus needed an emergency appendectomy? Ever hear of a carrot hung out with bad company in the Tenderloin?

Wirt was mumbling a little, nipping at the fried buffalo strips and metabolizing the meat danger with a sunny glass of brandy, a whole French hillside in convenient form. Jerry was listening closely, picking up a little dialogue. He leaned forward, watching Wirt's lips move, very intent. I had never seen him so silent, but then I had never seen him locked into conversation with a theorist like Wirt. As I slipped by, he gave me a hooded flick of the eyes. I had also never before seen anyone not take the opportunity to break off a conversation with Wirt, but Jerry didn't seem eager, memorizing the news of *Anyfood Poisoning*, the title of the book Wirt was writing, planning to write, working out the details before he found some terrific writer to tell it to—could be a hit movie, also.

Just as Sherrie thought I was wonderful, a person to be congratulated, maybe Jerry thought I was responsible in some way. In my heart of hearts, I was more on Jerry's side, although I wasn't sure why. Other people had fallen in love with Suki, too. The darkness that overcame Peter must have begun creeping upon him long before I ever met his mother on a Valentine's Day at the Old Spaghetti Factory & Cafe. Should I blame myself for that?

Also, I didn't feel myself in love with her now. But then I didn't feel very much these days, either love or not-love.

"He's still sort of Jewish," Nella was whispering to Sherrie, indicating Jerry Whiner with a sudden sharp bob of her head, "but I don't think he'll be Jewish all his life. He's a communicant at the Marin Ecumenical Temple, Notre Dame de la Torah."

"You're talking about me?" Jerry asked, waking from his trance with Wirt, who worked his spell on people. "Hey, catch you later, Wirt, don't want to stuff myself in front of you, be a disgrace to chlorophyll, man—you just go get something to not eat and I'll be right back. Got to have a snack and a word with my buddy Frank Curtis here."

We both watched Wirt shamble off, looking for a fresh ear to gnaw on.

"Wow," said Jerry. "I spose everybody got a passion. My deal, I decided to go commercial with a vengeance. This is a confession. I'm writing a new western, a cowboys-and-Jungians plot."

"Sounds like a real revenge against the form," I said.

"That's only the plot, the story tells about caring and sharing on the modern frontier. I cannot do a plot without a story—need it as an anchor, Frank, to being how I am. Take your average bankable star or director—doesn't give a shit, all he wants is the next vehicle. I'm not in the business of providing vehicles, I didn't go to mechanic school. I'm a person in my own right with a track record. And that, when you come right down to it, is what the poor kid lacked, you think?"

"Who?"

"Peter, who else?"

"I didn't know we were—"

"You're right, kids go through a real good identity crisis at that age, sometimes they can't deal with not having one, the anima goes off, the karma is in turnaround—hey, did that lady say *communicant* about me?"

"Everybody," I said, "has a stupid solution to other people's problems."

Jerry took a deep breath. He looked me straight in the eyes, focusing for greater comfort, as he had learned, on the bridge of my nose. "I'm sorry you're upset. I really am. I can understand that. You want to talk about it person to person, I'm ready anytime. We've never had a real talk, Frank. Just call and we can have lunch." He paused, still steaming. "But I'm not sure you're really ready for it, Frank."

"Okay, sorry, sorry, you mean okay."

Jerry searched within and found what he was looking for. He forgave. A man of power, which he aimed to be, had infinite forgiveness capacities. He thought he might practice on me, even before our lunch. He peered closely into my nose and lowered his voice. "Do you think maybe you're having an emotional difficulty about this incident that happened?"

"Possibly," I said.

" 'Snothing to be ashamed of. Only thing be ashamed of is when you don't *feel* the pain and shame and guilt—"

"That's considerate of you, Jerry."

"—'cause my therapist is dynamite with folks who have none of the normal human feelings. Want his number? The kid decapitated his granny in Atherton was one of his clients, so I think he's got a free hour all of a sudden. That kid exited the growth mode and entered the criminal justice mode, leaving Dr. Idnalson two free hours per week, 673-7161, that's his service, call him. Part of it's usually covered by your insurance, since I know you're not in big-bucks journalism, decided to take it easy and humble down from the treadmill—"

Involved in person-to-person intimacy, we hadn't noticed that Nella and Sherrie wanted to get in on the movie talk. They were frequent hostesses when film companies came to San

Francisco. Jerry wasn't a star, but he was an actual local working member of the Industry, deserving of respect. They paid their homage in the form of opinions about things.

It was not to be. With heavy eyes they watched Jerry slide off. They hadn't meant for this to happen at all, leaving them alone with a person, me, who was totally out of the ravishing part of the social world, except that he happened to be present when the star of this particular afternoon killed himself. Nevertheless, it didn't seem right, social grace-wise, to bring up the event to a bystander, me, who may have been peculiarly connected with the incident. The matter wasn't even under option; Sherrie and Nella weren't up for it yet.

"Didn't I read in Pat Steger how Jerry was having conferences with Terry Tuna?" Sherrie asked. "Didn't you read that?"

"I don't read the superficial social pages," Nella said. "Herb Caen is enough. But people come into the tavern, they catch me up on Pat Steger sometimes. So what about Jerry and Terry?"

"Terry Tuna got a new project, and he was discussing with Jerry," Sherrie told Nella. "You know how the last one opened wide, *bam?* Flat! No legs, no *body*. A jillion dollars down the tube."

"Just proves virtue is rewarded," Nella remarked abstractedly.

Sherrie looked a little lost at Nella's response.

She paused, and then plunged on. "But now, on a script he developed, just naked paper, Jerry for rewrite, they're financing him again. He comes in under budget."

"And loses money," Nella said.

"But how many triple hyphenates come in under budget?"

Since I was there, I put the question. "What's a triple hyphenate?"

Sherrie was patient. "A writer-director's a hyphenate. A *producer*-writer-director adds one more—I don't know the word—so I call that a triple hyphenate."

"A triplefate?"

She made a little thoughtful mouth.

"Okay, Frank, I may not be so good with the vocabulary, but I always know what I mean."

"That's important," said Nella, "unless you're just fucking around, which you're usually not. In the tavern business, too, a person's got to know what the drinker means, the cops, the city, the inspectors, even the crooked bartender, but the important thing, I always tell my fellow ladies in the businesses that used to be totally controlled by a male mafia is what *I* mean. I think triple hyphenate is terrific, Sherrie. Personally, that's what I feel like—a woman-businessperson-human being."

Watkins, the law prof from Davis, who must have been a highly formered escort to Suki—he carried too much weight for her—was chatting up one of the pretty manufactured-Greek caterer sisters. Yes, they were ethnic, she explained once again; Mama from Sweden, not Stockholm but Malmo and a lot of bleaching time north of the Arctic Circle; Daddy from Dahomey via five generations in Georgia, Detroit, and finally San Francisco. "That makes us Greek," she giggled (she had thick reddish hair and, like Watkins, a slightly full figure for Suki's circle). Her baby sister added, "We always say, and then we say we don't generally date the folks when we work a party."

"This isn't a party," Watkins said.

"A wake, a funeral, a memorial service, we don't date them either."

"But you're nice, Mr. . . ." She studied the card he had handed her. "Mr. Watkins." And then she carefully put the card in the dish with the used shrimp tails.

Watkins flushed, moved off, and the Greek sisters rolled their eyes at each other. They were strictly business today. In honor of grief they were serving exceptional, memorable gourmet snacks: fried buffalo strips, bacon bits in cheese balls, cold hard-fried eggs with a smear of mustard on each one. They wanted to try some new things. They wanted to invent a tradition. They were treating us to a Tenderloin theme funeral. I thought I detected Filipino lumpia, pink Thai coconut and pork in cold intertwining, pale Vietnamese finger vegetables—there, in another platter, where big Watkins was tasting and licking his fingers, oiling over the sorrows of rejection from a fellow hefty. The Greek caterers were expressing themselves creatively; Suki hadn't given detailed food instructions for today.

Watkins, his hands clasped behind his back, was studying the Dufy prints on the wall—a Nice series, Promenade des Anglais, Jardins Quelquechoses, La Plage, Les Voiles. I wondered if he was now far from Nice, telling himself he was better off for losing Suki; if he saw trouble and pain ahead for her, more than anyone could anticipate. I did. Now Watkins turned from the flapping sails in the Nice harbor and stared at Suki with a look that might, to another, have seemed to be desire and regret. I was sure he was only searching for the evidence.

Barbara, the design consultant, was watching Watkins watch Suki. Sometimes Barbara seemed merely to help fill the space at Suki's parties, but I could see her shrewdly figuring out, maybe correctly, that Watkins realized he was better off. Barbara strode toward him; she knew an opening when she saw or hoped for one. She had some new menu ideas to share with Watkins. She wanted his opinion about this year's fruit, soy fantasy, and the new cholesterol-leeching after-exercise drink developed by a team of Brigham Young University scientists especially for teenage athletes and mid-life design consultants. It came in Sparkling or European, according to your taste.

Just because a son was dead, which must happen all the time, was no reason for normal life to stop. People have to eat, an addiction harder to treat than heroin or smoking because you can't just quit cold turkey. And if you only cut down, there's still a problem.

"Uh, Wirt," said Watkins in response to Barbara's menu probe.

"Wirt what?"

"Maybe he has the answer for you. He's a Breatharian."

"Oh, but he's *anorexic.*"

"That hasn't been proved, according to him. He just says he doesn't eat because it's his philosophy and he throws up if he does."

Barbara closed her heart to Watkins. It had only started to open. This was not how a man talked to a person when he was up for a little flirtation. Just because Suki's son had died was no reason for him to treat Barbara to this unpleasantness à la carte. But Barbara had grown accustomed to loneliness; she went to check in the kitchen and see what new snack secret the caterers might choose to share with her.

Inexorably the universe was thickening for Barbara. No matter how many walls and pillows and lampshades for which she prescribed creamy shades, done over in pink, the night came and the darkness fell and she woke with a start to remember that the refrigerator stood humming and welcoming and offering butter, frozen rolls, cheese, cold meats. It did no good to leave her refrigerator empty except for Perrier, because then she just went to the cabinet with a

spoon and had peanut butter with Perrier, or
opened a can of sardines, or gnawed on something, anything, whatever was stowed there in
case of earthquake or atomic war or a visit from
her nephews.

Watkins saw me watching the space where
Barbara had been. He shrugged. He looked
gloomy. He may have been pleased at his good
luck in not being required to comfort Suki more
than her other friends. An average amount of
sympathy was acceptable. But he was still sad
about her son. The Greek caterers didn't really
count for him. Watkins' gloom was of the steady
sort that concentrated on the endless distress of
existence; you could count on it; he had room to
include Suki's midnight loneliness in his view of
things.

"How's your back?" I asked Ted Keneally.
The brace was off. He stood with a kind of alert
stiffness and a fixed smile on his face, a man who
had been through pain. His buttery hair was
shellacked down with fresh gel.

"Much better, good as it'll ever be," he said.
"And I learned from the experience, so who
knows if it was the disaster I thought it was?"

I wondered what he had learned. In California
we learn just like other people that life stops and
life goes on; people get sick and people die; people fall in love, out of love, wear love out. Some
people even get older. For those things it's just
like anyplace else in the world.

"Hey, Frank, you didn't ask me what? Aren't you going to ask me what?"

"Sure thing."

"Okay," and the fixed smile gave way to a boyish twinkling one, the one he used when he got soft with juries, the one that gained him his victories with the help of the secretaries, widows, and older non-Oriental women whom he tried to place on his juries. "What I learned, fella, is look in the pool first and make sure there's water before you dive."

Things were different with Ted since I'd seen him last. He was easier with Alfonso; he wasn't resentful and jealous. He was easier with Suki; he had given up. A broken back seemed to have cured his struggle for certain inaccessible things —to be a six-footer, to win Suki. "You know, I saw a black orthopod," he said. "Does basketball players, football kids, and now me. Says I got the spine of an athlete—what's left of it, anyway, couple unfused vertebrae. The spine of an athlete who jumped into the pool with mucho liquid in the subject but none in the object."

Some people who drink," Nella said, "don't get in trouble so much. That's what I've noticed in the tavern business. For example"—she lowered her voice—"for example, Peter isn't . . . oh dear, *wasn't* . . . a youthful offender in the drinking field. I mean, if he got a heat on with, say, *beer*, like a normal adolescent, wouldn't that make—have made—everybody happy?"

I leaned forward to hear her low whispers.

Ted leaned stiffly backward to stop hearing them, and then checked out for the pain-relieving section, the bar. He had a right.

"I want you to know I don't believe you did anything necessarily bad, Frank," Nella was saying. "I hold you almost blameless." The whisper didn't fit with her high-heeled strut through the room to inform me of my innocence. Her tavern in North Beach, only slightly remodeled to decorate the old Italians out, was making money. *Got a beat on* was a phrase left over from an earlier life.

I want you to know I hold myself nearly blameless, too, I wanted to say to her. Before Nella, I had had a prior argument with myself.

Rattling their connections with each other, chanting their lonely arias, Suki's friends and lovers gathered for the afternoon. Some of them wished they had taken an extension course in how to be sad; they sought to develop their talents. It was required on this occasion. Not many folks these days had the opportunity to lose an only son. The rules of the play were not clear. Sherrie was looking to access her pain; Wirt wanted to etherealize himself above it; even the Afro-Swedish Greek caterers, industrious and professional, felt the obligation to be different from what they were, although what they were seemed to work out, most of the time. Watkins' non-specific gloom didn't help him; he too would like to offer something special. Alfonso just went on, whatever came through, whatever was right.

I was only an amateur in this place. The living needed something, but I didn't know what it was, no more than I knew what I could do for the dead. Suki hadn't asked, hadn't given me an inkling. Yet in the thin dry air of her routines, her persistence in sociability—even in the style of this celebration to the memory of Peter—I could hear a howl of motherhood, a screaming and rending, silent and deadly in the air like escaped microwaves.

Just now at the door there was a little disturbance, a rustling and sideways shuffling, as if a new creature had found its way to the watering hole. Harry, the skinhead boy who used to ride behind Peter on his homemade cycles, stood holding a towel and rolling it in his hands. He had worn it on his head like a Sikh turban as a protection against the elements. Alfonso was talking softly with him when I walked up. "You looking for something?" Alfonso asked him.

"Wanted to sort of say hello."

"Hello," Alfonso said.

"Like, just say hello."

"Hello again," Alfonso said, bellying closer to him.

The kid turned and walked away. There were sweat patches on his black leather. He must have walked here from downtown.

Alfonso said to me, "Sorry for the kid, you know that? I think he's really discouraged."

"Yes," I said.

"But what can a person do?" Alfonso asked with his broad heavy purplish smile. "I'm just a dick, I do my dick things, you got any better ideas for me?"

"No," I said.

Watching Harry, Suki had stood near a table covered with plates of food, her hand over her mouth, a blue vein throbbing across her forehead. The outlines of the hand seemed to fuzz and fade for me, but the vein stood out clearly. If Harry had stepped forward, past Alfonso, and Alfonso had let him, there was no way to tell whether Suki would have urged him to fill a plate, take something to eat, or whether she would have leapt upon him, shrieking and scratching. We would not have the answer to this question, either.

Alfonso and I stood at the door until Harry disappeared, shambling down the sidewalk toward the corner, walking in his duck-footed way, his hands in his pockets, the towel over his head. He was looking from side to side. There was a bus stop two blocks away and maybe he hoped to turn lucky, this could be Harry's good day after all, he might find a transfer.

We turned back to the celebration. Everyone here had good manners. After the momentary lull, everyone went back to normal business, nourishing themselves, refreshing themselves, talking quietly.

"I'll tell you a secret," Alfonso said. "That

woman is depress. Crying don't cut it for me no more, and we notice she ain't crying, but that woman is depress." He looked at me with his face puckered into a purplish frown. "I guess sadness cuts it for me."

Cal, the Chapter 11 software genius, his wife, and their son and daughter—frightened little girl in organdy with puffed sleeves—stood in a little semicircle together in the garden, silently guarding each other, and then Cal looked at his watch, and then they moved slowly, cumbersomely, an eight-legged entity, from the garden where they had been staring at the growing things—"Nice, very nice, outstanding," said Cal's wife—to the door. Suki ran up to her former husband and he allowed her to put her arms around him, while his wife still seemed to be mouthing the words, Nice, Nice, Outstanding; and then he put his arms around Suki and his wife seemed to be mouthing different words or perhaps none at all, her lips merely twitching; and then he made a little bow and the entity left. Suki saw them to the door. She watched until they were safe at the curb, still moving together toward their Honda hatchback.

Suki tapped on a glass and everyone fell silent, some in the middle of sentences. Her face was white and frail. "I would like," she began, then stopped. "I wish." And stopped. And again: "I must say a few words to my friends about my son whom we . . ." And again: "Whom we wish to remember because I . . ."

And stopped. "Because I loved him."

"Peter," she said. "My boy. My son."

I pushed past Nella and Sherrie, and as I went by Alfonso he tapped me twice on the shoulder. I stood alongside Suki, feeling the avalanche of heat falling from her body, consuming her flesh, feeling her fingers intertwining with mine, burning, letting go. She was making no claim.

"Peter was . . ."

In the sudden silence there was the deep-sea bubbling of a coffee maker, the breathing and waiting. I could smell the heavy damp from the open doors leading into the garden. Alfonso's thick fingers were folded together over his belly and he was staring at the floor.

Suki said, "Peter was my son."

Somehow Harry had come back and around and was standing outside in the garden, staring defiantly into the house, his jacket wet, his face gleaming. He had climbed a wall to get there; his hands were bleeding. Alfonso hadn't stopped him.

Alfonso saw him and gestured with his paw, bringing him inside. The boy stood between Alfonso and me as Suki waited there in the silence for more words to come.

"He was my son."

Harry looked at Alfonso for permission to do something. Alfonso shrugged and gave it. Tears were rolling down Harry's face.

SEVENTEEN

Later in life people begin to recalibrate their heads and hearts when their friends disappear, wives and husbands die, the disasters happen. They'd better. They have no choice. Maybe an old guy comes to think of disappearing with the others; letting the disaster happen to him. Comes to want only not to feel it too much. That might be the ticket.

For me it was still too early to sink without a trace of myself. Yet there was darkness and solitude in there, a yawning heaviness in my arms, legs, and head. I met my classes at the university; the young woman with the Alzheimer's project was headed for a good career; I put my time in; it was something to do. Sometimes sleep was a problem, but at least I had a reason to get up, an obligation to get up for, and I got up, often thinking I hadn't slept. But I had slept. The shadows across the wall had shifted; it was dawn. I had merely dreamed of sleeplessness and this was tiring in itself.

During that afternoon and evening of Suki's celebration for Peter, I thought, Yes, it's right that she celebrate her son, that's the only way. I hung about the house as the Greek caterers were cleaning up. So did some others—Norrie, Sherrie, Watkins, Alfonso—until Suki suddenly seemed to notice us, looked up from taking a whisk broom to a rug with a spilled ashtray. She was astonished to find us still there. "Hey, you guys! You're in the way! We're sweeping—watch out for the vacuum! Party's over!"

"You want me to go, Suki?"

And with a quick glance, and then a quick turn, she used her fists to hit the pillows on the couch to plump them up. "I just need to get this house cleaned up, okay?"

The others were leaving and finally I left with the last of them. Evening had come, that unwelcome darkness when an afternoon party has gone on too long. The day was all used up.

Alfonso and I made a promise to keep in touch. Maybe there was a Sunday magazine profile to be done about the clever overweight detective with the night school law degree and a nice, burly, rumbly way of handling things by letting them work themselves through until they finally went away. We planned to have dinner one day, no specific day, Monday through Friday, maybe escalate to the weekend—fishing off some cop's boat, a few beers—one of us would call the other.

A few nights later I wasn't sleeping, I thought, yet I was awakened by the phone that must have run through its routine a couple of times before I heard it—"Unnh?"

"Oh, Frank, I'm sorry, I know I shouldn't do this to you—" It was ten to two. "But they still didn't come to pick up the stuff, it's just sitting there in the garage—"

Suki was calling in the middle of the night to tell me Huckleberry House had neglected to bring its truck to carry off Peter's clothes and equipment.

"It's just been there, Frank, it's just sitting there and they *promised*—"

"Okay, put the lights on, make a pot of tea, I'll be right over."

I dressed, brushed teeth, pulled a bottle of wine out of the refrigerator. I wiped the windshield of my Fiat, which was fogged and wet. I drove through the nighttime streets of Berkeley and across the Bay Bridge and down Lombard in San Francisco at an hour when the loudest sound was the clicking of the traffic lights. This was the famous twenty-two-minute commute—twenty-two minutes at two-thirty in the morning. After the traffic lights, the loudest sound was the clinking of the bottle of wine in the glove compartment as it knocked back and forth. This is for medicinal purposes only, Officer, I practiced saying; notice it is not opened yet, sir, and also notice I'm only carrying it to a needy friend. Please notice the lack of wine flush on my cheeks, Officer, and also the lack of burglary tools as I drive through the streets at this odd hour. Just making a house call, Officer.

Although it was the middle of the night, the lights had not all gone out on Suki's block—the anti-prowler spots in the gardens, the dim glow through windows of baby and geriatric watch lamps, a bathroom or a kitchen left bright in other houses. America, folks. Ruby reflectors burned in the Neighborhood Security Patrol markers. Soon a cruising cop car would come around, making its circuit.

I was entertaining myself with nervousness. At home in my bed this was one of the hours when I started awake, feeling the bachelor chill, and tried to make out the welcome graying of the shadows, which meant pretty soon dawn, pretty soon sunlight and obligations. And then tried to will myself back to sleep because it was too early. A person can't always find snug harbor, but I preferred to be inside and not to answer questions.

Suki's kitchen was the one that was lit up. No one else on the street was cooking at this hour. Her garage light was on above the place where the basketball hoop had been unscrewed. She couldn't have expected the Huckleberry House pickup at this hour, but it was waiting for them. Down the driveway I could see that the garage door was open, see the pile of bicycle, sporting equipment, clothes in a ski bag labeled "Peter Crowell"; and I could also see no point in telling Suki that this was an invitation to burglars. People do a lot of telling each other what they already know.

Here came the cop car. He slowed down in that peculiar ostentatious official way. He shined the spot on my paper bag that contained the bottle of wine, looking like a bag of state-of-the-art intruder's tools. I was a goner. Then Suki opened the door, wearing a pale robe, and I could hear the cop laughing as he turned the spot briefly onto the upper-story bedroom, whirling it giddily back and forth across the curtains, and then switched off and went gliding away in his Ford into the darkness. She didn't need the bozo with the paper bag. If those Pacific Heights ladies got horny during the night, a person could always radio for a brother officer to come cover for him for how long it would take, maybe ten-fifteen minutes if she turned into a really serious romance where you take off the shoes. A joke on a person's appointed rounds; a bit of distraction on the goddamn night shift.

Suki stood there a moment, not moving, blocking the door, as if considering whether to ask me in.

"What's that?" she asked.

"Bottle of wine. It's not early enough for coffee yet."

"Am I being foolish? Are you making fun of me?"

315

"Don't think so, Suki. Are you going to let me through the door?"

She was thinking and she didn't move. She said: "I don't know to turn on all the lights or turn them off."

There was the lamp where I was standing like a visiting swain at the dinner hour of the evening. There was the spot of yellow at the garage, where the consignment for Huckleberry House was waiting. I took her hand and led her back into the house. "Why don't we switch off the garage light?" I said, and when she didn't answer, I kept her hand and led her to the kitchen and did so. I also hit the kitchen switch. There was enough glow from the street and sky and dim appliances—digital-counters flickering—so that we could see each other. I put the bottle of wine on the table and sat facing her. We didn't open the bottle. I could wait for dawn if necessary and then make coffee.

After a while she spoke. "I want to go back."

"Back where?"

She didn't answer. Maybe she did, but she waited so long that I wasn't sure it was meant to be the answer. "I might rest if everyone leaves me alone."

"Do you want me here now?"

She sounded puzzled. "I don't know."

"Do you want to talk?"

"I don't know. I can't sleep."

I might have said that time would help. I

might have suggested just letting herself go. I knew enough to say nothing.

"I called you," she said.

"That's why I'm here. I'm glad to be here."

"Trouble is, that was inconsiderate of me."

"I care for you, Suki. It's no trouble."

"Why?" she asked. "Why did it happen?"

I thought of the awful privacy of his yearning and need, and the loneliness of his clever, unformed, and empty life, and the strangeness of his gift for devices, little motors, video equipment, things that buzzed and poked and pried, and the father he did not have, the father I couldn't be for him either, the mother whose life he secretly shared and did not share, this beautiful and clever and yearning woman who was looking into my eyes and waiting for me to speak. I thought of his vindictiveness. I thought of his despair.

"Explain it to me, Frank. I know you can tell me something, it won't even have to be the truth, you don't even have to be nice to me, I won't even care if you're mean—"

I remembered her saying to Peter, *You used to be kind. You were a kind child.*

I was trying to remember when she said that, and how to recall it to her, and she was watching the way I was laboring to say something that might help her to understand or to pass the time until she could give up trying to understand. I think I was going to say that he didn't have a chance to grow into his kindness, but I'm not sure if I could have said that. It would not have helped.

Before I could speak, she put her hand on mine. "Probably there must be a reason. There always is. What was it?"

"I don't know how you feel, Suki. Nobody does. I know you feel awful, maybe a little crazy—"

"You think so? Crazy is supposed to crowd out sad. That's what Alfonso said. I wish it would."

I could hear the pulsing of the refrigerator. I could hear her heart. Her breathing was a soft and pumping machinery.

"This isn't what you expected from me, Frank. When we played together how we did. The way I did. Why do you suppose they didn't come for the pickup?"

"Huckleberry House? It's not a business. They have to count on people who . . . I don't know what I expected from you."

"Not this. Couldn't."

I stood up and found the corkscrew above the sink. I opened the wine, which was still chilled, and poured her some in a water glass. I took the same amount for myself and drank; she only held her glass, forgetting what to do with it.

"Not this," she said. "You could be warm in your bed or maybe someone else's—"

"I'm here," I said. "I want to be here."

"He was very bright. He had a talent with tools. He scored off the graph on mechanical aptitude. When he was a child, Frank, he wasn't unkind."

"It can't be justified, Suki."

"He was just a baby. Don't some people call on God?"

"They do. They try to."

"For what? To make it better? Maybe for revenge, do you think so?"

"Not appropriate this time, Suki. I wish I could help."

"Thank you for getting up in the middle of the night. Do you want to go to bed?"

"No, I'm happy just to sit here." The glow of street and sky and white kitchen things made me squint, as if under glare, although the lights in the house were out and it would be an hour or two before dawn. And we sat there. She didn't drink the wine, but she held the glass. Her skin shone bluish in the white darkness.

"I suppose I could take you to bed. Would you like that?"

I might fall asleep if we did that, but I knew she wouldn't sleep.

"Would you, Frank?"

"Let's just talk a while."

But then she said nothing. She sat and another sound was added to the motor of the refrigerator, heartbeats, breathing. It was the soft catch and release, catch and release of her sobbing. I tried to understand what she wanted from me. I waited.

At last she asked, "Do you really want to stay here, Frank?"

"Yes."

"This isn't going to be fun."

"This is where I want to be."

"It didn't start out like this. If you liked me then, this isn't what you liked."

"People change."

"You might be making a mistake, Frank."

"I suppose so. But it doesn't matter."

"They do matter. Mistakes do matter."

"This is the one I want to live with."

"Should we walk? Should we drink? Should we try to sleep? Should we make love?"

"We don't have to decide now."

She turned to the right and to the left; she turned and peered out the window toward the garage, where the light was turned off but the door was still open and the mound of possessions was untouched. "Is it getting to be daylight?"

"Not yet, Suki."

Not yet.